A Christmas Love Song

ANDEE REILLY

CHAMPAGNE BOOK GROUP

A Christmas Love Song

Published by Champagne Book Group
2373 NE Evergreen Avenue, Albany OR 97321 U.S.A.

~~~

First Edition 2021

eISBN: 978-1-77155-999-7

Cover Art by Jack Reilly

www.champagnebooks.com

Version_1

For Carol.

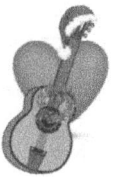

Chapter One

"We looked out at the city lights that night / The connection we both felt, it seemed so right / We looked above to the stars that shined so bright / Sharing in each other's dreams was pure delight."

Jake Wilder held the microphone out to the crowd. "You know the words," he said. "Now let me hear you!"

Thousands of adoring fans sang the chorus in unison. Their voices lifted into the night sky, and in that moment, they were a synthesis of sound and energy.

The 55,000-seat stadium was packed to the rafters. Fans spilled out into the aisles. They danced and shared in the experience of seeing their favorite band live. A mixture of cheers and hollers reverberated through the crowd. Girls perched on their boyfriends' shoulders and waved their arms to the rhythm of the music. People embraced and linked elbows, swaying like branches in the wind.

This was his favorite moment during his concerts. For a short time, he owned the hearts and souls of his devotees. Like electric current, the music pulsed through the fans' veins. "City Lights" was the number one song in the charts for thirty-eight weeks in a row. Everybody would remember it. Their first date. Their first kiss. Their first child. Their first concert together. Jake's song would be the soundtrack to their lives, and he would live on in their hearts.

They would never, ever forget him.

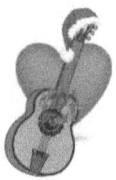

Chapter Two
Ten Years Later

"This could be an incredible opportunity to introduce your music to a whole new generation of fans," said Annie, the television producer Jake agreed to meet with.

She was young and so polished and professional, he felt like a shaggy old dog in comparison. He was used to dealing with music people in torn jeans and messy hair. This woman's bun was pulled so tightly his head ached just looking at it.

"We've been thinking a lot about the title of the show, and we believe *Has-Been House* has a certain ring to it."

He didn't mind the one-hit wonder label because it wasn't true. Despite having several hits, being called a *has-been*, even after all these years, still hurt.

"Sounds promising." He forced himself to keep an open mind. "Sort of like *Celebrity Big Brother*."

"Oh, no, no," she said. "This is *much* different."

Jake wasn't sure how different the shows could be. The concept sounded exactly the same, but he pretended to agree anyway.

His manager had arranged the meeting at a trendy outdoor café on the Sunset Strip. Jake eagerly attended, always up for a new way to reintroduce his music to the world even if that meant leaving the privacy of his cozy Hollywood Hills home and driving through rush hour traffic. In the old days, he took limos everywhere and barely noticed the hordes of cars jamming the streets of Los Angeles.

"I've been working on some new music." He stretched the truth. It had been years since he'd written anything decent but didn't want the television producer to believe he'd lost all his motivation even if he was stuck playing at small venues in the area singing the same old songs.

At a nearby table, three teenage girls stared at him. One got on her phone, perhaps to Google him. Did they even know his name? The title of his song probably sat on the tip of their tongue… "City" something or other. Maybe they heard it last at their favorite clothing store in the mall. Being recognized these days was a luxury. He was always polite to fans who struggled with his name or garbled the lyrics to his songs in an attempt to place him. He smiled, signed what they put in front of him, and posed for selfies.

The girls passed the phone among them. They must've found a match. An old headshot or a picture from the night he accepted a Grammy for best new artist. He diligently recreated the mysterious, angst-ridden look he'd been known for because he had a reputation to keep, even if few remembered his name.

"I think the show sounds great." He returned to his conversation with producer Annie. "All of us *has-beens* living under one roof."

"Terrific." She didn't seem to notice his sarcasm.

"Would we perform our songs on every episode or take turns?" He softened his tone. Earlier that morning his manager reminded Jake they needed the paycheck. A television show wasn't too shabby of a way to earn recognition *and* money.

Annie shifted in her seat. She smoothed out her fitted pencil skirt. "Not all the artists will get to—"

"I don't mean to intrude," one of the girls from the nearby table interjected. "But my mother is your biggest fan, and she'd kill me if I didn't get an autograph."

He took the pen and napkin from her. "Who should I make it to?"

She toyed with a lock of hair and told him her mother's name.

These comments about appealing to *parents* stung. When did he become so…old? He was only in his early thirties. His whole life was supposed to be ahead of him. Though he appreciated all fans, he ached for his favorite type of fan. The I'm-Your-Biggest-Fan Fan. Many of the originals still showed up to support him at his shows, but even they, along with the gigs themselves, were getting fewer and far between.

After the teenager left with the autograph, Annie took a sip of her chardonnay, perhaps to gather courage. "As I was saying, not every artist will have the chance to perform." She flushed, either from the alcohol or the discomfort of finally admitting the truth. "They have to survive challenges and evictions first."

"Evictions?" He prayed another fan would interrupt, even welcoming the "Hey-Don't-I-Know-You- From-Somewhere?" fan.

"The experience will be fantastic. Everything you do and say will be under surveillance and broadcast to a potential audience of millions. We encourage high drama, so expect a lot of fighting and backstabbing. The audience loves that kind of thing." She clapped her hands together as if she'd enjoy the commotion even more.

He'd seen these reality shows and sympathized with the contestants when their housemates ganged up against them. If he couldn't sing, what was the point of humiliating himself in front of millions of strangers?

"Sure. Loads of fun." He tugged at his shirt collar. The sun was hitting him from behind. "In episode one, we'll all become great pals before we start fighting to the death."

She gave a mirthless laugh. "I wouldn't say it's to the *death*. The show's all about survival."

"Survival," he said, jiggling his foot under the table. He knew what it meant to survive when everybody he cared about abandoned him. When the phone stopped ringing, when the music producers didn't want to work with him because his music had become passé. When everyone moved on to the next Big Thing. He dug in his heels and did what he needed to do to pay the bills. To *survive*.

Jake tossed the napkin from his lap onto the table. "I'll have my manager get back to you."

Disappointed but relieved, he headed back to the sanctity of his home nestled in the hills.

~ * ~

"I didn't know man," said Bodhi. Jake's manager helped himself to a slice of leftover pizza from his refrigerator. "She promised every artist would have an opportunity to perform. I didn't think you'd have to fight for the privilege."

"I hate to break it to you, but that pizza's way over its prime." Jake slid the promotional materials Annie gave him across the kitchen island to Bodhi. A ridiculous picture of the future cast was Photoshopped together like they were lifelong friends.

Bodhi dumped the half-eaten slice into the trash and picked up the picture. "Good looking group," he said.

Jake raised a brow. "I'm more likely to be a contestant on *Dancing with the Stars*."

"I tried," said Bodhi. "Believe you me, I tried."

"We at least have the Troubadour gig coming up." The place was one of Jake's favorite old venues.

"They cancelled." Bodhi opened the refrigerator and searched for his next entrée.

"Don't you eat at home?"

"Hardly," said Bodhi. "Being a confirmed bachelor for life means I go hungry half the time."

He didn't mean to harass Bodhi. They'd been friends for years, and the truth was, he stood by Jake after the whole industry pushed him aside. Representing him wasn't exactly good for Bodhi's career, but he stuck it out anyway. The last two standing on the sinking ship that was Jake's career.

"The booking agent from the Troubadour called and said they rented out the entire place. A private party of some kind."

Jake feared the truth was they couldn't sell enough tickets to his show. Most of the big Los Angeles venues were pay-to-play. Bands sold their own tickets, but the local clubs made an exception for him and paid him a nice little sum at the end. The decline became obvious, even to him. The crowds were dwindling.

"I had an interesting call from one of the record labels just before you came home," said Bodhi.

Jake perked up. "What've you been waiting for?" The news buoyed his spirits, but he remembered to lower his expectations. When anyone from his old label called, it usually was something to do with rights or taxes—business stuff he loathed. He left that up to Bodhi.

"Hear me out," he said.

"Uh oh." Jake sank back into his chair. The proposal already sounded suspicious.

"The president of Satellite Records is feeling festive this year. He wants to put out a Christmas hit—a new song people will be singing every holiday season from here on out. Right up there with 'Jingle Bell Rock' and 'Here Comes Santa Claus'."

He suppressed a laugh. The idea was ludicrous. He wasn't exactly the Christmas type, but he thought of all the artists who'd sung Christmas songs before him. Elvis Presley, David Bowie, Taylor Swift. The concept wasn't so farfetched.

Perhaps encouraged he didn't kick him out of the house right then and there, Bodhi continued, "Think about it. Your own original Christmas hit."

"You mean, I'd have to write it?" Jake panicked.

Writing something new sent him into a tailspin. It wasn't for the lack of trying, but every time he sat at the piano, notebook by his side, he broke into a sweat remembering the day he'd gone to his old label with a demo of his latest work. They practically called security to escort him out.

"The deal's not exactly that simple." Bodhi was elbow deep in a tub of hummus Jake didn't remember buying.

"Here we go." He was thankful to be free of the obligation. Yet, he had to do something big to get back out there. He wasn't ready to drop off the face of the earth yet.

"The word has gone out to several other artists. The Satellite Records president has a soft spot for retro artists." Bodhi knew better than to say *has-beens*. "He'd like to see someone make a comeback with a Christmas hit. Whoever has the best song wins the contract."

Another challenge and elimination game. Two in one day. Jake didn't have the stomach for it.

"Christmas is only three weeks away," he said. "How do they plan to produce a record in time?"

"They've got it all figured out. The winner will debut the song on a TV Christmas variety show called *A Poppin' Christmas*. It'll be huge."

"But they'll need the song sooner than that? How much time do I have?" Jake hated deadlines.

"Let me worry about the details," said Bodhi.

Jake glared at Bodhi.

"A little more than two weeks," Bodhi finally admitted.

"Perfect." Jake threw up his hands and wondered when he should break the news that he hated Christmas. Bodhi should know better than anyone why Jake avoided the holiday at all cost.

If Jake Wilder was going to survive, he'd have to find the Christmas spirit even though it left him long ago.

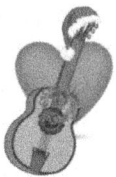

Chapter Three

Mackenzie Stone stormed into her editor's office at *The Sunrise Press*. "Mr. Hughes, you do realize I have a degree in journalism *and* political science."

He let out a harsh breath. On several occasions, he'd asked her not to raise her voice, especially in front of the rest of the staff. Not that he'd ever fire her. She was hands down his best reporter.

There were exactly two things she hated: being told what to do and getting assigned fluff pieces.

"I've said it a million times." He looked up from the plant he was watering. She admired his green thumb since she could barely keep her Chia pet alive.

"The political news comes straight from *The Associated Press*. Our focus is on community events and human-interest stories," he said.

"And you think what's going on in the rest of the world isn't of human interest?" She slapped her hand on the desk for effect. He jumped. Too gentle to be in the cutthroat business of big league journalism in her opinion. Though *The Sunrise Press* was hardly big league. How he lasted over forty years at the paper was a miracle.

She took in a deep breath. Her father always said her temper would lead to trouble. There was also the whole red-headed stereotype. More than once she'd been called hot-headed and told it had something to do with her flaming red hair. This narrow-minded assumption usually irritated her even more.

"All I'm asking for is a serious story. I need something with grit."

Mr. Hughes set down the watering can and scratched his head, pushing his gray hair so it stood up in all directions. She stopped herself from smoothing the wayward strands and, while she was at it, straightening the sagging shoulders of his cardigan sweater. He was like the unkempt, sweet old grandfather she wished for as a kid.

He finally said, "Take it easy, Lois Lane. You'll get your chance at the Pulitzer someday."

She brushed off the Lois Lane comment. Profiling Superman would be a lot more interesting than the story he had assigned her. "The whole world's going to pot, and you want me to profile some washed-up pop star named Jake Wilder?"

"Everybody loved him. You know that song," he said. "'We looked out at the city lights that night'," he sang. "'The connection we both felt, it seemed so right'."

Not bad. She was getting too distracted and needed to drive the point home that nobody would care about this story. "Yeah, well I had to Google him, and so will the mere handful of people who may want to read about him."

"Believe it or not, young lady, pop music didn't begin with Lady Gaga, or whoever it is you're listening to these days."

"But there are plenty of washed-up stars to profile. Why him?"

"I think the term you're looking for is *retro*."

She imagined that's how Mr. Hughes referred to himself as well.

"If you Googled him, then you should know the answer," he said. "He's a local boy. Born and raised in Pasadena. Probably grew up right down the street from you."

Her family knew everybody in their private, very exclusive neighborhood. She would've heard if they had a celebrity, even a former one, in their midst.

"He hasn't even cinched the deal." She'd been informed earlier about the details of the contest. Jake Wilder was only one of several artists competing for the shot. "His Christmas song could be a disaster and the story a huge waste of our time."

"Let me worry about that," Mr. Hughes said.

"This is so lame." She slumped into the chair across from him. For five years she'd been compiling a portfolio of important stories that might land her a job at one of the major newspapers. This Jake Wilder nonsense wouldn't make the cut.

"I got a call from Jake's manager today. He said we'd have exclusive access to the whole process—from Jake accepting the challenge, to writing the song, to waiting for the call," he said, punctuating every stage with an animated hand gesture. He was excited about the story, and she knew she'd lost the battle.

"I don't even like Christmas." She hoped he wouldn't remember her desk was covered in Christmas decorations.

He leaned his head back and laughed. "Everybody around here knows the truth. You're crazy about Christmas. You've driven Ross

Overton to ban all Christmas music in the office until at least one week before the twenty-fifth."

"I don't sing that badly, do I?" The thought of Ross controlling her life, even in the smallest way, burned her up. "What does Ross know anyway?" she shouted.

"Did you call?" He swung open Mr. Hughes's office door. Ross was older than Mackenzie, but he reminded her of a twelve-year-old boy in his father's suit. His eagerness to please Mr. Hughes made Ross even more boyish.

"No," she said. He was a major pain in her neck. On top of being pushy, he was always trying to scoop her stories. She only put up with him because he was the publisher's grandson.

"I'm assigning Ms. Stone a profile piece. Unless—" Mr. Hughes paused. He knew she despised Ross. "She wants to let you have it."

"No, thank you." She headed for the door.

"Who's the story about?" Ross's phone was at the ready to take notes or research pertinent information.

"Nobody you know." She waited at the door to make sure Mr. Hughes didn't give Ross the story instead. That wouldn't be the worst thing in the world, but she suddenly felt possessive of it.

"What makes you so sure?" He swallowed hard. His forehead was wet with perspiration. "Maybe we can grab a cup of coffee and think of an angle."

It took everything she had not to roll her eyes. "I have work to do," she said, excusing herself from the office.

~ * ~

"I'm sorry I'm late." Kacey Flores dropped her large black portfolio into the empty chair beside her.

The people at the table behind couldn't stop watching her as she settled down. She was a magnet for attention. Her dark long hair and deep brown eyes were enough to stop traffic, but the paint-splattered clothes she usually wore around town garnered the most compliments. One woman even offered to pay two hundred bucks for a pair of colorful, but worn-out jeans. Mackenzie adored Kacey's T-shirts with their randomly patterned handprints.

"How'd it go?" asked Mackenzie.

"Guess who's having her first solo exhibition at the Stella Lee Gallery?"

"Hmmm, let me think." She playfully tapped her fingers on her chin.

"Me!" Kacey screamed. Now she had everybody's attention. She didn't notice or care. "Should we order an entire coconut cake to celebrate?"

From their first year in college together, Mackenzie and Kacey had been inseparable. Nobody would ever guess at first, they couldn't stand each other. When Mackenzie walked into their shared freshman dorm on orientation day, she figured she'd merely have to tolerate her new roommate. For starters, Kacey had already chosen her side of the room and tossed clothes all over the tight space. She even had the audacity to cover the walls with her original abstract art. Mackenzie would never admit it now, but she hated Kacey's paintings back then.

Mackenzie complained to anyone who would listen she had nothing in common with her roommate. Kacey, one to never mince words, told Mackenzie studying politics was a waste of time. She thought the same about a degree in art. They argued more than they agreed. They were complete opposites: Kacey was a night owl, up all night painting and studying, while Mackenzie woke at seven AM sharp every morning to hit the gym and go to class.

When they'd outgrown their tiny dormitory, they knew they couldn't live without each other and searched for an apartment off campus. They thrived from the banter. Though they disagreed about most everything, there was one thing not up for debate. Gerrard's, the French bakery down the street from their apartment, made the world's best coconut cake. Some might even say she and Kacey put up with their over-priced, crammed apartment for all these years because of its proximity to the bakery.

"An *entire* coconut cake?" she asked.

"Maybe we'll start with just a slice." Kacey typed on her phone. "I'm sorry. I have to tell my parents."

"They'll be thrilled to know their investment in your art education wasn't a complete waste."

"*Cállate.*" Kacey threw a packet of Splenda at Mackenzie.

"You shut up. But not before you tell me everything."

Gerrard brought them extra-large slices of coconut cake and both dug in.

"When's the exhibition?" Mackenzie asked.

"In the spring." White coconut flakes coating Kacey's lips. "I'm terrified. I've got a ton of work to do."

"I'm so unbelievably excited for you." Joy filled her. "I want to know all the details."

"There's not much to tell yet." Kacey's eyes beamed with pride.

Her dream was coming true, and this motivated Mackenzie to work even harder on achieving a significant career in journalism.

Kacey continued, "Once we get closer to the opening, the gallery will put out the marketing materials. Maybe I'll even get some good reviews."

"Are you kidding? Of course you will. You'll be the toast of the town."

"Anyway," said Kacey, brushing away the compliment. "We've got plenty of time to talk about me. What's going on with you?"

"Unless you count Ross from work asking me out for coffee, not a heck of a lot."

"Girl, I could show you some self-defense moves that would put that guy in a sling."

"Easy tiger. He is the publisher's grandson. A royal pain but completely harmless. Besides, I've got bigger problems."

She dropped her fork onto the plate mid bite. "What?"

Always the dramatic one. "It's not a big deal," said Mackenzie. "Finish your cake."

Kacey crossed her arms across her chest. She looked like a schoolgirl refusing to eat her vegetables.

"Fine." Mackenzie gave up. "You know how hard I've been working to get clips together so I can work at a *real* newspaper. A big one—here in the city or New York or Washington DC. I want to report serious news."

"What did Mr. Hughes assign you now? A report on Ziggy the waterskiing squirrel."

"He retired."

"Mr. Hughes?"

"No, the squirrel."

"How does a squirrel *retire*? Did he die?" Kacey finished her cake and was eyeing Mackenzie's slice. "How do you know that anyway?"

Her shoulders sagged. "I reported the story. And you'll be glad to hear Ziggy is alive and well and enjoying his retirement."

They giggled.

"Does the name Jake Wilder ring a bell?" she asked.

"Of course! 'We looked out at the city lights that night / The connection we both felt, it seemed so right'," Kacey sang. "I loved him."

Again with that song. "Then you're gonna love this. He's up for some kind of Christmas song-writing competition. The winner will be featured on a TV Christmas special called *A Poppin' Christmas.*"

"How fun. And you get to write the story?"

"Get to? Mr. Hughes is practically forcing me to. It's so superficial." Mackenzie didn't want to sound like a snob, but it was the only word that came to mind.

"Only if you write it that way."

"Who cares about a washed-up popstar?"

"It's the classic underdog story. I can see it now." Kacey stared off into the distance as if she was watching it play out on stage. "Down and out popstar makes a comeback celebrating hard-nosed journalist's favorite holiday."

"Wait a minute. How'd I get involved? I'm the reporter, not the story." Mackenzie bristled at the idea Kacey was on to something. She hated to admit it, but maybe Kacey was right. There was a story there. Mackenzie only had to dig it up.

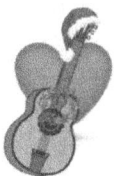

Chapter Four

Jake tucked a strand of hair behind his ear. He was thankful to still have his signature full head of loose waves. They called him the pretty boy of pop, and the crowd used to go mad when he ran his hand through his hair. The gesture was a nervous habit, but Bodhi encouraged Jake to play up his looks and took credit when he made *People* magazine's sexiest man alive. Embarrassingly enough, the title meant way more to him than it should have. The recognition had once validated him, but that was a long time ago. Now, he only wanted to play music.

He peeked out from backstage to see how many people were in the audience. Bodhi gave a thumb's up to indicate there was a good crowd. They had started communicating in code—thumbs up or down, head nods and shakes, shoulder shrugs and winks—after Jake developed stage fright a few years ago performing at an Indian Casino in Palm Springs. The gigs had always gone like clockwork. After the whole record industry had forgotten about Jake Wilder, he pulled himself up by the bootstraps and got back out there to sing the songs that made people happy. He waltzed on stage, struck the right chord, and sang. Song after song, the loyal fans still loved him.

That night, out of nowhere, everything went wrong. He stumbled when he came on stage. His throat went dry, and he forgot the lyrics to songs he had sung thousands of times. Collapsing after just two songs, he was rushed to the hospital. It turned out only to be the flu, but afterward, he questioned everything about himself as a performer. His once-natural talent became forced, and the inability to write or perform anything new, paralyzed him with fear.

As the audience size shrunk, the more nervous he became. He feared the intimacy. A smaller group of people could physically get closer to him. Could they see sometimes his right shoulder hurt from years of slinging a guitar or that his voice cracked on the high notes? The latter was hardly true since he practiced with his voice coach once a week and never touched a cigarette a day in his life.

He forced himself to look past Bodhi and his positive thumbs-up into the crowd of about fifty people standing in front of the stage at the Bakersfield Winter Festival. In the early-evening light, Jake watched the people gather on the small grassy field. Some of those people might even be his biggest fans with their children now in tow. The December California weather was warm enough for the band to comfortably perform outside.

Bodhi gave Jake the okay signal and stepped up to the microphone. "Ladies and gentlemen, put your hands together for the Jake Wilder Trio."

Jake inhaled, chanted a few self-affirmations, and casually walked on stage into the spotlight.

"Hello, Bakersfield," he said into the microphone. "How y'all doing tonight?"

A few people hollered in return. The energy was low. His breath shook. He nervously ran his hand through his hair. A woman in the front row whistled and yelled, "I love you, Jake Wilder."

He pointed to the audience. "Love you back."

"Ready?" He checked in with his bandmates.

The drummer, Mike, who he'd been playing with for the past few years, held his sticks poised and ready. Everybody called him Mikey the Meatball for his culinary abilities and love of Italian cooking. He and his wife practically catered all their gigs. Phil, a loyal friend and excellent bass player, was an original member of Jake's old band Beyond Millennium. Phil had gone out on his own after the band broke up but said he never found the same chemistry he had with Jake. They were like brothers, bonded in their rollercoaster experience of the rise and fall of fame.

He wrapped his fingers around the neck of the guitar. His arms felt clunky and stiff. Afraid to hit the wrong note, he closed his eyes and repeated the mantra, *this too shall pass*. The guys knew what was going on with him and learned to work with him to ease his stage fright. Nobody was in a rush. They kept the vibes mellow, but years of experience told them the show must go on. They had to start paying sooner or later.

"Ah one, two, three, four," Mike counted from behind the drum set.

Innately, Jake's body knew what to do. If he let himself go, playing became as natural as breathing. He strummed his guitar and sang to the small but adoring crowd below. They looked at him as if he could do no wrong. For a while, he also believed he was invincible. He only needed to understand he was capable. His talent hadn't abandoned him.

As he performed song after familiar song, the butterflies in his stomach subsided. An older couple embraced and danced. Arms on shoulders and hips, they faced each other and spun around like high-school students at a formal dance. The merriment caught on, and several couples followed suit.

Jake delighted in the moment. He'd come home.

The band played hard, and he offered to treat his bandmates to some classic carnival food afterward. His mouth watered envisioning his favorite, a deep-fried Twinkie. He'd have to run an extra mile the next day, but the time on stage had burned enough calories for him to earn the warm, crunchy and gooey treat. Escaping into the crowd would also allow him to avoid Bodhi. The entire drive up to the gig, he pressed Jake about the darn Christmas song. Bodhi asked fifty different ways whether Jake had come up with anything.

No! He had wanted to yell. *I haven't written anything new in years, and I don't know if I ever will.* Instead, he swallowed the unspoken words and said he was mulling over a few ideas.

There were plenty of old notebooks filled with music and lyrics. He recorded a few of the songs in his studio. At the height of his career, he installed a custom recording studio in his Hollywood Hills home. He was all set to cut a new album, but hired musicians failed to show up and people flaked on him left and right. At first, he thought he could make the album all by himself. Who needed hired musicians when he could play all the instruments? Bodhi even set up a meeting with one of the record labels. They practically laughed in Jake's face. Eventually he gave up.

Not only did he have zero inspiration to write a new song, the truth was he hadn't celebrated Christmas in years. He felt like a phony attempting to write a song about a holiday he avoided at all cost. Reveling in the season was fine for other people—those with families and children—but he was a loner. He preferred to escape to Hawaii or Miami, bury his head in the sand, literally, and wait for the celebrations to pass. He was the last person anyone would want to write a song that was supposed to become a classic.

After changing from his stage clothes into more comfortable jeans and a T-shirt, he put on a baseball cap and moved freely about the fairgrounds. Recognition didn't come his way all the time, but he was in a hurry to pick up the Twinkies and get back to the guys and wanted to avoid the interruption. Requests for autographs and selfies, while flattering, took up too much time.

He smelled the deep-fried confectionaries before he found the stand. A line of about twenty people waited to make their way to the window. Jake relaxed his shoulders and looked at his phone. There was a text from the *Has-Been House* producer. Annie said the house was filling up quickly. If he wanted a spot, let her know ASAP!

Delete—he clicked away the message. Bodhi already told Annie Jake wasn't interested. This put even more pressure on him to win the Christmas song challenge, and the worst part of all, he wasn't allowed to get help from the rest of the band. They wanted a Jake Wilder only creation.

A young couple waited in line in front of him. The guy put his arm around his girlfriend's shoulder. "Did you like the band?"

"They were okay. I remembered a couple of their songs."

"See, I knew you would." He removed his arm and faced her. "My older brother worshipped Beyond Millennium."

Jake hoped he wouldn't be recognized. He was all too happy to play the fly on the wall. To hear true fans talking about the old days was a real treat.

"He made me learn all the drum parts so he could play along on the guitar." The guy played an air-drum solo to demonstrate.

"You're silly." She kissed him on the cheek after he finished. "Don't you think—" She hesitated.

"What?" The boyfriend hung his once-drumming hands by his side. His forehead creased, as if he guessed what was coming next.

"The guy's kind of pathetic," she said.

Jake's stomach sank. The boyfriend looked like he took the insult as hard. Jake would leave the line if she elaborated any further but worried they might notice him. Instead, he froze—a deer in the headlights.

"I mean, like, has Jake Wilder written anything new in the past ten years?" The girlfriend played with her hair. "I don't think so." She pulled her phone from her purse and immersed herself in the glowing screen.

He marveled at how casually this stranger was able to obliterate his entire existence while she scrolled through Instagram.

"It doesn't matter what he's written lately." The boyfriend was intent on defending Jake's honor, and he was grateful. "He was a great artist."

"Key word: *was*." She slid her phone back into her purse. "And all those women screaming at him. That could've been my mom out there."

"Then your mom has good taste." The boyfriend crossed his arms.

"Let's not fight," said the girlfriend, snaking her arm around her boyfriend's waist. "Jake Wilder is amazing," she said. "Is that better?"

The boyfriend nodded. "Better."

Jake stepped out of line. Suddenly the smell of the deep-fried Twinkies made him sick. They were right. He was a has-been. If he didn't write something new, and *soon*, he wouldn't be able to look himself in the mirror.

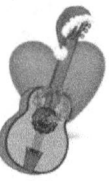

Chapter Five

Mackenzie hated to admit it, but she was lost. Even the vocal instructions from the map app on her phone proved useless as she wound her way through the Hollywood Hills. It didn't help the convertible top was down. The traffic noise drowned out the automated voice giving her directions, and she had clearly missed a turn along the way. The road was too narrow and busy to pull over so she could check her phone. There was also the map Kacey had so painstakingly drawn for Mackenzie. Kacey didn't want to give Mackenzie any excuse for missing her first meeting with Jake Wilder.

"He better be worth all this trouble," she said aloud to nobody.

She must change her attitude if she was going to accomplish anything productive. *No use going in with a closed mind.* She went over the plan again. First, she needed to find out the details of the contest. How many other artists were up for the job, and could Jake Wilder really pull it off? According to her research, he hadn't written anything new in some time. Based on his lack of radio airplay on stations that play current hits, she didn't need to do any more investigation. His better days were behind him.

Writing an original Christmas song was not going to be easy. Many of her favorite popstars put out their own version of Christmas hits, but to come up with something truly original seemed monumental. It might be pessimistic of her to wonder how someone like Jake could possibly win the contest. Even a popular singer would struggle against such odds. Worst of all, if he didn't win, would there be a story? She was good, but she was no magician. To pull something meaningful from thin air would be next to impossible.

She unclenched her jaw. The anxious downward spiral of her negative thoughts got the best of her again. The night before, she tossed and turned trying to come up with an angle. The only hope was her self-confidence, and that was starting to wear thin. She sat up straight. *If anyone can do it, you can.* She told herself this over and over. The affirmation might sink in sooner or later.

The traffic thinned as she drove higher into the hills. She breathed a sigh of relief and pulled to the side of the road. Sometimes she wished she drove a newer-model car. One with GPS and Bluetooth.

The classic Mercedes Benz convertible was a gift from her mother after graduation. It was the only expensive gift she would accept and satisfied her mother's need to spoil her daughter. Her mother didn't understand Mackenzie's desire to live modestly when she had access to a healthy trust fund left to her by her grandmother. Mackenzie wanted to make it on her own—a matter of pride only her father appreciated. He'd had a modest upbringing and worked extra hard to become a successful architect.

Kacey's map was hardly helpful as Mackenzie searched for any familiar landmarks she may have passed. It was pretty, that was for sure, but she couldn't find anything that told her where she was or how to get to Jake Wilder's house. She turned the map upside down.

"That won't help." A male voice came from the sidewalk.

A guy in shorts and a mustard-gold T-shirt stood next to her car. A baseball cap and sunglasses obscured his face, but she guessed he was somewhere in his thirties. He was tall and lean with nice teeth and wavy brown hair that brushed his shoulders. A beagle stood faithfully by his side.

"You look lost," he said.

"In more ways than one." Should she be talking to a complete stranger? She wasn't helpless, but a person can never be too careful.

"Can I help?" he asked.

He might offer the directions she needed badly, so she handed him the map. "Be my guest."

The dog whined. "It's okay, Peterkins. We'll get you home soon."

Peterkins. Mackenzie's heart melted. Growing up she begged her parents for a dog. They gave her a stuffed Snoopy dog instead. A beagle like Peterkins.

"Beautiful map. It's color-coded." He handed it back to her.

"My roommate made it for me. She's an artist." Kacey would be disappointed Mackenzie failed to properly follow the directions. The streets lined with trees and shrubs Kacey had so intricately drawn hadn't helped a bit.

"I know right where this is," he said. "You could follow me."

"Is it far?" she asked, unwilling to offer him a ride, but the idea of tailing him in her car for blocks was awkward.

"We're almost there." He patted Peterkins on the head. "Ready to go, boy?"

"So, how do you know Jake Wilder?" he asked, walking along her car.

"I don't." She supposed everybody in the neighborhood knew which celebrities lived where. "My newspaper's doing a story on him."

"That's interesting," he said. "Are you a reporter?"

"I am." He was probably going to ask her details about Jake's story. It wouldn't bother her much if he were nosy. Most outsiders wanted juicy celebrity gossip. The problem was she didn't have anything to tell.

"I'm sorry to hear that," he said. "I was starting to trust you."

Trust her? Where did that come from? He was the one wearing dark sunglasses and a hat so nobody could identify him in a police lineup.

"That's your mistake." She tried to remain calm. "You don't even know me."

"Reporters are all the same," he said under his breath.

Too bad for him she possessed excellent hearing. "And what's your problem with journalists?" She didn't appreciate the insult to her or her profession. Guys like him probably got their news from unreliable sources, which annoyed her to no end.

"Nothing," he said, unconvincingly. "You're okay, I suppose."

"You suppose?" She raised her voice. She couldn't help herself. If she wasn't so lost and late, she'd drive away and take her chances with Kacey's map.

He laughed. "Relax. I was only joking, but you have to admit, as soon as a person's down on his luck, if there's an accident or a fire, here come the reporters. "I mean... *journalists*," he said, mocking her title.

Mackenzie slammed the brakes. "Look buddy, I don't know who you are or what your problem is, but I do know I work hard and am very serious about my job. We're not a bunch of vultures, or whatever it is you're making all reporters out to be."

A car pulled up behind her, and the guy waved it around. He had a smile on his face, despite her obvious anger.

"And furthermore," she continued, her face growing hotter by the minute. "Where would you be without the news? For instance—" She searched for something relevant to say, but he made her so mad, she couldn't think straight. "There might've been rain in the forecast, and you're wearing shorts because you knew it would be 72 degrees and sunny thanks to your local weather report."

"This is southern California. It's always 72 degrees and sunny."

She considered balling up Kacey's map to throw at the guy. He was so infuriating. But that would be a waste of a good work of art.

"Or," Mackenzie remembered Kacey's words about the possible story she could pull from Jake Wilder's Christmas songwriting contest. "Sometimes we report profiles in courage—a heroic fireman or police officer. We may even write something about the down-and-out, underdogs, making a comeback."

"Underdogs?" He seemed to process that concept for a moment. "Look, I'm sorry," he said. "I've had a few bad experiences that have left me a bit jaded. Nothing personal."

To her, her job was *very* personal. She might've told him where he could go if she had more time. "Just because you have some kind of hang up, you don't have to smear my profession and the good people I work with." *Besides Ross.* But this guy didn't need to know the details. For the most part, everyone she worked with was honest and decent.

His shoulders slumped, and his head cocked to the side. For a moment, she couldn't get over how much he looked like a sorry puppy dog. Maybe because Peterkins was whining to get home.

"I'm sorry to get bent out of shape," he said. "It's hard for me to accept criticism when I'm only trying to create things of enduring value. To realize a vision. And the critics slam your work as mediocre."

Her stomach sank. Who exactly was this guy she was having an argument with in the middle of the street?

He checked his watch. "We better get going. You're late."

She hadn't told him what time the appointment was, had she? "How do you know when my appointment is?" She feared she already knew the answer.

The guy took off his hat and sunglasses. "I'm Jake Wilder. My cottage is around the corner."

~ * ~

If this was considered a *cottage*, her two-bedroom apartment was a shoebox in comparison. Mackenzie curved her way around the circular cobblestone driveway and parked in front of Jake Wilder's English Tudor revival. At least three chimney stacks jutted out from behind several steeply pitched roofs. The herringbone brickwork alone was gorgeous. A thatched-roof guest quarter sat right of the main house. Did somebody else live there? His housekeeper, maybe? Or perhaps he rented it out for extra income.

"That's my studio." He gestured toward the guesthouse.

Considering his career was on life support, she didn't think of him as an actual *recording* artist anymore.

"Don't look so surprised." He opened the front door to the main house. "I might have a few songs left in me after all."

If she were to give him a fair shake, she'd have to get rid of the negative assumptions. He was once a mega star and probably recorded his best hits in that studio.

Her face warmed again. This time from embarrassment rather than anger. Saying the interview started off on the wrong foot was the understatement of the year.

Peterkins barged past them, almost knocking Jake over on the way. The dog flopped on one of several Persian rugs. He yawned and let out a big sigh.

"Guess we overdid it," he said.

She laughed and stuck her hand out. "Can we start again? I'm Mackenzie Stone, reporter from *The Sunrise Press*."

He took her hand. "Nice to meet you, Mackenzie. Let me show you around, and we'll get started."

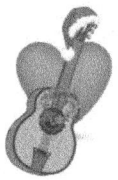

Chapter Six

"What an amazing view," said Mackenzie.

They were outside watching the busy metropolis go about its business. Buildings of all shapes and sizes dotted the horizon as far as the eye could see. Lines of traffic zigzagged through the streets. Everybody was in a hurry to make a deal somewhere in Los Angeles. She and Jake looked down from high on top of their perch.

He loved his home in the hills. At least he'd done *something* right by securing this retreat, a small slice of tranquility in an otherwise chaotic environment. He could write music or read books by the pool, indulging in more of the latter much to his manager Bodhi's chagrin. Sometimes the reading led to napping. Hours passed, and Jake hadn't accomplished anything productive.

"Is this a black-bottomed pool?" she asked. "It's gorgeous."

He put in the custom-designed pool after receiving his first check from the record company.

"You should see it at night." He hoped she didn't take the comment the wrong way. It wasn't like he was asking her out on a future nighttime date by his pool. "It reflects the city lights." He could kick himself for saying "City Lights" out loud. It sounded like he purposely referenced his most famous hit to impress her.

She didn't let on if she noticed. Wiggling out of her shoes, she stuck her foot in to test the water. "Warm."

"Next time we'll go for a swim." He seriously doubted Mackenzie Stone, uncompromising journalist, could ever let loose long enough for a swim with somebody she was profiling.

He reminded himself not to let his guard down. To her, he was a subject to scrutinize.

Jake squirmed like an insect under a microscope when he had given her a tour of the house when they first arrived. She had peppered him with questions about the contest. Namely, was he up for it? When he said *of course* in an overly enthusiastic way, she seemed skeptical. That made both of them.

"I'd love to." She slid her shoes back on. "I mean, sure. Maybe someday," she added, as if remembering why she was there, for business not pleasure. She tucked her hands into the pockets of her perfectly-tailored blazer.

"Honestly?" He expressed more surprise than he intended. Mackenzie seemed like a nice enough person but not his type at all. Attractive, yes, but he liked a more free-spirited woman. These relationships never resulted in anything serious, however. The women he dated always flitted right out of his life like the free birds they were.

Even one ex-girlfriend broke up with him on the way to the airport. She called to say she loved him but needed to find herself first. Unfortunately for him, that so-called *self* she was looking for resided in London. When he offered to meet her there, she admitted to falling for another man.

Mackenzie's shoulders tensed. "Why not? I like to swim as much as the next gal."

"How'd that happen?" He gestured toward her forehead to a tiny scar above her right eyebrow.

She touched her face. "Mountain biking. I hit a rock and went flying over the handlebars."

"Ouch." He was sympathetic but impressed. "That's why I like my bikes nice and stationary. No helmet necessary."

"I can't stand exercising indoors," she said. "I get bored so easily."

"I didn't take you for the outdoorsy type."

"I guess I'm full of surprises. I didn't take you for the wimpy type."

That hurt. He might've made too many false assumptions about her. She was getting even.

"Hey, who you calling wimpy?" He mockingly puffed out his chest and flexed his muscles.

"Impressive." She chuckled and tucked a loose strand of hair behind her ear.

"Who am I kidding?" he said. "You're right. These hands are for strumming musical instruments not pumping iron."

"I would think so. I heard you're pretty good at it."

"I'm okay." His ego needed more stroking lately. He didn't dare refute the compliment.

"Wait a minute," she said. "You're trying to derail me from my interview."

"Why would I do that?" Annoyed when Bodhi shared his so-called amazing idea to have the press cover Jake's possible comeback, he had been guilty of avoiding her. Writing a new song pressured him enough, let alone a Christmas song. He didn't need somebody dissecting his every move.

"Because you're afraid," she said. "But I believe there could be a great story here."

Jake felt empty inside. *If I were in her shoes, what would I write about me?*

He remembered something she said earlier. "I'm down-and-out making a comeback."

Her eyes glinted with hope. If he won the contest, he could make that comeback, and she'd be right on the money.

Earlier he read some of her articles and was impressed by her ability to humanize almost every story. Even reporting the lighter events like the opening of a bowling alley in downtown Pasadena became a reflection piece on hometown values and the need for human connection in today's world of social division and self-imposed loneliness.

"I have to admit. I don't know what the story will look like yet." After pausing a moment, she straightened her posture and put her hand over her heart. "I'll come up with something good. I promise."

If he could somehow see her as an advocate rather than an enemy, it would benefit both of them. He had to trust her. They were in it together now. He hoped they wouldn't regret their professional commitment to one another.

"Now take me to where the magic happens," she said.

Perplexed by her request, he scratched his head in contemplation. There had been an absolute lack of magic in his house for years. He froze, unsure where to go next.

"Your recording studio." She snapped her fingers in front of his face.

"Of course," he said, waking from his stupor. "That's the next stop on the tour."

They went back through the house and outside to the studio. Anxiety filled every part of him. Not many people were allowed in his sacred space—even he rarely entered. Metaphorical cobwebs awaited him in a place where he attempted to go everyday but found reasons not to.

The strong, pungent smell of sage greeted them as they crossed the threshold. The cleaning lady believed she could purify the space and help him overcome his writer's block with her ritualistic cleaning. She said something about changing the ionic composition of the air. It sounded a little too new-age for him, but he was up for anything.

"I've never been in a real recording studio." She gravitated toward the piano in the middle of the room.

"This is where it all begins." He followed but stopped short of sitting on the bench. *She might expect me to start writing the Christmas song right here and now.*

"You compose on the piano?" She pulled a pad of paper and pen from her purse. "I assumed you started with the guitar."

As she kicked into reporter mode, he reminded himself not to clam up. They needed to work together to succeed.

"A piano provides a richer environment for writing a song. It's easy to hear what sounds good, and I go from there adapting it to other instruments. Then I write the lyrics."

She jotted down something, as he forced himself to sit behind the piano and pluck out "Jingle Bells."

"C'mon, 'Jingle Bells'? Is that all you got?"

"What's your favorite?"

"'Winter Wonderland,' of course." She sat on the sofa and crossed her legs like she was sitting in front of a campfire.

He started playing. "Aren't you tired of Christmas songs yet?"

"You'd be surprised." She rocked back and forth. "It's Christmas music all the time for me now."

She snickered as he sang every other word to the song. Obviously, Christmas songs weren't his specialty.

"Sing along." He transitioned into a melody of other Christmas carols.

"No, you don't want to hear me sing." She waved her hands in protest. "Trust me. A guy I once dated said I might be tone deaf."

"That's not nice."

"No kidding." She pouted. "Practically scarred me for life. I only sing alone in the car and the shower."

He couldn't resist playing "Blue Christmas." He had listened to the Elvis Presley Christmas song again and again as he and his ex-fiancée planned their wedding. It was Samantha's favorite.

The painful memory jolted him back to reality. He would be happy to skip the month of December entirely. The irony he might be the artist selected to write a Christmas song was almost too much to bear. The holiday season made him too sad to celebrate and too hopeless to create.

She started to sing softly. Barely audible, but singing, nonetheless. He didn't want to react or she might stop because she hadn't realized she was singing in the first place. It would be like waking her from a pleasant dream.

He finished the song and closed the lid to the piano. "Is there anything else you want to know about the contest?" There was no use avoiding the nitty-gritty details any longer.

Jolting to attention, she sat upright and frantically patted the sofa. "I've misplaced my notepad."

"You got carried away in the music."

"Here it is." Fishing the pad of paper from between the cushions, she proceeded with the interview ignoring his last comment.

Winning her over was going to take way more effort on his part.

"From what I understand, the contest involves several retro artists." She studied Jake, perhaps to see how he'd take the term.

"Has-beens you mean." He corrected her.

"I was trying to be diplomatic about it," she said. "Besides, retro sounds—"

"Less pathetic?"

"Maybe."

Jake was surprised by her honesty, but he appreciated it in a town where he'd heard too many lies and false promises.

"Anyway," she continued. "Several *retro* artists have been selected to write a Christmas song and submit it to the record company who will choose one. The winner will debut it on a television Christmas special."

"That about covers it." Phrasing it so plainly made him wonder why he'd been worried in the first place. Chances were slim he'd win, but that pesky hopeful voice inside him kept rearing its annoyingly optimistic head. *What if my song won? That would change everything.*

"But that's only in a couple of weeks." A muscle in her jaw twitched. She looked panicked, which struck him as strange since he was the one with the deadline.

"I'm sure you've started it by now." Her shoulders slumped, the disappointment palpable. "I thought I could be in on the entire creative process."

"It wouldn't be that interesting from your perspective. It's boring. I tap out a few notes on the piano, drink lots of coffee, and jot down lyrics on any available piece of paper." He successfully avoided telling the truth that he hadn't even committed to doing it yet.

"What will be your inspiration? Have you always loved Christmas?"

"Oh, that isn't really the issue." He could see he was in trouble. Looking for motivation behind the song was dangerous territory. He'd have to reveal he was a phony. "I'm like anybody else."

Her brows knitted together. She wasn't buying his non-answer answer. "Care to elaborate?"

"Honestly, I find it a little overwhelming. It's become so commercialized. Christmas has lost its meaning." He hoped this cliché would satisfy her and prepared himself for another question. Instead, she waited for him to continue.

"You know what I mean?" he asked, dying for an out.

She shook her head. "Lost meaning for everybody else or you?" She wasn't going to make this easy for him.

"I suppose I could fall into that category." He felt like a politician scrambling to think of ways not to answer her questions directly.

"I see," she said, writing in her notepad. "So I don't misquote you. What you're saying is, you don't like Christmas?"

"That's not what I'm saying," he said. She had it exactly right, but he needed to spin it. "It's the commercialization I don't care for."

"But you want to win this contest so you can sell your song?"

Open mouth, insert foot. He was blowing it and sounded like a jerk to boot. "Let me start again," he said. "Some of my favorite musicians have made Christmas albums. What I'm trying to say is I've never enjoyed celebrating Christmas, but I respect those who do and want to add my voice to the festivities."

He bounced his leg, nervous she'd get to the truth. Writing a Christmas song was the last thing he should do.

"Hmmm." She took some more notes. "That's inspiring."

She didn't mind inserting her opinion. He thought reporters were supposed to stay objective. "Does it matter whether I love Christmas or not? It's about reaching the audience and getting *them* to love Christmas."

"Sorry to be so naïve." She sighed. "When I sing along to my favorites, I imagine the musicians are happy to be right there with me embracing the holiday spirit."

He was exhausted and exasperated. Writing a song didn't always come with so much baggage. "Well," he said as he stood up. "I guess I better get to work."

She gathered her things. "I'm looking forward to hearing your song anyway."

"Yeah, me too," he said. He escorted her to the door.

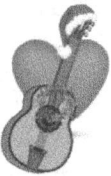

Chapter Seven

Mackenzie typed furiously. If she didn't send the email immediately to Mr. Hughes, he might assign the story to Ross.

She called Mr. Hughes again. He didn't answer. Sending a text message was out of the question since he owned the last flip phone in America and refused to pay extra for texting and data.

A local councilman had just been indicted for insider trading. Apparently, he sat on the committee of a tech company that lost its funding and was going belly up. He sold his stocks immediately and advised the rest of his family to do the same before the news was announced to the shareholders.

Her paper would cover this story and give her a chance to prove herself. This byline would be an important addition to her resume and a boost to her career.

"Knock knock." Kacey hovered in Mackenzie's bedroom doorway eating a giant chocolate chip cookie.

"You're a wonder of science," she said. "Eating anything you want without gaining an ounce. I hate you."

"Love you too." Kacey wiped her hand on a pair of purple pants smeared with blue and green paint. "Wanna bite?"

"No thanks. I'm trying to cut out sweets"

"Why?" Kacey licked her lips.

"Because I'm cleaning up my act."

"Okay, that's weird." Her face scrunched up in disbelief. "Are you working on something?"

"I hope so." An email arrived from Mr. Hughes. "Give me a sec." Mackenzie scanned through the response and sighed. He assigned the story to a freelance writer. Some big shot from the city who promised Mr. Hughes he had connections and could get exclusive details.

She closed her laptop. "I'll take some of that cookie now."

Kacey broke the cookie in half and sat on the edge of

Mackenzie's bed. Under normal circumstances, she would've scolded Kacey for getting paint all over the bedspread, but Mackenzie didn't have the energy. She was tired of fighting the uphill battle with Mr. Hughes and couldn't rely on him to help her score that big story she so desperately needed.

The cookie was perfect. Just the comfort food she needed. Kacey waited patiently for Mackenzie to finish eating.

"What's up your sleeve?" She could tell Kacey wanted something by the way she was tidying up Mackenzie's bedroom. Her friend could barely put away her own clean laundry let alone fold someone else's.

"Nothing. Can't I help out a friend without her getting all suspicious on me?" Her smile looked duplicitous to Mackenzie. Sweet and devious all at the same time.

"Spill it."

"I talked to Bodhi today."

"Jake's manager?" Mackenzie tilted her head. Kacey never interfered with her stories. Something wasn't right.

"He sounds cute. I *love* British accents."

Mackenzie relaxed. It only had to do with a guy. They were always throwing themselves at Kacey. She humored the lucky ones with a date or two then let them down easily by saying she was way too busy breaking into the art world to make a serious commitment.

"He called to see if you wanted to watch Jake perform tonight," she said. "I sort of invited myself along too."

"He called on our landline?"

"Apparently we're listed in the directory."

Mackenzie planned to go to one of Jake's upcoming gigs. It would be good for the story, but she hoped she'd be too busy writing a more important story, like the one about the indicted councilman. Besides, if she wanted to see the Jake Wilder Trio perform, there were plenty of videos on YouTube.

"He wants you to see Jake in action. Bodhi's afraid of what you might say in your story." Kacey gave up on putting Mackenzie's clothes away and rifled through her closet instead.

"I only write the truth." That was going to be a challenge considering Jake's unwillingness to share everything with her. He kept his cards close.

"That's exactly what worries him." Kacey held a black dress up to her body and examined herself in the mirror.

"Yes, you can borrow it." Mackenzie knew Kacey wanted to wear the dress to Jake's gig. When she put her mind to something, there was no use fighting it.

Mackenzie resigned herself to going. *It's not like I have a pressing deadline and important story to cover.* The corrupt city councilman feature was another line she wouldn't be putting on her resume.

Kacey handed the dress to Mackenzie. "You're wearing it."

"No, thank you." She pushed the slinky dress away. "This is not a social occasion, and I don't want Jake getting the wrong idea."

"You are wearing it, and you'll look fantastic. Don't tell me you're gonna wear one of your serious reporter outfits."

"Maybe." Mackenzie had pondered a dark pantsuit.

"Plus, when you look great, you'll feel great."

"We'll see."

"Trust me on this. I'm right, and you know it." Kacey bounced out of the room.

"You got paint on my bedspread," Mackenzie yelled after her.

~ * ~

"I can't believe his band is playing at a corporate party." Kacey pressed her lips together and shook her head in disapproval. "Isn't that like selling out?"

"Hey, you're the one who wanted to come." Mackenzie tugged the short, tight dress down her thighs. The fact Kacey talked Mackenzie into wearing it only proved how persuasive her best friend was.

"I wanted to go to one of the cool music venues in the city, not the Sheraton near the airport."

"You should've cleared that up with your best friend Bodhi."

Kacey intercepted a waitress carrying a tray of sliders. "I'll take one of those."

"We're not guests." Mackenzie was mortified and nervous they'd be called out for crashing the party. She snagged a napkin from the tray. Kacey always made a mess.

"Excuse me, one little hamburger is not going to break the bank."

If Mackenzie wasn't afraid of making a scene, she might've engaged in the bickering they'd become famous for. Kacey's mom said they reminded her of an old married couple.

"Never mind," Mackenzie said. "Let's find Bodhi."

Kacey flashed one of her megawatt smiles and waved at someone standing by the buffet. "There he is."

The guy waving back was gorgeous. Tall with thick, dark hair, just Kacey's type. *Anyone's type really.*

"Is that Bodhi?"

"Yep," Kacey said without taking her eyes off him. She was obviously smitten, and Mackenzie couldn't blame her.

"How do you know that's him?"

"I have a sense for these things," said Kacey. "Do I have lipstick on my teeth?" She faced Mackenzie.

"Nope, just a huge piece of lettuce stuck in between your two front teeth."

Kacey panicked as she frantically searched her handbag for a compact mirror. "I'm going to kill you," she said, examining her perfectly clean teeth.

"He texted you his picture, didn't he?" Mackenzie wasn't sure how Kacey managed it, but guys became putty in her hands. She probably asked him to send a picture, and he spent an hour getting the right shot.

"You want a good story, don't you? Everybody knows the first step in getting close to an artist is to cozy up to the management." Kacey spoke with such authority, Mackenzie wondered if her expertise came from experience and pictured Kacey hobnobbing with agents and public relations people all over Los Angeles. A secret double life she maintained while Mackenzie let all the great stories slip through her hands.

"Trust me for once in your life," said Kacey. "I know what I'm doing."

She didn't have time to find out the details of Kacey's insider industry knowledge because Bodhi was on his way over. Kacey probably envisioned him floating in slow motion. The handsome stranger meeting the girl of his dreams.

"Glad you could make it." He held out his hand to her. She tilted her head in the same flirty way Mackenzie had seen many times before.

She repressed the urge to remind them both she was there on business. This kind of nonsense only interfered with the story she was supposed to write. Though it didn't seem right to get all sanctimonious when they were trespassers at a corporate party sponsored by a company she'd never heard of.

Once the guests had eaten and the food cleared away, the master of ceremony, a boisterous man of about fifty, took the stage. She guessed he was some mid-level manager. Someone in the company might've said, "Bill's got a great personality, let's give him the microphone."

Bad idea. He told one corny joke after another.

Bodhi approached the front of the room. She hoped he'd intervene and get the show rolling, imagining Jake on the side of the stage waiting patiently... or not so patiently. What was he thinking? She made a mental note to ask later.

Before Bodhi had a chance to make it to the front, the Jake Wilder Trio came on stage. A group of women rushed to the front. Kacey grabbed Mackenzie's hand and pulled her toward the crowd. They pushed their way forward. She wasn't sure why they needed to be so close until her friend screamed and hollered like a dedicated, life-long fan.

The band started with their hit, "City Lights." Some of the women practically lost it. Even Kacey spread her arms wide and belted out the lyrics.

His music lifted Mackenzie's mood. She sang along with the crowd and let go of all her inhibitions. The other night she listened to his old albums and recognized how great he had been. His songs were mostly about love lost and found again or love lost forever only to be replaced by a deeper understanding of one's self and human nature.

A music professor once told her we never grew tired of the songs we loved because they tapped into a shared heritage of human experience. Whatever the reason, everybody around her buzzed with so much energy, as if they'd all experienced painful break-ups, and the songs made them feel less alone.

Jake caught her eye and winked at her. Her stomach fluttered. Was she attracted to him? He wore slim black jeans, a white crew T-shirt, and a casual navy blazer that hugged his body. His hair looked freshly cut with a bit of length left on the top and sides so it moved with him as he strung his guitar. How had she missed his charisma before?

The first time they met, he made her so angry all she could see was an adversary. Now as he grooved to the music, he seemed different to her. The less-guarded and vulnerable Jake Wilder was the person she needed to capture for her article.

After the show, she was exhausted from dancing. It had been too long since she'd been to a good concert, even if the show was technically a corporate sponsored party.

Bodhi tossed Jake a bottle of water when he came out to the lobby where they'd been waiting for him.

"What a great show." Kacey's eyes glittered like a star-struck groupie. "I've already got hundreds of likes on my Instagram post." She held her phone up to Jake so he could see the selfie she had taken with him in the background.

"Wow," he said, squinting at the picture.

Mackenzie could tell he was merely being polite by the way he raked his hand through his hair. That seemed to be his tell. A gesture he did when he was holding something back or even distracted.

"What did you think?" he asked Mackenzie.

"Amazing," she said, and she meant it. "You made every song seem so fresh, as if they were brand new."

Bodhi laughed nervously. She hoped she didn't say something wrong. The truth was their songs were old, but maybe she didn't have to be so blunt.

"The concert was so good. You were perfect," she added, attempting to erase the insensitive comment. "Everybody loved it."

"Even you?" Jake asked.

"Especially her." Kacey pushed Mackenzie forward like a stage mother trying to get her child noticed by a Hollywood casting director.

She hung her head and felt silly, even a bit shy. She was a reporter, darn it, and Jake was nothing more than a celebrity she was profiling.

"I can't wait to hear your Christmas song," said Kacey. "Did you know Mackenzie is a Christmas song aficionado? In fact, she loves absolutely everything about Christmas. Every year after Thanksgiving, she turns our apartment into the North Pole. I can barely navigate the living room without stepping on a tiny porcelain villager."

Mackenzie crossed her arms over her chest. Jake and his manager did not need the intimate details of her life.

"I had no idea." Jake grinned.

The whole conversation made her uncomfortable. "Jake hates Christmas."

The group went quiet.

There I go again. She would have to remember to count to three every time she had a thought.

"He does not," said Bodhi.

Jake's jaw clenched. "What I said is I don't like the commercializing of it. Oh, never mind." He threw up his hands. "Guilty as charged, but I'm working on the song."

She wasn't sure she believed him.

Kacey's face lit up. "I've just had the best idea."

"I thought I saw smoke coming out of your ears."

She ignored Mackenzie and continued, "Since Christmas isn't Jake's thing, and it's totally Mackenzie's, why doesn't she help write the song?"

Mackenzie practically doubled over with laughter. "Yeah, right. 'Cause I know nothing about songwriting in case that matters to anyone."

He studied her. "You do *love* Christmas. That's a start."

"You can forget it right now because that is never going to happen," she said, mortified at the idea.

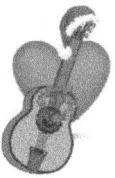

Chapter Eight

Bodhi picked a Starbucks near Kacey's apartment. He didn't want her stuck in traffic only to arrive late and grumpy. The meeting was too important. If Jake only understood the distance Bodhi went to assure his client's success. All morning he worked on his charm offensive. He wasn't the suavest guy in the world and became anxious around someone as beautiful and captivating as Kacey.

After the show at the Sheraton last night, he texted her to see what she thought. She was thrilled by Jake's performance, but Mackenzie still wasn't convinced he could write a Christmas song, especially under such a tight deadline. That negative attitude was exactly what Bodhi sought to change.

He ordered a chai tea for Kacey and a grande house blend for himself. She struck him as the type to enjoy tea. Artsy, smart, and sophisticated. Maybe she was a heath fanatic. He panicked. Should he have ordered something with less sugar? He'd blown it already.

She breezed in twenty minutes late. Her long, dark hair was twisted around a flowing blue scarf. She wore her jeans rolled up and flip flops on her feet. Her bare toes revealed several stacked toe rings. It may have been December, but she looked like she'd come from the beach.

"Was the traffic bad?" He'd chosen the place specifically because there wouldn't be any on the way but wanted to give her the benefit of the doubt.

"Not at all." She casually dropped her sunglasses into her purse. "I cruised over in a few minutes."

He fought the urge to ask why she was so late and reminded himself not to start out with accusations and tension.

"Thanks for coming," he said instead. "I hope you don't mind I texted you last night." He didn't want her to think he'd overstepped any boundaries.

"I'm a night owl. Besides, I'm used to it."

What does that mean? He guessed she had her fair share of guys calling and texting. There was no denying she was a catch.

"May I?" She removed the lid from the tea and inhaled.

"It's a chai tea."

"Perfect." She blew on the steaming drink before taking a sip.

"I'm glad you enjoyed the show last night?" he said. "Jake was thrilled to see you both."

"I had so much fun." She brushed a loose hair from her face. "Jake Wilder is awesome."

Now, if she could only convince Mackenzie of the same. "Jake's too humble to ever admit this, but he could easily win this Christmas song competition."

"You're a tad overconfident."

"I believe in him, that's all." Bodhi took another sip of his coffee. This was his third cup of the morning. He'd have to cool it if he didn't want her to think he was a jittering, nervous wreck.

"I'm no expert," she said, "but isn't writing a new Christmas song kind of hard? Most of the ones I hear on the radio are covers. Today's popstars singing the same songs from the 1940s and 50s."

"No doubt, that's the challenge. But if you knew Jake the way I do, you'd see he has it in him." What he left out was Jake had forgotten what he was capable of accomplishing. Over the years, his confidence tanked. There were only a few people, Bodhi one of them, who still believed in the magic of Jake Wilder.

Kacey looked wistfully out the front window. They were on a busy street. Cars whooshed by and dozens of people walked briskly past on the sidewalk. "I wish I had somebody believe in me the way you do in Jake. It's sweet."

He appreciated the compliment. "Mackenzie mentioned you have a solo exhibit coming up. *Somebody* must believe in you and your work," he said, imagining Kacey painting in a studio filled with loud music. Maybe she wore a beret and drank red wine. He shook the image from his mind. What an obvious stereotype.

Her face lit up. "It does feel good to have a gallery represent my work, and I can relate to Jake. It's easy to have doubts when you're making art. On one hand, you're creating only for yourself, but on the other, you seek approval, or at least acknowledgement, from an audience. It's easy to get stuck in a vicious circle of caring and not caring about what everyone thinks."

He appreciated how upfront she was about her emotions. Few artists copped so readily to their insecurities. He tried to be a good manager and friend to Jake. His job included booking gigs, but it also meant supporting Jake when he endured rejection. Cheering him up when nobody would book the band. Or encouraging him to go on stage when he developed stage fright.

"I hope Mackenzie understands the doubts artists can have."

"Mackenzie and I support one another. That's for sure, but we don't interfere with each other's work. She doesn't tell me what to paint, and I don't tell her what to write."

"I didn't mean to insinuate anything." Bodhi tried to be subtler. "I thought you, as an artist, might be able to express the whole insecurity issue to her."

Kacey's eyes narrowed.

He feared she'd leave unless he changed the subject fast. "Are you a dog person or a cat person?" It might not have been the most clever question to ask, but it was the first thing that came to mind.

"What kind of silly question is that?" Her face scrunched like he was speaking Martian.

"Dog or cat? Which one?"

"Pig," she said.

"You can't have a pig as a pet," he said.

"Who said anything about a pet? But yes, you can have a pet pig. Once when I was in Hawaii, I saw woman walking her pig on a leash. I'd get one today if my apartment allowed pets."

Was she messing with him?

"They're very clean animals," she continued.

"Okay, enough about pigs." She'd beaten him at his own game.

"You didn't ask me to meet you for coffee so we can talk about dogs or cats," she said. "So, what gives?"

~ * ~

From the moment Kacey received the text from Bodhi last night, she suspected he was up to something. While he struggled to answer her question, she sized him up.

He was great looking. No question about that. She imagined he had plenty of practice sweet-talking women.

Not this girl. She figured she'd meet him for coffee, but she would never let him use her as a way to get to Mackenzie. *Could he make it more obvious?* And the sad thing was, he thought he was being so smooth about it.

"Honestly," Kacey said. "I grew up with cats, but I love both." She threw him a bone, so to speak, and answered his ridiculous question.

He glanced around the store, as if he might find his next subject somewhere in the bins of Starbuck's paraphernalia for sale. "I only want to make sure Mackenzie's article takes a positive spin on Jake. Is it so bad a friend looking out for another?"

Kacey considered this. She'd do anything for Mackenzie, and Mackenzie would do the same. "I guess not."

"See," he said. "I'm not so bad." He produced a sheet of paper from his backpack and slid it to her. "Here's a bullet-pointed list of Jake's career highlights. I was thinking you could pass it along to Mackenzie."

"Seriously?" Kacey wanted to stand and leave. He had a lot of nerve. "Why don't you give this to her yourself?"

"I thought it might be too much coming from me. I don't want to unfairly influence the piece."

"You want *me* to instead?" She glanced at the list. If one overlooked the giant ten-year gap, she had to admit, his résumé was impressive.

"If you don't mind."

She pushed the list back. "I do mind. If your boy Jake can't deliver, there's nothing I can do about it." Bodhi was getting on her last nerve. This guy couldn't be any less interested in her. Not that she needed to be the center of attention, but she didn't like being used either.

"You're right." He tucked the piece of paper into his pocket. "I'm sorry. This is an extremely big deal for us, and if Jake fails, I'm afraid it'll be the end of his career."

"No more gigs at the Airport Sheraton?" The question sounded more sarcastic than she intended.

"Believe it or not," Bodhi said. "That was an important show for us. Corporate gigs pay well."

"We're in Los Angeles, for crying out loud. You'd think Jake could sustain a career playing his old hits."

"It's not like it used to be," he said. "Most clubs make the bands buy tickets to their own gigs. If they want to recoup the money, they have to find their own audiences to sell the tickets to. We've been lucky, but I'm afraid even that's coming to an end."

Jeez." She wondered how clubs were able to book so many musicians. The reality was the musicians were paying to be there. "Clubs charge musicians? What a racket."

He sighed. "It's tough. I'm afraid I'll have to find some new clients to represent or leave the profession all together."

His obvious frustration caused her to soften her tone. "How did you become a manager, anyway?" She could use one herself, but such a role didn't really exist in the fine art world.

"A lot of teenage boys fantasize about playing in bands. I used to play a mean air guitar."

"Girls too. I sang into my hairbrush every morning when I got ready for school. Drove my brothers crazy." She could hear them pounding away at the bathroom door trying to get her out so they wouldn't be late for school.

"I did that too. I had absolutely no talent, though. My parents gave me guitar lessons, but I was terrible no matter how hard I tried."

"I know what you mean." She wasn't the best singer, but unfortunately for anybody around her, she loved to belt out the lyrics.

"But I was good at math, accounting, anything in the area of business and economics," Bodhi continued. "My parents thought I would go on to be some rich hedge fund manager. Boy, they were disappointed."

"But there was the love of music?"

"Right." He flapped his hands, as if he were amped from too much caffeine, but she enjoyed his enthusiasm, nonetheless.

"I figured out how I could merge the two when I saw Jake performing at the House of Blues for the first time."

"That's how you met?" She loved hearing stories of discovery and fame.

"Jake was this awkward nineteen-year old. I wasn't much older or any less awkward, but I wasn't on stage trying to woo an audience. Anyway, he would barely look up from his guitar. He had the most beautiful voice, and the songs… They weren't polished yet, but they had potential."

"And the rest is history." The story was a nice one, but she wasn't swayed enough to interfere with Mackenzie's work. It would be up to Jake to convince her he was worthy enough for a positive profile.

"Jake's a great guy. Talented, smart, and generous."

"I'm sure Mackenzie will see all that. She's the ultimate professional, and always fair in telling her stories."

Bodhi sloshed his coffee around in the cup. Kacey wondered if he even liked coffee. The idea he got her there under false pretenses—a real date—annoyed her all over again. She was ready to leave when he stood up from the table.

"Excuse me a minute." He reached into his backpack and pulled out a large plastic baggie. Inside was a roll of quarters, a toothbrush and toothpaste kit, shampoo, a razor, a pair of socks, and a few granola bars.

He approached a man sitting at a nearby table. Judging by the bags of clothes on the floor, he looked homeless.

"Here you go, brother." Bodhi handed the man the large plastic baggie.

They shook hands, and the man said he was grateful. He

explained how he'd recently lost his job and was trying to get back on his feet.

When Bodhi returned, he said, "So, where were we?"

"That was kind of you," she said. Only a minute before, she had been ready to hate him again.

"What?" He didn't seem to expect her to make a big deal over what he'd done, which made him even more honorable in her eyes.

"You always carry that stuff with you?"

"Just in case. Gotta do my part."

Her heart soared. He was a good guy after all.

"Now, about Mackenzie. How can we get her to write something positive about Jake?"

She threw her hands up. "You're incorrigible."

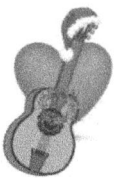

Chapter Nine

Jake waited on a bench outside, hoping the rain would hold off until they were at least inside a store. Had it been such a good idea to invite Mackenzie to meet him at the outdoor shopping promenade? She wanted to do another face-to-face interview before the deadline, just over a week away, and the last place he wanted to talk was his studio. She'd probably ask to listen to the demo. He may have *accidently* let her believe the song was finished. Without intending to lie, he let her assume he must be wrapping up by now. The misunderstanding was easy to pull off. He simply didn't respond to most of her emails.

Really, his non-reply was more like a lie of omission, which he justified was better than an outright lie. He imagined his fifth-grade teacher Mrs. Morris, hands on hips, chastising him for knowing better. A lie was a lie.

The promenade was decorated like a Christmas wonderland. A large Christmas tree towered at the front entrance and greeted shoppers as they passed. Light posts were draped with holiday banners wishing all a happy holiday season. Lights twinkled and danced to everyone's delight. The enchanted environment was sure to soften Mackenzie to his cause.

At first Kacey's suggestion Mackenzie help with the songwriting sounded ludicrous. How could a reporter, the *enemy* he believed most journalists to be, help with the biggest challenge of his life? Her disdain for his humbug attitude was clear. In her mind, he might as well be Ebenezer Scrooge. When it came to Jake Wilder, her Christmas spirit froze like an icicle. She was not going to help him if he was insincere. She made that plenty clear.

He was lost in making plans to win Mackenzie over when he noticed her heading his way. She was carrying a Starbucks cup.

"Sorry I'm late," she said.

"None for me?" He gestured to the single cup in her hand.

"Hope you like cream and sugar." She handed him the coffee. "I've already had mine."

"Thank you." He took the coffee, embarrassed he might have seemed ungrateful when he was only teasing. His hand shook as he sipped.

What was it about Mackenzie Stone that made him so unsure of himself? It was as if she could tell he continually hid behind a wall of half-truths. He only wanted to be his best around her, and concealing his flaws was necessary if he were going to make a good impression. Nobody was interested in the real Jake Wilder.

"You mentioned something about buying your niece a birthday present? Should we walk and talk?" she asked.

The sternness in her voice alerted him she wanted to get right to business.

"There's a toy store down the way." He gathered his jacket from the bench, careful not to spill the coffee. He'd have to discreetly dispose of it as they walked by a trash bin since he'd already drank his share of caffeine for the day.

It started to rain lightly. She picked up her pace. "Not a good day for outdoor shopping."

He opened his compact umbrella and held it over her. "Good thing I'm prepared. I read the weather report today. Did you?" he teased.

The corners of her mouth turned up. "85% chance of rain."

To his relief, she remembered their first conversation where she tried to convince him of the importance of staying informed.

She motioned for him to come under the umbrella. "I don't bite."

"Are you sure?" He was probably on thin ice, as he hadn't proved to be the most corporative subject.

"Only when provoked." She raised an eyebrow. "Like when someone avoids answering my questions."

He ducked underneath the umbrella. "Will you give me another chance?"

"Depends."

He practically ran to keep up with her. "On?"

"I want complete honesty."

"You don't ask for much." He wanted to disappear on the spot. In his mind, the deal was to write the song and make the comeback. Baring his soul hadn't been part of the arrangement.

She stepped into a big puddle of water, soaking the bottom of his brand new jeans. Had she done it on purpose?

"All right," he conceded. "Total transparency from here on out."

"That's what I thought." She smirked and handed him back his umbrella.

Once in the toy store, she headed straight for the aisle filled with dolls and Barbie's. "I imagine like most girls your niece is obsessed with princesses."

"I'm disappointed in you." He pursed his lips and mustered the best Mrs. Morris matronly-teacher expression he could.

"What?" Her eyes went round. She might be outspoken, but it appeared Mackenzie Stone didn't like to let people down.

"Of all people, I thought a strong career woman like yourself wouldn't make such assumptions." He couldn't resist playing her a bit longer. "As it happens, my niece wants to work at NASA. Ever since I took her to see the movie *Hidden Figures*, it's all she talks about."

"You're right. I stand corrected," she said. "So, what are you thinking? A rocket science kit or a telescope? Or even a planetarium projector?"

"A planetary what?" He was lost in the jargon.

"You don't have a clue what I'm talking about." She shook her head. "And you were the one who was disappointed in me."

Jake threw his arms in the air. "Hey, I'm just a music guy."

Even calling himself that was a stretch these days. An amazing opportunity practically presented itself to him on a silver platter, and he hadn't even started. He'd gone to the studio several times the past week and tried to come up with something. Anything. His recycle bin was full of balled up paper to prove his efforts amounted to nothing.

They finally found the science-based toys in the middle aisle of the store.

"This is a planetarium projector." Mackenzie pointed to the box on the shelf. "I had one when I was a kid."

"Perfect." The gift could've easily been ordered online and sent to his niece, but shopping in-person with Mackenzie was so much better. Besides, he wouldn't know a planetarium projector from a disco ball.

As they made their way up to the cashier, she asked, "Have you thought about what you might do if your song isn't selected as the winner?"

"I appreciate the confidence."

"I'm a realist," she said. "I like to plan for all possibilities, and you'd be smart to do the same."

He brushed off her reprimanding tone. "Let's imagine I write a winning song." He inhaled and tried to work up the courage to convince her to help him with the competition. "It could be possible with your passion for Christmas. You'll be my muse, maybe even toss out a few festive lyrics here and there."

She was already shaking her head before he could go on. "First of all, I have no musical experience."

"That doesn't matter." He sounded desperate but couldn't afford to care at this point. "I only need your Christmas spirit and enthusiasm."

"Plus, it would be completely unprofessional if I became part of the story." She was unmoved. "I'm profiling *you*, remember?"

"Do you mind a minute?" he asked the cashier who waited patiently as he continued his campaign.

"I understand your concerns." His scalp prickled with shame. Winning wasn't worth losing his dignity. "You can't possibly help when you're supposed to maintain an objective distance."

"Exactly," she said. "Besides, you're so talented, you don't need me."

He was stunned. Was she actually complimenting him again? "Thanks," he said. "It was my famous hair flip at the Sheraton that won you over."

"Nah, Kacey told me I had to be nice to you because you were a legend."

"Now I feel about 150 years old." He grabbed at his chest like she'd broken his heart.

"You know what I mean."

"I'm afraid I don't, but you can make it up to me by sprinkling some Christmas fairy dust on me."

"It's something you can't force. Either you have it, or you don't." She eyed him suspiciously.

He definitely didn't have it. "You're being stingy."

Her phone rang before she could respond. "Hello," she answered, as she disappeared down one of the aisles.

"I'm going to write the most Christmassy Christmas song you've ever heard," he called after her.

As he paid for the projector, he thought for a moment she might be talking to her boyfriend. He scolded himself for caring. Her personal affairs were none of his business. She was entitled to privacy. Only she'd never mentioned a significant other while she felt free to pepper him with questions about his life. This intrusion was the price he'd pay if he wanted to return to the spotlight. Everybody wanted the intimate details of his life, but he was expected to remain aloof and uninterested in others.

She came out of the store, a worried expression on her face.

"Everything all right?" Again, he held the umbrella above her. The rain poured on them even harder than before.

"Do you mind if we reschedule?" She already had her car keys in hand.

"Is there anything I can do?"

"My sister's been in a car accident with my nephew at our family home in Lake Arrowhead. She says they're fine—a few bumps and scrapes—but I need to drive up there to see if I can help."

"I completely understand," he said. "But this weather…"

They both looked up at the dark sky. Thunder crashed in the distance.

"I'll be careful," she said. "My parents are out of town, so I'm all Abby and her son have right now."

He pictured Mackenzie racing up the wet, curvy mountain road in her tiny convertible. She was too determined to be dissuaded, and the weather wasn't letting up anytime soon.

"Let me take you." He had planned to spend the rest of the day fully concentrating on writing the song, but what the heck. He wouldn't be able to work if he was worrying about her anyway.

"My knight in shining armor?" She looked at him skeptically.

She was so infuriating. "No," he said. "Just a guy with an SUV."

"Fair enough. We can be up and down the mountain in no time."

The terrible weather report had been all over the television. Storm watchers were scattered across Southern California waiting for the biggest winter storm of the season.

"Sure," he said. "I'll pick you up at your place in an hour."

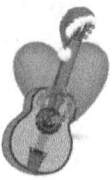

Chapter Ten

By the look of awe on Jake's face, Mackenzie realized she should've prepared him for the opulence of her family's Lake Arrowhead home. On the ride up, he had asked if the cabin was near the lake. She said yes, failing to mention the estate was more like a 3,800-square foot luxury log cabin *on* the lake.

He whistled when he got out of the SUV. "Some place. Didn't you call it *cozy* on the way up? I pictured a little two-bedroom cabin. Not this chalet."

"It's my parents' house," she snapped, sounding more defensive than she intended.

She didn't want him to think she was a spoiled princess incapable of taking care of herself. People made assumptions about her life based on her family's wealth. Some even asked why she bothered with a career. They believed she worked at the newspaper because she was bored, not that she needed a job or wanted to be a successful, important journalist.

"Either way, it's not too shabby," he said.

It took about two hours to get to Lake Arrowhead. The traffic was light despite the bad weather, and they quickly wound their way up the two-lane windy road to the San Bernardino Mountain community. The fact that in California a person could drive from the Pacific Ocean, the farthest point on the western continent, to a quant mountain village in an afternoon never ceased to amaze her. She appreciated her home state, but if a newspaper on the east coast hired her, she'd go in a New York minute.

She spent most weekends in the mountains as a child until weekends turned to summer then Christmas breaks only. Her father, a well-known architect, designed the house. It and the surrounding community reminded her of her parents. They spent most of their time abroad now, and she missed them. A certain longing hit Mackenzie on the rare occasion she visited the mountain house. She pictured their afternoons fishing on the lake in the summer or sledding down the snowy hills in wintertime.

By the time they reached the foothills, the rain had stopped, but the day was chilly. Almost near freezing. She zipped up her jacket. "It might snow," she said, steering the subject away from the lavish house. Though once inside, Jake would be impressed once again.

"I hope so." He removed a sock hat from his jacket pocket and pulled it over his head.

His floppy brown hair covered his eyes. She missed seeing his warm hazel eyes. The affection she felt for him startled her, and she quickly pushed it from her mind.

He hadn't noticed her momentary lapse of judgement. A weak heart wasn't going to get him the song he needed or the story she desired.

She imagined Kacey rubbing her hands together in sheer delight. The nosy little matchmaker had teased Mackenzie back at the apartment as she waited for Jake to pick her up.

"Admit it," Kacey had said, peeking out the window. "There's chemistry between you two. I know about these things."

"You ought to," Mackenzie said. "The girl who leaves a trail of broken hearts behind."

She brushed Kacey off, but Mackenzie had a nagging feeling her friend was on to something. She started tuning in to classic rock stations waiting for a song by Beyond Millennium. If they played "City Lights," her heart skittered as she imagined Jake singing directly to her.

"Brrr." He shivered.

She snapped back to reality. "It's beautiful when it snows, but I don't know if you can deal with the cold weather."

"What do you mean? I've got my hat." He tugged it down even tighter.

"And a leather jacket? Not exactly snow gear, Wilder." She teased him, shaking her head to make the point he just didn't get it. He was a real Southern California city boy.

He wrapped the jacket around his body as if to protect it from her scrutiny. "I'll have you know it's vegan," he said. "And possibly waterproof."

"I'm sure it is."

Though she was anxious to see Abby and Dylan, she took a moment to admire the house. It was spectacular. Mackenzie imagined seeing it as if it were the first time, remembering the builders stacking pine logs so high she was scared they'd tumble over and marveled at how they attached them to walls of glass—giant viewing windows into the lush forest beyond. Her father's lifelong vision was to blend rustic with modern and create this architectural masterpiece.

"I'm so relieved to see you." A woman's voice coming from behind startled Mackenzie.

"Mrs. Kinley, you scared me." She placed her hand across her chest.

"I didn't mean to sneak up on you, but I was about to check in on your sister."

The Kinleys owned the house next door and only recently became full-time residents.

"Thank you. I was upset when I heard," she said. "Though I talked to Abby on the way up, and they're okay."

"That was nice of you to come anyway," said Mrs. Kinley.

"Actually, she told me not to make the drive. You know Abby. The tough one of the family." When they were kids, Abby bossed Mackenzie around. The older sister who played the teacher role to Mackenzie's disobedient student.

As if noticing Jake for the first time, Mrs. Kinley froze in place. Her star-struck face revealed all.

"This is Jake Wilder." Mackenzie resigned herself to the fact she was no competition for a handsome celebrity.

"Oh, I know." Mrs. Kinley clapped her hands together.

"Nice to meet you," he said.

"Please, call me Penny." She smoothed her already-perfect bob. "I can't believe it's you. I still find myself singing along loudly to 'City Nights,'" she said. "When I'm in the car, people stare at this crazy, old lady."

"You're not old. Just old enough to know better."

Her face lit up.

Mackenzie was surprised by Mrs. Kinley's reaction to him. Beyond Millennium didn't seem like a band she would've listened to. People's tastes always surprised. As a reporter, she learned early on not to make assumptions. She remembered Mrs. Kinley's children. They were teenagers ten years ago. Maybe Jake Wilder posters had covered their walls.

"Okay, Penny it is," he said.

Mackenzie noticed how polite he was to his fans. She'd remember to get that tidbit into her article.

Mrs. Kinley didn't wave her phone around and ask for a selfie, much to Mackenzie's relief. She was anxious to get inside.

"We've got to get going if we're going to make it home at a decent hour." She struggled not to sound too ungrateful. "I'll tell Abby you stopped by."

"You're not thinking of driving home tonight?" said Penny. "It's almost dark now. Much too dangerous to drive these roads at night."

Was it inconsiderate of Mackenzie to ask Jake to get back in the car for another two hours? Spending the night, on the other hand, would be a huge inconvenience for the both of them. They had work to do, and besides, it would sound like she wanted him to spend the night *with* her.

"There's snow in the forecast," Penny continued.

He pointed toward Mackenzie. "It's up to the boss."

"What about Peterkins?" Maybe his trusty pooch could save her from the awkward predicament they were in.

She wondered if she made a mistake letting him drive her all the way up to the mountains. Accepting favors from people had a price. Nothing in this life came for free, her business-minded mother always told her. He was only being polite though. As the deadline inched closer and closer, he had the most to lose by staying the night.

"I guarantee as we speak that spoiled baby is on his back, legs in the air, getting his belly rubbed by his favorite sitter. I'll call and ask her to stay the night with him."

"Are you sure?" She wondered how much a celebrity paid his pet nanny. "I could drive us back anyway." She hoped it would be an adequate compromise.

"Nonsense," Penny said.

Jake laughed. "You tell her, Penny."

"I wouldn't dream of keeping Jake Wilder from his work. He's got a very important Christmas song to produce." Mackenzie dished it back out. His least favorite subject was the song, and she imagined Penny would be the last person he felt like explaining it to.

"A Christmas song!" Penny clutched her hands together in delight. "Wait until I tell my kids about this."

He rocked back and forth and glared at Mackenzie. "It's not official yet. I have to write the thing first."

"I'm sure it will be wonderful," said Penny.

"You tell *him*, Penny." Mackenzie always had to have the last word.

As soon as Penny left, the front door to Mackenzie's house flung open.

"I told you not to—" Abby stopped abruptly as soon as she saw Jake. Her eyes widened, and her face flushed.

Mackenzie suppressed a laugh at her sister's overreaction. *Way to play it cool, sis.* She hadn't seen Abby this *verklempt* since they thought they saw Ryan Gosling at the Beverly Center.

"You didn't tell me we have company." She spoke with a polite southern drawl.

Mackenzie had no idea where that came from. Both her parents were from the east coast before moving to California.

Abby patted her hair. A few pieces of her short pixie were sticking up as if she'd been lying down.

"Abby, this is Jake—"

"Please," she cut Mackenzie off. "I know who he is." Abby bounced on her toes. "This is so exciting! Why are you here with my sister?"

"It's a long story." Mackenzie wanted to check on her sister and nephew and get back on the road. She didn't have time to deal with a sister who acted like she was on her way to starting her own Jake-Wilder-Tween Fan Club.

He kept his cool. "We heard you got into an accident."

"It was terrifying." Abby placed the back of hand to her forehead as if she could faint at any moment.

"But you're okay," said Mackenzie.

"Barely." Her eyes practically bugged out of her head. "We escaped with our lives."

Her usually-resilient sister was playing the damsel in distress. The effect he had on people fascinated Mackenzie.

"Anyway, enough about me." Abby turned to him. "Jake Wilder! You're amazing. I'm your biggest fan."

Mackenzie tried to remember if that was true. There was a six-year age difference between them, and Abby shut her little sister out of a lot of her teenage years.

"How's Dylan?" Mackenzie steered the conversation back to the accident and her nephew.

"Who?" Her sister snickered. "I'm kidding. He's great. The accident was more of an adventure to him than anything else. You know twelve-year old boys." She spoke directly to Jake.

"I'm afraid I do. I was once one myself."

She doubled over as if it were the funniest joke she'd ever heard.

Mackenzie raised an eyebrow at her sister. *Back off*, Abby, she wanted to say.

Abby took the hint. "Let's go inside. It's freezing out here."

They found Dylan reclined in his grandfather's favorite chair. He beamed when his gaze fell on Mackenzie. She marveled how much he resembled his mother more everyday with his auburn hair and rosebud lips. "Hey, buddy. How are you feeling?"

"Mom's making a big deal over nothing." He set the book he

was reading aside.

"It's not nothing. You and your mother were in a serious wreck," she said.

"No big deal."

"I'm glad to see you're reading. That looks relaxing."

"Mom says I have to for thirty minutes every day." He shot his mother a dirty look. "It's so unfair when I'm on vacation."

Mackenzie smiled inwardly. Her parents had placed the same daily requirements on their children during school breaks.

"I'd rather be sledding or doing something fun with my friends," he said.

She sat on a chair beside her nephew and squeezed his hand but really wanted to snuggle him like they used to. At his age, he'd only tolerate a little physical affection. "Considering what you've been through, I think you're doing the right thing by hanging out at home."

"Mom's only freaking out because they smashed the back of her minivan."

"I'm not freaking out." Abby appeared at the doorway with her hands on her hips. She'd been giving Jake a tour of the house. "We could've been hurt."

"Your mom's right," said Mackenzie. "Then who would I take to see the Dodgers this season?"

"Seriously?" His eyes lit up.

"Yep." She tried to get tickets to at least a few games every season and hoped to take him to his first World Series.

"Dylan, you'll never guess who Auntie Mac's friend is."

Dylan glanced in Jake's direction but didn't seem the least bit impressed.

"A big time famous musician. Isn't that neat! I used to have his posters all over my walls."

Shoot me now. Her sister was exaggerating. If she had been such a mega-fan, Mackenzie would have remembered when she was assigned the story and called her sister right away.

Dylan lifted his chin in Jake's direction. "What's up?"

When did he become such a teenager?

"Not much." Jake put his hands into his pockets. He looked uncomfortable. Mackenzie needed to cut in before Abby invited them to stay over.

"It's much too late to drive home," said Abby. "I insist at least you stay the night."

Too late. Mackenzie had to admit making the trek home would be risky with the possible snow and dipping temperature.

"There's obviously plenty of space for you to both crash here tonight," said Abby.

"The house is certainly big enough." Mackenzie resigned herself to the fact they were staying over. "I hadn't mentioned it earlier, because I didn't want to take up anymore of your time."

"I've got nothing but time." He winked. They were both in on the joke. "What's another day?"

After dinner, Mackenzie and Jake sat in the living room with its vaulted beamed ceiling and granite fireplace. The room flowed toward the outdoor spacious viewing deck and faced the lake. Abby and Dylan had gone to bed, and the house was finally quiet.

"Do you really think you can do it?" Mackenzie asked. "Write a winning song by next week?"

The clock was ticking. First, there was the deadline to submit the song to the producer. Then, if the song was accepted, he would appear on *A Poppin' Christmas* a few days later. The schedule was impossible as far as she was concerned.

"I wrote 'Between the Seasons' in one night." Something like wistfulness shone in his eyes. "Woke up in the middle of the night with a melody in my head and wrote lyrics to match. The next morning I'd forgotten about it until I found the completed song on a notepad by my bedside."

She took a sip of the herbal tea she'd made for them and held back the concern that snaked through her. His success was her gain too.

"Don't worry," he said, as if he could read her mind. "I'll get something soon. If not for me, then for Bodhi. He's at his wit's end."

"Trust me. I'm not worried." She lied. "You'll either write the song or you won't." Her own harsh tone surprised her. Maybe her reaction was a defense mechanism that someone was getting close enough to sense her thoughts. She hadn't let a man get into her head in a long time, and it surely wasn't going to be Jake Wilder.

He raked his fingers through his hair. "What do you love about Christmas songs anyway?"

He was obviously trying to change the subject. *Okay, I'll bite.* "Where do I start? Everything! I love the way they make me feel. Warm and nostalgic and hopeful too. The light ones lift my spirit, and the spiritual ones lift my heart." She hadn't intended to go on like that, but the subject moved her to continue, "They voice humanities best qualities: our generosity and brotherhood."

"And don't forget sisterhood," he added.

"Of course not." She appreciated his sensitivity to equality. Did he have sisters? She forgot to ask when they were shopping for his niece.

"I've loved Christmas music forever."

Mackenzie thought back to when she was a little girl. Her grandmother gave her a small porcelain Christmas tree. It was no taller than six inches and covered in plastic colored lights that lit up when she placed it over the base with its mounted light bulb. A young girl dressed in a red cape trimmed with white fur sat in prayer position next to the tree alongside her pet lamb.

She cherished the gift, and every Christmas, placed it by her bed. Tuning into a station that streamed Christmas songs twenty-four hours a day, she contemplated the sweet Christmas moment that seemed frozen in time until she could no longer keep her eyes open and drifted off to a peaceful sleep.

"You must be remembering something nice." Jake interrupted her thoughts. "You were grinning."

"It's nothing." She wanted to keep the remembrance private. "Only listening to the music in my head."

"Can you let me in?" He gave her a puppy-dog look. "I could use the inspiration."

Lust blindsided Mackenzie, and before she had time to process the emotion, a shot of anger exploded through her. This back-and-forth between attraction and frustration was infuriating. Never before had she been so bewildered by a work assignment. The line between personal and professionalism was being crossed in an uncomfortable way.

She turned away from his gaze and realized she felt guilty. Was it her fault he was there with her instead of at his home studio hard at work? Refusing his offer to drive her up to the mountains had been an option, but she wasn't thinking straight. Her sister and nephew meant the world to her, and if he got her to them safely, she had no problem accepting his invitation.

"I'm not the person you should be looking to for inspiration," she said.

He shoved his hair away from his face. "Don't give me some cliché line about needing to find the answers within myself."

"I'm afraid so. I doubt a magical Christmas fairy will flutter in here just because you need this song." *And I need the story.*

"Wishful thinking." He smirked.

It took everything in her not to comfort him. That wasn't her job. Her obligation was to report the story as it unfolded.

She looked at her watch. "It's getting late."

"It was nice talking to you." He offered his hand to shake.

She gripped it firmly. *This relationship is all business from here on out.* "Goodnight."

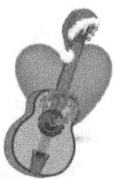

Chapter Eleven

Jake slowly opened his bedroom door. Everyone else was clear on the other side of the house, but he was careful not to wake them up. As he walked down the hallway, the wooden floor squeaked. He stopped and listened. Nothing. Continuing to tiptoe toward the kitchen, he needed a cup of coffee something fierce and would try not to clang around in the kitchen looking for the right ingredients and equipment to make a pot.

Years of bachelorhood taught him many lessons, the most important being how to make a good cup of joe. Even the Stone's precision brewer was no match for his skills. Mackenzie would be impressed the way he carefully measured the beans. The desire to please her caught him off guard. Why should he care what she thought of his coffee? He wanted her to like and respect him, and if that meant appreciating his mean brewing skills, so be it.

The blue and green flannel shirt he wore was actually comfortable though not really his style. She had lent it to him from her father's closet because, as she phrased it, his city slicker clothes wouldn't cut it up in the mountains. He didn't realize she was such an outdoorsy type. The fresh air and nature suited her even though twelve hours ago she was navigating the streets of Los Angeles like an over-caffeinated urbanite late for a meeting.

Outside, the snow covered the ground in thick drifts, and the windows were frosted a pure white that made him want to reach for his sunglasses. The morning was bright and beautiful, but the mounds of snow also meant they were stuck. Being the city boy he was, he didn't have a whole lot of experience driving in the snow, even if they had chains for his tires. They would have to wait for the weather and the roads to clear.

Inside the kitchen cupboards, matching sets of china and every day dinnerware lined the shelves in perfect order. The pristine alignment was to be expected in a kitchen like this. The appliances were high end, and he wondered if they'd ever been used. They gleamed as if brand new. Either that or somebody worked diligently to clean and buff every surface until they could see their own reflection.

A hardworking housekeeper must have kept their ship running tightly. Mackenzie probably grew up with all this lavishness, yet she seemed so down to earth. His family struggled to pay for the private music lessons and had never stepped foot in a mountain cabin, let alone a luxurious log cabin like this one. Fortune came later for him, and as Bodhi reminded, was not sustainable at Jake's current rate of decline. Good thing he hadn't gotten too used to this kind of living.

Steaming cup in hand, he padded back through the foyer and to the library. Bookcases lined the walls. From floor to ceiling, neat rows of books on every subject, including a massive section on art and architecture, obviously the Stone's passion, filled the shelves.

Climbing up on the rolling ladder, he pulled out a thick history book. An entire lifetime could be spent catching up on the art, history, philosophy, and science he missed as a teenager in school. There was even a small section dedicated to journalism and politics. He opened one of the books and saw Mackenzie Stone's name penned neatly inside the cover. A textbook from one of her college classes, no doubt.

In his imagination, she sat attentively in the front row of a Journalism 101 class, probably wearing glasses she didn't need because they made her look studious and thoughtful. She tucked her hair behind her ears and took copious notes about what it took to be an effective journalist and why the news mattered in the first place. Joy bubbled up in him remembering how she'd schooled him on the subject when they first met.

He slid the book back into place and gravitated toward the beautiful grand piano in the middle of the room. For a quiet moment, he appreciated the grandeur of the object rather than seeing it as a source of stress. He eased himself on the bench and lightly tapped out a few tunes, careful not to wake anybody up. Resting his fingers on the cold keys, he relished the soft, familiar touch. So much potential laid within that keyboard.

Music and lyrics, that's all it is.

As if he'd awoken something deep within, his hands moved across the keys. It was Tchaikovsky's "Swan Lake Theme," the song he played at his first recital. The audience clapped loudly in appreciation; his parents gave him a standing ovation. The joy had rushed all the way from his fingertips, up through his scalp, and down to his toes. At that moment, he was hooked. Playing simply as a hobby was not enough. He was meant to perform professionally.

Being on stage was as natural as breathing. When audiences rejected him for the next one-hit wonder, he had been devastated. He'd lost his purpose, a dragon slayer without a dragon to slay. That was when the stage fright took hold.

He glanced outside to clear his mind. Every time he started composing, bad memories crushed the good ones. Frustrated and annoyed, he let the unpolluted white field of snow become a metaphor for the clean slate that could be his mind.

Jake stretched his legs to get the creative juices flowing. From his pocket, he unfolded a piece of paper. It was probably a note he was supposed to give to Bodhi. To his surprise, the scribbles turned out to be a melody Jake had written in the middle of the night. Having woken from a dream hearing music, he wrote it down and stuck it into his pants pocket so he'd find it the next day. He'd completely forgotten about it.

Not half bad. He hummed the tune and tapped it out on the piano. His mind scrolled through the Christmas song canon like a jukebox filliping through its record selections. Settling on "Silent Night," he played the world's most popular Christmas song. He remembered his piano teacher told him in Austria, the song's birthplace, "Silent Night" was only played on Christmas Eve to preserve its sacredness.

Next, he played "White Christmas," hearing the words. "Just like the ones I used to know," he whispered the lyrics. The song was sad, melancholic, and full of longing. Did he want to create that sort of mood?

Then there was Mariah Carey's "All I Want for Christmas is You," a fun, pop song about the love and happiness Christmas could bring. He had a terrible experience in that particular department and pushed the thought aside before he gave up completely.

Jake accidently kicked the pedal. The old discouraging feeling of defeat snaked through his body. *A throbbing big toe and a bad attitude does not a Christmas song make.*

He needed fresh air and found a jacket, heavier than the vegan leather one Mackenzie made fun of and a pair of gloves. Careful not to lock himself out, he unlatched the door and went outside.

The cold air prickled his face. He wasn't used to freezing like an ice cube the moment he stepped outdoors. Even his eyelashes collected snow. He blinked several times to keep his eyelashes from sticking. Was that even possible? Seeing his breath as he exhaled was a rare phenomenon in his world. It got cold in Los Angeles but nothing this frigid.

He thought about what to do once he was outside. The lake was only a few steps away. Strolling around it would take too much time, and Mackenzie might wake up and wonder where he'd gone. She'd worry he'd taken off back to the city. His car was in the driveway though. Maybe she'd be glad to have a few moments without him.

Last night they'd run out of wood for the fireplace. She said there was more in the shed next to the house. He walked around the perimeter, hoping he didn't run into Penny. She wasn't a bother, but he didn't want to interact with anyone right now. He needed to keep his head clear for the next inspiration.

The shed was on the side of the house. He figured he'd bring in a few logs and start a roaring fire. Mackenzie would appreciate his efforts, and it would put him in the holiday mood so he could get back to songwriting. The snow would keep them there longer, and he'd be able to complete his song. Maybe he was being selfish. She did have a full life, separate from him, after all.

He opened the shed door and discovered the wood wasn't bundled together neatly like he might find in Home Depot. Big, heavy tree trunks were piled high to the ceiling.

Was he supposed to chop the wood himself? She would get a kick out of that. The last time he'd swung anything was a mallet at his hometown's annual carnival. Let's just say the puck didn't exactly strike the bell on the high-striker game. He was lucky to make it past the weakling level.

He had seen wood chopping depicted in movies and on television, envisioning the scenes but nothing technical came to him. As a lifelong musician, he was fit but not exactly bulging with muscle.

His current circumstances made him laugh. There he was in the mountains, facing a pile of wood that needed to be chopped. Perhaps he'd luck out and not find an axe. He looked around, but not with too much effort. Pushing aside hundreds of pounds of wood didn't sound appealing, but then, unfortunately, he spotted the axe. The sun gleamed brightly off its metal blade challenging him to pick it up and swing like a hero he believed he could be.

As he rolled one of the logs to an open spot outside of the shed, he inhaled deeply. With all his might, he swung the blade into the block of wood. It stuck, neither splitting the log nor dislodging from the wood very easily. He struggled to free the axe and try again. Apparently, brute force wasn't the answer.

Stepping back from the block, he paused to think about the task logically. He had tried to split it right in the middle, the most solid part of the wood. It would probably be much easier if there was a crack already in the log itself. A vulnerability he could exploit. Putting it that way, he agonized over destroying the piece of wood. He examined the log and found several places he could strike.

Again, he raised the axe and hit one of the cracks. To his amazement, it worked. A piece of wood fell off to the side. He did it again and again. Once he got it, the rhythm was easy and natural.

Chop, chop, chop, the sound filled the air.

He could've sworn he heard sleigh bells off in the distance. Did people up there travel by sleigh? He laughed off the silly notion. His imagination was working overtime.

How refreshing. It'd been a long time.

The chopping rhythm, the sound of sleigh bells, and the melody he'd come up with in the middle of the night all coursed through his mind.

Jake was lost in the budding song when he noticed a long, dark shadow hovering over him. His heart skipped a beat as he imagined an angry bear ready to pounce. *What is he supposed to do in this situation? Run? No. Slowly walk backward.* As if he could help darting like a terrified cat.

"Mom likes the logs tied in small bundles so she can carry them."

He jumped at the sound of Dylan's voice.

"I didn't mean to scare you." Dylan, wrapped in a coat and scarf, held out some twine.

Embarrassed by his skittishness, Jake shrugged it off as if he'd known Dylan was there all along. "It's cool, dude." He wondered if kids still called each other dude. They did back in his day.

"Want some help?"

"Sure." Jake told himself letting kids do chores around the house was good for them, but the truth was he didn't want to mess up this simple task. During the past several years, he hadn't been practicing his outdoorsman skills. He could fix a few things around the house, but major work was better left to the pros.

Dylan wrapped the cord around a small stack of logs. His bright hair shone in the sun.

"Thanks," he said. "I usually buy my firewood chopped, tied, and ready to go."

"It's okay." Dylan produced a pocket knife from his pocket and cut the rope. "I've been doing this since I was a kid."

He refrained from suggesting Dylan was still a kid even though when Jake was twelve, he thought he had it all figured out. Dylan looked like he might be able to survive a few nights in the forest while Jake, more than twice his age, startled over a shadow in the snow.

"You've been coming up here that long?" He gathered another small stack for Dylan to tie.

"Yep."

"Do you have a lot of friends here?" Jake had been a loner himself in middle school. It wasn't until he started a band in high-school people noticed him.

"Some," said Dylan. "There's a few who come up for winter break like us, and there's the local kids."

"That's good. I've never been great at making friends." Jake felt comfortable admitting his shortcomings to Dylan. Nobody was infallible, especially Jake. He was no superhero.

"Not even after you became famous?"

"Even then. You can't trust everybody." Was the advice helpful or did he sound like a cranky old man? "Friends are good, though."

Dylan nodded, as if he had years of experience in the department of friendship and betrayal. He quietly piled the wood by the back door.

"I Googled you," he said when they were finished.

"Oh, yeah? Don't believe everything you read." The last tabloid he'd seen about himself suggested he'd fled the country after running out on his recording contract and keeping the big cash advance.

"I like your songs." A blush crept up Dylan's face. "You were pretty famous."

Were, being the operative word. "There's more to being a successful musician than fame."

"It sure looks fun playing your guitar in front of thousands of fans. I watched you on YouTube."

The memories delighted Jake. "There were some good times for sure, but I'm still out there playing. You should have your mom take you to one of my shows."

"That'd be awesome. Can we go backstage too?"

There wasn't much of a backstage to speak of in the tiny venues his band played now. "Sure."

They'd been outside a good hour. His feet were numb, but he didn't want to rush Dylan. He seemed to be enjoying Jake's company, and he could use the distraction.

"I've got a guitar up in my room," said Dylan. "Want to see it?"

"Absolutely, you any good?"

"Not really."

"It takes a lot of practice." Jake speculated about how Abby handled endless hours of Dylan hitting the wrong chord before he finally got it right.

"I can't get my fingers to go in the right places."

"I can show you a few tricks."

"Cool!" Dylan's face lit up. "I've only got a few days—" He

stopped himself short as if he wasn't sure what to reveal.

Story of my life. "A few days?"

"It's kind of stupid." Dylan kicked the ground.

"Believe me. I've heard it all." *What's stupid is me, of all people, writing a Christmas song.*

"It's for the tree-lighting ceremony. I need to learn 'Jingle Bell Rock', or they're gonna kick me out."

"That's harsh." The music business was rough all over. "Of the ceremony?"

"No, out of the band," said Dylan. "I can't get the hang of it…and there's this girl."

"It's always about a girl," said Jake. "Though it shouldn't be," he added for good measure to be a suitable role model.

Dylan fidgeted with the zipper on his coat. "Her name's Sophia. I really want her to like me."

Jake wasn't sure advising a pre-teen on his love life was his territory. "What's your dad say?" Abby or Mackenzie hadn't mentioned Dylan's father, and Jake didn't want to pry.

The boy's expression sobered. "He died when I was six."

"I'm sorry." Jake felt even more compelled to help. "Let's go over the song a few times. Soon, you'll be playing it like nothing."

"Thanks. You're awesome."

"We'll see about that."

Dylan and Jake gathered the logs to take inside. He was on the verge of facing an even bigger challenge: getting Mackenzie to stay long enough so he might help Dylan learn his song *and* finish his own.

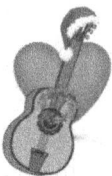

Chapter Twelve

Mackenzie peeked through the bedroom blinds. The snow blanketed the mountain overnight and clung to the pine branches, forming perfect dangling icicles like Christmas tree ornaments. The scene was breathtaking, yet it only made her miss her parents more than ever. They spent snowy winter afternoons skiing at the local resort and sledding down the nearby hills and drinking hot chocolate by the fireplace afterward. It had been picture perfect. The kind of winter vacation her Los Angeles friends watched on television. Though they were only a few hours out of town, the mountains were another world. One filled with enchantment and the blessings of family.

She missed them at Thanksgiving. Her mother dreamt of taking a cooking class in Italy, and Mackenzie encouraged her to go when she'd been accepted into a prestigious culinary academy for a six-week course. They'd begged her to join them in Europe, but she declined. Too much work, she'd said, secretly fearing Mr. Hughes would give Ross all the newsworthy stories while she was gone. Staying vigilant sometimes meant staying lonely.

Speaking of work, she wanted to get back to the office in case something big broke. She opened her laptop and checked road conditions. According to the Caltrans website, the highway patrol now required all vehicles to either be equipped with snow tires or chains to get down the mountain. Jake's SUV probably didn't have the mandatory tires. His four-wheel drive didn't look like it had seen much in the way of mountain terrain or driven over snow and ice. Her father kept a spare set of chains in the garage. She'd be relieved to get back, and he was probably as anxious to start working on his song.

She didn't mention it to him, but it was only two days until her birthday. It wouldn't be the usual Stone extravaganza—last year her parents hosted forty-eight guests—but she was still looking forward to it. When Kacey's mother learned Mackenzie's parents were out of town, she insisted Mackenzie celebrate her birthday with them. They were like a second family to her, so being with the Flores family was a no brainer, especially since she hadn't wanted Abby and Dylan to make the drive down the mountain. Mackenzie looked forward to their small, intimate dinner.

At half-past eight, she finally made her way to the kitchen. Her sister and Dylan would probably be up, but she imagined Jake was still asleep, used to the rock-and-roll lifestyle of late nights and sleeping in past noon. That they'd stayed in the same house felt awkward. She had to admit, her parents' home was more like a bed and breakfast than a tiny cabin in the woods. It had only been for one night, and she definitely wasn't going to mention it in his profile. Readers would never understand the lengths to which she went to get her story. From now on, all of their interactions would be strictly professional.

"Morning." Jake greeted her with a cup of coffee. "Hungry?" He gestured to a plate of golden waffles topped with blueberries.

Dylan was already scarfing down his. Abby, fully made up and picture perfect, sipped coffee.

"Thank you." Mackenzie wrapped both hands around the coffee mug and embraced the warmth. "What's this?"

"What does it look like?" Jake beamed, clearly proud of himself. "I hope you don't mind I whipped up a little something."

"He's talented in the kitchen too." Abby batted her long lashes.

"You didn't have to." Breakfast was Mackenzie's favorite meal of the day. She was starving but imagined they'd grab something to eat on the way out of town.

He picked up the plate and a set of silverware. "Follow me."

Dylan stood up to follow too, but Abby touched his shoulder. "You're on clean-up duty, young man."

He flopped back in his chair. "Okay."

"What are you up to?" Mackenzie reluctantly let him lead her to the library. "That's a nice fire." The tall flames danced and crackled. "I thought we were out of firewood."

He placed her plate on the coffee table. "Not a problem when you have a big strapping mountain man at your service."

She grinned. "You chopped all that wood?" A pile of freshly cut logs was stacked by the fireplace.

"You don't believe me?" He pouted, playing like he'd been insulted. "You should've seen me. I'm a regular Paul Bunyan."

"I hope you didn't hurt yourself. Those hands hold the key to our future. I expect a great song from you so you can win the contest, and I can write my story."

"Then, you're going to like this. Sit and eat before your food before it gets cold."

"Don't mind if I do." She sank into the sofa.

He sat at the piano. He ceremoniously stretched out his fingers and played. "Recognize this?"

"Of course. It's 'White Christmas.'" She adored Bing Crosby and played the song at least a hundred times this season.

"Irving Berlin wrote it in 1942. It's so wistful, it breaks your heart, doesn't it?" He sang some of the lyrics. "Imagine our boys deep in the thick of World War II. They could only dream of a white Christmas back home."

She thought about not only the service men and women away from their families at Christmastime but about all those who didn't have enough money for a proper holiday meal or presents to unwrap. Then there were those poor souls without a home in the first place. She hoped to give a voice to those people in her career as a journalist.

"Just like the ones I used to know," Jake sang.

She fought back tears. The morning was not proceeding as planned. As a person of to-do lists, she focused on completing intentional steps all pointing directly toward carefully-considered goals. Jake and his rendition of "White Christmas" threw her way off target.

He switched it up and played "Winter Wonderland." "And there's always your favorite."

She was grateful he lightened the mood.

"For what it's worth, this isn't technically a Christmas song."

"It is so," she said, genuinely insulted, as if he committed blasphemy by accusing her favorite song of being an imposter.

"It's not," he insisted. "Sure, it's a wintertime song, but there's no mention of Christmas. Only building a snowman and walking in snowy meadows."

"I don't care." She folded her arms across her chest. "It's about snow and love and makes millions of people happy."

Despite the absurdity of it, she was actually defending a holiday song. It was like she was fourteen-years old and arguing the merits of a Beyoncé song to her parents. Also, the argument was a terrible one anyway, devoid of logic and verifiable evidence. Her debate professor from college would've never let her get away with it.

"Ah, love," he said. "Another great theme of the Christmas song."

She agreed. Not that she had been an expert in the area of romance. There had been only one serious boyfriend in her life. She and Alex both interned at *The Sunrise Press* during college. He was satisfied to run errands as she worked her way to a permanent staff position. Alex said he was more interested in television journalism anyway and applied for jobs across the country.

In the meantime, they'd become pretty serious. At least she thought so. Her mom made plans for a springtime wedding, despite Mackenzie's protests there hadn't been a proposal yet. She wanted a future together—she a topnotch journalist and he a successful television anchor.

One afternoon Alex said he'd been offered a job in Des Moines as a special assignment's reporter. He wanted her to go with him, but when she said she'd wait to find a job first, a small chasm opened. He moved away, and they eventually drifted apart. When he was promoted to evening anchor on the local news, she was truly happy for him though it left her lonely and desperate for her own success.

A melody she didn't recognize broke her from her memory. "What will be the theme of your song?"

Jake didn't answer and continued to play. The song started slow and plaintive but became bright and cheerful.

"What's that one?"

"Do you like it?" he asked.

His eyes twinkled, and his whole body filled with something she hadn't seen in him before. Confidence? Inspiration, maybe. *Could this be a Wilder original Christmas song?* She resisted running to get her reporter's notebook, fearful the disruption would break the spell.

"Very catchy," she said.

"I believe this is the one," he said. "I've had so many false starts, but this feels right, as if it's been waiting for me to discover it all along."

"It's wonderful." The melody captured both the nostalgia and the love themes they'd talked about earlier. "Have you written the lyrics?"

"Not yet. But the way I'm feeling, they could come at any moment. There's something about this place. It's magical."

He wasn't exaggerating. Her parents' house in the mountains was mystical and dreamlike. Many days she'd been inspired there herself.

He stopped playing and faced her. His face brightened. "When I was outside chopping wood, it hit me. How could I possibly write a Christmas song in the middle of all the Los Angeles smog and traffic? I need snow-covered hills and roaring fireplaces. I need to feel it deep in my bones and in my soul."

That made perfect sense to her, but there was one problem with the scenario. She wanted to go back to the city even though she'd checked her email before breakfast, and Mr. Hughes hadn't contacted her about any breaking news he wanted her to cover. Jake's story was the only assignment she was working on. It was unfolding right in front of her. Asking him to leave this perfect place of inspiration seemed counterproductive for both of them.

She weighed her options. One would be to return to her apartment and sit by helplessly while he slipped back into the same writing slump where she found him.

"Don't you have to get home to Peterkins?" she asked.

"Are you kidding? The old mutt's happy to spend as much time with his nanny as he can. I told you. She spoils him rotten."

"I don't know." Though he hadn't officially asked to stay, the request was hanging out there. If she acquiesced, could it hurt their professional relationship? If she said no, he probably wouldn't finish the song and any chance she would have for maintaining a profession in the first place.

"Look," he said. "The conditions aren't great to drive home anyway. And what about Dylan?"

"My nephew?"

He nodded solemnly. "He's asked me to help him learn a song on his guitar to win over a girl. You don't want to ruin the poor kid's life."

She sized him up. "Now you're playing me."

"If it's not too much to ask, give me two days," he pleaded. "Then, come what may, we're on our way down the mountain."

"I suppose this might give me an opportunity to start writing our story."

"Bingo."

Worry gnawed at her. Was she making a huge mistake? "It's my birthday in two days, by the way."

Jake started to play "Happy Birthday."

"I have a party to get to," she said. "And I can't be late."

He stopped playing and offered out his hand to shake. "I'll have you home in two days. Deal?"

"Deal."

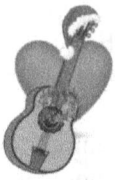

Chapter Thirteen

Jake tapped out "Chopsticks" as fast as he could. He did this whenever writer's block took hold. His childhood piano teacher showed him this technique to let go of tension and free up his mind. Sometimes meditation worked too. Lately he'd fallen asleep instead of focusing on his mantra. The other day Bodhi found Jake curled up on the floor underneath his piano in the studio. Bodhi laughed so hard Jake nearly hit his head when he jolted awake. Bodhi wouldn't let Jake live that one down anytime soon.

For the most part, he was satisfied with the melody. A few tweaks here and there, and his Christmas song was on its way. The tricky part was getting the lyrics right, and he played the opening again. He wondered if anyone else was getting sick of the repetition. Mackenzie was in the next room working on her laptop and probably looking for another story to cover that had nothing to do with has-beens and comebacks.

As far as lyrics, there was a whole grab bag of Christmas-like words and phrases to work with: snow, sleigh bells, presents underneath the tree, lights twinkling. The list went on and on. At one point, he was tempted to put these words on strips of paper and randomly stick them together like the magnetic poetry game he'd seen on Bodhi's refrigerator. Maybe it would be a good exercise, but it certainly wasn't going to get Jake into the Christmas song hall of fame.

He had to be thoughtful about the process and imagined what she would write. She enjoyed the Christmas spirit and believed in the splendor of the holiday season. He wished he could say the same for himself. That train left the station long ago.

The Stone's beautiful home and the winter atmosphere had put him in the right headspace, but to think it would erase years of insecurities was naïve. The day before he had been so optimistic. It only took a mere twelve hours for the doubt to come creeping back.

He dropped his head into his hands and imagined being a kid again. On Christmas morning, before their parents were awake, he and his brother and sister would sneak downstairs to see if Santa had eaten the milk and cookies they'd left for him. If he cleared the plate, there'd probably be lots of presents under the tree. One year his sister thought Santa needed to slim down and left fruit instead. Santa ate the orange slices, and based on their haul, seemed perfectly content with the low-calorie treat.

Christmas song lyrics played in his mind over and over again. The repetition drove him mad. He'd become completely useless as a songwriter and doubted he was the same person who wrote those hits years ago. How did he do it then? It came so naturally before. It seemed as if he was being punished for early success and fame. He would happily give that past all up in exchange for a steady flow of inspiration and motivation.

Jake paced the room, pausing to gaze outside. The snow had stopped falling, but there was enough to make driving down the mountain difficult. He was glad Mackenzie agreed to stay a few more days. It would give him more time to work on the song and help Dylan.

Seeing all that snow trigged the line "In the meadow we can build a snowman." Ever since she revealed "Winter Wonderland" as her favorite, it had become a constant earworm. Jake wasn't sure how helpful hearing the same song play was to his process, but since she liked it so much, he found it charming.

He couldn't control the flood of familiar lyrics from becoming a noisy loop of chaos and confusion. Words and melodies crowded his mind, making it impossible to create anything original. Maybe he needed a walk. Perhaps she would join him. He glowed inside at the prospect of them building a snowman together even though he didn't have the first clue how to go about it. She'd probably laugh at the silly idea anyway.

He sat back at the piano and pounded out a maniacal version of "Chopsticks."

"If I have to hear that song one more time—" Mackenzie appeared in the room so swiftly and suddenly it startled him. "Somebody's gonna get hurt."

The corners of her mouth curved into a smile. If she'd been annoyed, he wouldn't blame her. He usually played these little ditties in the privacy of his own studio.

"I'm sorry if I'm disturbing you." He'd imposed on Mackenzie's time and generosity, keeping her away from the office for the sake of finishing the song. The progress he experienced earlier had come to a screeching halt.

She gave a dismissive wave. "You're not. I can't seem to focus anyway."

"Am I disturbing your sister and Dylan?"

"Penny took them into the village to run a few errands."

"I completely understand why they'd want to leave the house. I'm sure you can tell I'm killing it in here." He dangled his arms at his side. "I should give up. Pack it in and call it a day."

"Maybe we both need a break," she said.

"That's a good idea." He was grateful she was the one to suggest it. The last thing he wanted was to inconvenience her more than he already had. "How about a walk?"

Layered in so many undershirts, he could barely lift his arms. She rolled her eyes. All he could do was ignore her and wiggle his fingers and toes to keep the circulation flowing.

"It's not that cold, Wilder," she said, prancing her way down the snow-covered path to the lake.

He was shocked at how quickly she acclimated to freezing temperatures. Like a princess who'd been exiled in the city for far too long, she practically sparkled in the snow. He always thought she was pretty, but in this light, she was downright spectacular.

Fighting the urge to physically shake his head free of these romantic notions, he reminded himself she was only being polite and probably already knew his story was doomed to failure.

"What's the mopey face about?" she asked. They paused by the frozen lake to take in the spectacular view.

"It seems so overdone for an artist to say this, but I have doubts. I mean who am I to write a Christmas song?"

She scooped up a ball of snow from the ground. "Don't make me throw this at you."

Was she teasing him or merely frustrated? He put up his arms in protest. "Okay, I'm sorry. No more woe is me."

"Darn right."

"I deserve it. C'mon, throw it right here." He pointed at his head. "Maybe you'll knock the song right out."

"I don't want to hear that kind of talk," she said dropping the snowball. "You can and should write a Christmas song. Why *not* you? Millions of fans still believe in you." The corners of her eyes crinkled. "I believe in you."

Jake let the words linger. He didn't want to ruin the moment by saying something wrong or revealing how much he needed her encouragement. His despair might make them both uncomfortable. Whether she said it only to be nice or not, he wasn't sure. What he did know was appreciation for his music was a lifeline he sorely needed.

He eventually broke the silence. "Thanks to you, I can't get that lyric about building a snowman in the meadow out of my head."

"Hmm, we might have to do something about that." Her face brightened.

"Like?" he asked. "I'll crawl out of my skin if we have to sing that song once more." The fact she couldn't hold a note made it even more unbearable.

She gathered up snow and shaped it into a large ball. "Are you going to just stand there?"

"You know what you're doing? Maybe we should Google it." He pulled out his phone.

"Put that thing away. You are looking at Lake Arrowhead's three-time consecutive champion snowman builder."

"You mean snow*person*, don't you?"

This time she lobbed a snowball at him.

"Careful," he said, ducking in time. "You don't want to mess this face up. I was considered *People* magazine's sexiest man of the year."

While she formed the base, Jake worked on the head and body. He carefully shaped the parts, as if trying to coax this snowperson to life by his gentle touch and even asked him what he wanted to be called.

Jake named the snowman Mr. Noel. The end product looked downright professional. If snowman building was a profession.

"He needs a hat." He placed his beanie on Mr. Noel's head.

"That's one cool snowman," she said.

"No pun intended." They both laughed at her corny joke.

"Can I ask you a question?"

"It's your job, right?" He was nervous about answering personal questions, but he owed it to her. She was willing to stake her journalistic reputation on him.

"I tease you a lot about hating Christmas, but I see your face when you play the songs. Your eyes gleam with joy."

"Or tears." He deflected the inquisition. His reply was a kneejerk response, and he reminded himself to be more open. "Sorry, go ahead."

"There's gotta be a place inside you that loves Christmas."

"Most kids have some pleasant memories of Christmas." He glanced at Mr. Noel. His lopsided grin said, "Go ahead. Tell her the truth," as if he was ganging up on him along with Mackenzie. "I'm only tapping into a universal feeling."

"It's more than that." She was so sincere and earnest it made a small crack in his armor.

"Should we walk?" He felt too crowded. "Sorry, fellow," he said to the snowman. "I'm going to need this back," he said, lifting his beanie from Mr. Noel's head.

"Don't worry." She patted the snowman on his bare head. "I'll bring you another."

"If I tell you something, can it be off the record?" Jake was asking a lot of her. Perhaps his past wouldn't be an integral part of her story anyway. There were many angles she could take. If he believed what he was about to say might land in a newspaper for public consumption, he wouldn't mention it.

"Sure." She slowed her brisk pace so he could keep up.

"What you said earlier, about me loving Christmas. You're right. I used to love it." He fidgeted with his beanie. "When I met my ex-girlfriend Samantha on Christmas Eve, I thought it was fate. She loved the season so much too that when I asked her to marry me, it had to be a Christmas wedding."

Mackenzie listened intently. He understood she was too good of a reporter to interrupt.

"Sam planned the whole event right down to the real snow and reindeers. This was in Los Angeles, mind you, and that year we happened to have record-breaking heat. We both panicked, but with the help of some industry professionals, we pulled it off. There was white and green, red and silver and gold for as long as the eyes could see. The warm California evening transformed into a winter wonderland."

"I bet it was beautiful."

"You can say that again. An hour before the wedding, Samantha asked to see me. A bad sign. She was very traditional. It could spell bad luck for a groom to see the bride before the wedding. Sam, of all people, knew that."

He paused and gathered up the courage to continue. "That's when she broke the news. She couldn't go through with it."

"Why did she wait until your wedding day?"

"I think she intended to marry me, but at the last minute, couldn't do it. She said in the beginning, she was attracted to me because I used to be so successful. That showed her I had motivation to achieve greatness. When my career continued to spiral downward, she gave up hope and dumped me."

"That's why you hate all things Christmas," said Mackenzie.

He faked a smile. "Bah humbug."

~ * ~

Jake returned to the piano, refreshed but still without the lyrics he hoped to find outside with Mackenzie. The break hadn't gone quite as he intended. The frivolity turned too serious when he revealed why he hated Christmas. *I should've kept my big mouth shut. Way to ruin the holiday for everybody.*

He tapped out his melody a few more times when Dylan entered the library. At this rate, he'd never get anything done but welcomed the distraction.

"My mom said I shouldn't disturb you." Dylan waited near the doorway, holding his guitar by the neck.

"Come in," Jake said. "I'm stuck anyway."

"Is that the Christmas song you're working on?" Dylan stood next to the piano as Jake played a few notes.

"What do you think?"

Dylan shifted from one foot to another. "Good, I guess."

"With a little luck and a lot of perspiration, someday it might just be." Jake didn't bother to mention someday should've been *yesterday.*

"How's 'Jingle Bell Rock' coming along?"

"It's not." Dylan's gaze cast to the floor. "I can't do it."

"If you tell yourself you can't—" Jake reached for Dylan's guitar and strapped it around himself. "Then you won't."

Jake strummed it a few times. "This thing's way out of tune," he said, adjusting the guitar.

When the guitar sounded right, he inhaled deeply. "Sometimes you only need to relax. Let the song come to you." He should take his own advice. *See the song, be the song* was a silly mantra he used to repeat to himself to break free from writers' block.

Dylan crossed his arms over his chest. "I should quit. It's not worth embarrassing myself."

"You're right." Jake unstrapped the guitar. A bit of reverse psychology worked wonders on him. Bodhi played that game all the time when dealing with Jake's mood swings, and he always fell for it.

"Wait." Dylan waved his hand to stop Jake. "You don't want to at least try?"

"Sounds like you don't want to." He straightened out his scattered notes. If he'd learned anything through the years, it was how to act like he didn't care.

"I guess it couldn't hurt to go over the song a few more times."

"Are you sure?" Jake yawned.

"I'm sure," said Dylan. "I want to."

"Then, let's do this." Jake slung the guitar back on and played the intro to "Jingle Bell Rock." "This is a great song for the guitar. Start with 14th fret on the high E string." He played the beginning a few more times. "After the into, do a little bend and slide your fingers down the neck."

"You make it look easy," said Dylan.

"Now try it yourself." He handed the guitar back to Dylan.

He hesitated at first, but finally took the guitar. Imitating Jake, Dylan took a big breath and played the song, hitting a clinker right off the bat. "See, I can't do it."

"I can't tell you how many sour notes I've hit in my lifetime. Even right on stage. It was awful."

"What did you do?" Dylan's eyes widened.

"I kept going," said Jake. "That's all you can do. Now try again."

Beads of perspiration formed on Dylan's forehead. He inhaled and played again. This time, he didn't miss a chord.

"Good, now maybe a little more upbeat next time. This is a fun song not a funeral dirge."

The boy's forehead creased.

"Never mind," Jake said. "One more time. You've got this."

Dylan played it again. He laughed, maybe in amazement or maybe in disbelief he played the song almost perfectly.

"You sound like a pro," said Jake. "How long have you been practicing this song anyway?"

"The band asked me to join about a week ago." Dylan chewed his bottom lip. "I might've lied a bit when I told them I already knew the song."

"That's not a lie. It's called projection. You envisioned yourself doing it." Even Jake's fifth-grade teacher Mrs. Morris would approve of this justification since it was the motivational kind. "But I wouldn't mention this conversation to anyone." He winked at Dylan.

"No way. It's on a need-to-know basis," said Dylan.

"Tell me about this girl. Is she worth all the trouble?"

A shy smile crept over Dylan's face. "She's the prettiest girl around, but she doesn't know I'm alive."

"And you think if you really rock this tune, you'll get her attention?" asked Jake.

"It's better than nothing. I can't even talk to her. The other day we were all snowboarding. I'm pretty good. I wanted her to notice me and hang out. I asked her to do one more run with me, but she said her dad was coming to pick her up."

"It was probably true."

"I know," said Dylan. "I felt dumb anyway."

"I gotta be honest here. There are other reasons to pursue music besides winning over girls." Jake didn't want to give Dylan the impression making good music was about getting a date.

"Like what?"

Jake knew a lot of guys in the business who used their talent to chase women. Making music was so much more. It was about creating something out of thin air. One moment there was silence, next it was filled with a song you've written and presented to the world. The experience was awe-inspiring, addicting, and for him, it used to be downright fun.

"For one thing," he said. "It's exciting all that beautiful sound filling the space around you is coming from you and your instrument. Without you breathing life into it, this guitar would only sit silently. It's just waiting for you."

As Dylan looked at his guitar, it seemed he was seeing it for the first time. He turned it around in his hands and played the song again, this time with the soul it had been missing.

"There you go," said Jake. "Play the song with all your passion. If certain people notice you for it, great. But you want to be loved for what's in here and here." He pointed to Dylan's heart and head.

"I think I can do this," he said.

"I know you can." Happiness nearly made Jake giddy.

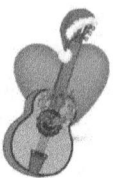

Chapter Fourteen

Mackenzie stared at her opened laptop and racked her brain for an approach to Jake's story that was less obvious than underdog makes a comeback. No doubt it was a compelling take, but there was no guarantee he was going to make a comeback at all. What then?

The who, what, when, and where was all there, but the story fell flat after that. Until there was a song, she was stuck. If the results didn't come out the way they wanted, if he didn't win the contest, would she have a story at all? Mr. Hughes had been a reliable mentor, continually pushing her to dig deeper, and she imagined discussing the story with him.

Maybe it's not the winning that counts, she'd say to him, but getting back in the game that matters. If the Christmas song didn't work out, Jake might become inspired to work on another sort of comeback that didn't have anything to do with the holiday. It was apparent he needed more than a professional revival. He needed a personal one too.

The idea of his fiancée leaving him at the altar. On Christmas, no less. With his history, why did he agree to this contest in the first place? So many people struggled during the holidays. It had to be tough seeing happy families when your own heart ached.

She didn't have a significant other but envisioned a future family Christmas photo where they'd all wear matching sweaters. Kacey would make fun of her, of course, but she'd probably end up in her own family photo.

Glancing back down at the computer screen, the blinking cursor taunted Mackenzie. She picked up her cell phone and dialed Mr. Hughes.

Ross answered, "*Sunrise Press.*"

A lump formed in her throat. Something was off. "Why are you answering Mr. Hughes's phone?"

"You didn't hear?"

"Spill it." She was too unsettled for polite conversation and wanted to get right to the point.

"Mr. Hughes had to leave on a family emergency."

"What happened?" He was married with grown children and grandchildren. She prayed everybody was alive and healthy.

"It's his mother. Poor woman fell and broke her hip."

"How awful." Considering his age, his mother had to be well in her nineties. "Will she make it?"

"The way I see it," said Ross. "This could be the beginning of the end." His tone struck her as insensitive. He seemed to relish in the drama.

"I'll be acting editor-in-chief until he returns," he continued. "*If* he returns."

"Why wouldn't he?" It seemed beyond rude to suggest his departure at a time like this.

"You know how these things go. Maybe he'll realize it's time to retire. Spend time with the family. Travel. The possibilities are endless."

In your dreams. "If there's anything I can do to help out. I can be in the office in a couple of days."

"Don't worry about it. Take as much time off as you need. There's no breaking story I can't handle myself."

She resented the insinuation she was taking time off. He didn't have a clue what she was up to. "I'm working on the Jake Wilder piece."

"That little entertainment profile. How's it going?"

She was about to tell him it had real potential to be a serious story about the emotional rollercoaster of celebrity in an era of the 24-hour news cycle where careers can be made and unmade in a matter of hours or within a single tweet.

"Mackenzie." Ross interrupted her thoughts. "I've got to go. Something's just come in."

He hung up on her. At first, she was too stunned to react. Was it denial? Anger? She moved through the grieving stages as fast as the reality hit that for the foreseeable future, he would be in charge of doling out the stories. She certainly wouldn't be at the top of his list.

Her options were limited. She could stay on the paper and cover trivial stories or continue working on the one she had and, with some luck, it would get syndicated. If other newspapers picked it up, her name would get out there at last. Suppose Jake won the contest, his song became a hit, and Mackenzie Stone was there all along to witness the birth of another Christmas classic. They'd both go down in history. She perked up again. Ross wasn't going to burst her bubble no matter what.

The sound of "Chopsticks" came beating into the kitchen. Her stomach sank. "So much for not bursting my bubble."

Was Jake ever going to move on from this exercise of his? It'd been hours since she heard him play the song. He was supposed to be working on the lyrics not manically tapping the same keys over and over.

Both of their careers relied on him finding the right words, and she had to do something about it. Staring at the blank computer screen wasn't helping the situation. What she needed was encouragement for them both. There was only one answer. The Village.

The road to town had been plowed, and the idea thrilled her until she remembered she didn't have a car. Neither did her sister after it had been wrecked in the accident.

She crept into the hallway, past the library. The house was suddenly quiet. When she peeked into the room, he was at the piano, eyes closed. Was he sleeping? Maybe he was meditating. In any case, he wouldn't miss the car or her if she stepped out for a minute.

As quietly as possible, she started the engine. After adjusting the seat and mirrors, she pulled onto the road. Exultation surged through her. It was as if she was sneaking the family car out for a joy ride. She turned on the radio and found a station playing the classic Christmas songs she loved.

Despite the recent snowfall and treacherous commute up to the mountain, the city was buzzing with activity. Locals and tourists alike went outside to admire the beautiful snow-covered landscape. Spotting tourists was easy because they often stopped their cars dead in their tracks to snap a photo. She wasn't annoyed since it only gave her a better opportunity to take in the sights herself.

~ * ~

"If it isn't Mackenzie Stone." Patrick Murphy unhitched the tailgate of his pickup truck and untied the thick rope wrapped around the freshly cut Christmas trees.

A few men stood by to haul the trees to the lot. The Murphy's Christmas Tree Farm was filled with trees of all shapes and sizes, festive lights, and lines of children waiting to get their pictures taken with Santa Claus.

The Stones had been buying from Patrick for twenty years. Except for one time when Mackenzie's father thought it'd be fun to chop down their own tree. Axe in hand, he dragged the family through the forest. Her mother worried it might be illegal to cut down a tree and hid behind a scarf and dark sunglasses.

Mackenzie and her father were excited by the challenge of finding the perfect tree until they saw paw prints in the snow. Mrs. Stone said she heard a bear growl though nobody else did. Nonetheless, she grabbed her daughters by the hands and ran to the car. Her father had no choice but to follow. They promptly drove to the Murphy Christmas Tree Farm where they've been loyal customers since.

"Where's the rest of your family?"

"Oh, here and there." She didn't have time to chat. "I've got a situation."

"Uh oh," he said, rubbing his chin. "Sounds serious."

"I need a good one." She scanned the few trees the men brought in but none seemed right.

"If you wait a second, I've got a beautiful Douglas Fir somewhere in the back of this old heap." He waved his men over to help pull the rest of the trees out of the truck. "Guys, we've got a Christmas tree emergency."

She couldn't help but laugh. It sounded a ridiculous when he put it that way. "I wouldn't say emergency, exactly. More like a crisis of Christmas faith."

The guys loaded Jake's car with the perfect six foot tree. Not too tall but full and lush. She would drag it into the house on her own and surprise Jake, never suspecting she'd go out and buy a tree on her own. The plan was to leave on her birthday, but she saw the error in putting another deadline on him. Obviously, he'd stressed himself into a complete creative block. She needed to take the pressure off for the sake of both of their careers. It was all purely a matter of professional persistence.

Instead, she would drive down for her birthday dinner alone, leaving Jake to finish his song. The next morning she'd zip back up, and it would be like she'd never left.

Mackenzie had to admit she was slightly nervous to see Kacey alone. She would take a good, long time questioning Mackenzie about the status of her relationship with Jake. Was romance brewing, she'd ask?

Kacey pretended she didn't care about romance, but Mackenzie knew better. Once Kacey made homemade heart-shaped peanut butter cups on Valentine's Day and distributed them to all their neighbors. They looked more like misshapen blobs, but they tasted delicious.

Jake and Abby stood at the front door as Mackenzie pulled into the driveway. She parked and exited the car, careful not to reveal her cargo. The surprise would be ruined.

"There you are," said Abby. "Poor Jake had no idea where you'd run off to."

"I was about to call the police." He tsked and shook his head.

Mackenzie widened her eyes attempting to look innocent. "I returned your car in one piece."

"Thankfully." He took a brownie from the plate Abby was holding. She'd become Betty Crocker since he arrived.

"I wanted Jake to try some of my famous salted caramel brownies." Abby lifted an eyebrow. "Aren't they delicious?"

"It's cold out here," said Mackenzie. "Why don't you two go inside? I'll be there in a minute."

Abby ignored her. "These will give Jake just the boost he needs to finish up his song. Isn't that right?"

"I'm doing fine." He sighed dramatically.

"Move past 'Chopsticks' yet?" Mackenzie got in a little jab after he threatened her with the police, teasing or not.

"Don't be mean," said Abby. "Give him a few days."

She'd invite him to move in if she had her way.

"I'm afraid we're leaving soon," he said.

"Maybe not," said Mackenzie.

He cocked his head. "No?"

"Since neither of you will go inside, you might as well make yourselves useful. Put down those brownies and help me get something out of the car."

The smell of fresh pine released from the car when she opened the hatch.

"What on earth?" he said.

"Did you know Mariah Carey wrote 'All I Want for Christmas Is You' in the middle of summer?"

"I love that song," said Abby.

"Imagine the luxury of having so much time," he said. "What's that got to do with me?"

"For inspiration, she brought in a snow machine and real reindeer to her house. She created her own winter wonderland. Christmas in July." Mackenzie gestured to their surroundings. "You have the snow and the deer, but maybe it's not enough. What you need is to feel the true spirit of Christmas. This tree's only the start."

His gaze softened. "I can't believe you did this, but we're leaving in less than two days."

"From now on, let me worry about details and deadlines." The most important one was one week away. They both knew that. "You focus on completing your song."

The three of them carried the tree to the house. Abby tried to get Mackenzie's attention by clearing her throat, but she refused to look at her sister. Probably dying to find out what Mackenzie had planned, Abby would not accept the it's-strictly-professional line Mackenzie had rehearsed in the car on the way back home.

Dylan," shouted Abby from the front door. "Help us with the Christmas tree."

When he didn't respond, she explained, "He's upstairs practicing that song. I think his body's gonna grow around his guitar before he turns thirteen."

"Let him keep playing," said Mackenzie. "Jake and I will bring the tree to the library. You set up the stand."

While they waited in the foyer, he asked, "Are you sure you want to do this? What if I can't—"

She waved her hand in the air, cutting him off. "Let's get the tree in place first. Then we can talk all about the what ifs."

"You're right. I'm sorry." His shoulders relaxed. "This is an incredibly thoughtful gesture, and I should be more appreciative."

I've got a lot riding on this too, she wanted to say, but refrained from putting more pressure on him. Instead she said, "You're welcome."

Once they put the tree into place, Dylan finally came to see what was going on. "Awesome," he said, followed by, "What's for dinner?"

"Don't you want to help decorate the tree first?" asked Abby. She seemed disappointed her son wasn't more enthused about the holiday season.

"But I'm really hungry, Mom."

"Typical man." Abby grinned at Jake. "Always thinking about food."

"He's a growing boy." Mackenzie ruffled Dylan's hair. "He's right. Let's have dinner then Jake and I will get started on the tree. You two can finish up tomorrow."

She hoped her sister would take the hint she wanted to be alone with Jake. This was her chance to build up his self-esteem and Christmas spirit. It was a half-truth. Being alone with him for one of her favorite Christmas pastimes secretly thrilled her.

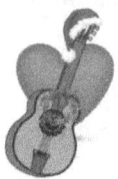

Chapter Fifteen

The green branches shimmered against the snowy white backdrop. Instead of inspiring Jake to write, the perfect atmosphere made him want to sip apple cider and help Mackenzie decorate the tree rather than struggle to find the right words that would make his song a hit.

Why didn't he collaborate with a lyricist, or better yet, accept he wasn't up for the job in the first place? Bodhi would be disappointed, but Jake was disappointing a lot of people lately.

"Stop being a sad sack," he sang aloud to the tune of his new song. She was in the garage gathering decorations, so he could sulk all he wanted. "You're nothing but a Christmas bummer and an all-around hack," he belted out.

He looked up at the Christmas tree. "You're not helping much." The lush branches mocked him. How could he compete with such beauty?

The thought of her loading the tree into his car by herself, filled his chest with warmth. She had enough faith for both of them; he couldn't let her down. The fact she was willing to sacrifice her time for him was enough kick in the butt to stop his bellyaching right in its tracks. When she finally admitted to Jake she had plans to celebrate her birthday at the Flores's house, he insisted they go back to Los Angeles together. She said not to worry about it.

He listened for her but didn't hear anything as he dialed Bodhi's number.

"Aloha," Jake said when Bodhi answered.

Considering he was surrounded in a world of snow and freezing temperatures, an island greeting seemed absurdly inappropriate. Bodhi couldn't know Jake was being ironic.

"Where are you?" asked Bodhi, a mixture of worry and anger in his voice. "Haven't you listened to my messages? I even called the pet nanny, but she wouldn't tell me anything."

"Client-pet-sitter privilege," said Jake. "A man and his dog need their privacy."

"I didn't know it worked like that." Bodhi exhaled, clearly frustrated at Jake's caginess. "The deadline's right around the corner."

"I'm aware." The last thing he needed was to be reminded of the ticking time bomb. It was all he could think about. He paced the room, keeping an eye out for her. He didn't have time to waste with chitchat.

"How's it going?" asked Bodhi.

He knew Bodhi was asking after the song's progress but didn't want to tell him writer's block had taken a deep hold. The lyrics remained elusive no matter how hard Jake tried. "Look, I've got the music down, and I'll play it for you as soon as I see you."

"I'm free today."

"I'm up at Mackenzie Stone's cabin in the mountains." He dropped the bomb casually, hoping Bodhi wouldn't make a big deal about it.

"With Mackenzie Stone, the reporter?"

"I'll explain later. I need you to do me a big favor."

"I'm worried," said Bodhi.

"Don't be." He worried enough for all of them put together.

"Is this like on the Infinity Tour when you requested we drape your dressing room in pink chiffon?"

"I was messing with you." The memory amused Jake after all these years. It had been fun playing the prima donna, if only as a joke.

Bodhi went silent.

Jake might be asking too much, but in the years since he'd known Bodhi, he proved himself ready for anything Jake could throw Bodhi's way.

"Name it," he said.

Relying on his friend was truly a privilege and blessing. "Call Mackenzie's friend Kacey."

"Of course." Bodhi agreed a little too quickly in Jake's estimation.

"Ask her to come up here with you for Mackenzie's birthday on Sunday. It's snowing, but the roads are drivable. Bring dinner, cake, balloons, the whole bit." Jake wanted her to have a big surprise party.

When he told Abby what he had in mind earlier that morning, she helped with the plan to invite everybody up to the mountain house.

Mackenzie's steps echoed in the hallway, so he quickly hung up with Bodhi. She entered the room carrying a large plastic container.

"Let me get that." Jake took the box from her arms. It was heavy. She was probably stronger than him and could chop the rest of the wood outside in no time.

"I tested the lights. They work fine, but my best train set and holiday village are back at my apartment."

"You have more than one train set and village?" he asked.

"Maybe." Her face smoothed into a poker face. "Don't judge."

"I'm impressed."

"If Kacey would let me, I'd run the train around the apartment all year long."

"I suppose you have to show some restraint." He pictured her working diligently on her train set, building terrain and bridges over creeks with actual running water. She was quirky, but he liked eccentric people, and she revealed more of herself every moment he was with her.

"I guess." She opened the container. Inside was the most colorful ornaments he'd ever seen. They ranged from purple and magenta to green and chartreuse to oranges and reds. Shards of stained glass reflected the afternoon sun.

He picked up a glass ball and turned it in his hand. It was smooth and delicate.

"Most of these are handmade from around the world," she said. "My parents collected them over the years."

"I don't trust myself," he said, placing the ornament gently back into the box. "I'll string up the lights instead."

"Nonsense." She begun unwinding an extension cord. "Let me decorate the tree. You write, and I promise I won't disturb you."

"I think I'm done for the day anyway."

"You can't be." She frowned. "Maybe you need another break."

Taking breaks was his specialty. "That's probably it," he said. "C'mon, let's do the lights."

He took the other end of the string from her as they wound their way around the tree, connecting more strings as they went.

"I like a lot of lights," she said, her face glowing.

"Me too." He tried not to stare at her, but she was dazzling beside the tree all lit up and waiting for its ornaments.

As they neared the top of the tree, they came closer together. The warmth of her body on his quickened his pulse. It took all his strength not to inhale her perfume. Every inch of him craved her. Neither let go of the string, and he waited for what seemed like an eternity for her to make the next move.

Should he drop everything and hold her close to him? Bury himself in her hair and neck and forget all about the song, Bodhi, and the never-ending expectation to revive his career?

Jake searched her eyes. What was she thinking? There was

nothing more he wanted but her at that moment.

Passion took hold of him, but he hesitated. Their relationship must remain professional. He had promised himself that, and anyway, starting a romance during Christmastime hadn't worked out well for him the last time.

She pulled away. "I never know what to do with the end of the cord once I reach the top."

Disappointment sagged through him even though she'd been right to reject him. A romantic relationship was a bad idea, and they both knew it.

"It's because you're too short," he teased her, hoping to lighten the mood. "I'll tuck it right behind this branch in the back."

"What were your family Christmases like?" She went poker-faced and removed one of the glass ornaments from the box, proceeding as if there hadn't just been a tense moment between them.

"Are you asking as a reporter or a friend?" He didn't mind the question but wanted to find out more about her.

"Both," she said.

"We celebrated at my Aunt Marilyn's. They lived in a small apartment. At least twelve of us were crammed into the living room. She went all out draping red tulle across the walls and attaching hundreds of tiny white lights on the ceiling. In the dark, it looked like a starry winter night."

"She sounds like my kind of woman."

"You would've liked her. Everybody did." His voice dropped at the memory of his aunt's sudden passing. Mackenzie must've noticed his sad tone, because she didn't press him for any more information.

"You know everything about me," he said. "What about you?"

"I'm the journalist, remember?" Her eyes narrowed.

"Of course." He threw up his hands. "But tell me something about yourself."

"What do you want to ask? I'm an open book." She fished an ornament from the box.

"Hmm." He thought for a moment not wanting to blow this opportunity with a simple question. What's your favorite color wouldn't do in the company of a journalist.

He gazed around the library and landed on her textbook collection. "Did you always want to be a journalist?"

"I wasn't sure what I wanted to do. I didn't want to be like some of my cousins, relying on a trust fund with absolutely no motivation to work."

He admired her independence. It was one of the first traits he noticed about her.

"My first two years in college, I changed my major at least three times," she said.

By the time he was twenty, he was touring the world and making lots of money. He thought about going back to school and admired people with the opportunity and courage to switch career paths. Not that he ever wanted to give up music. Sometimes it felt as though music had given him up.

"I was ready to quit altogether until I had an epiphany one afternoon at work," she said.

"At the newspaper?"

"No." She shook her head. Before I interned there, I worked part-time in a clothing store. Anyway, I already hated the job. The pay was low, and the work was hard. Not that I minded the challenge," she said defensively.

"Of course not," he said. "Hardest working reporter at *The Sunrise Press*."

She crossed her arms and eyed him suspiciously.

"Go on," he said. Why did he have to interrupt? Obviously interviewing wasn't his best skill.

"The manager wasn't nice and mistreated us. I usually held my tongue because I didn't want to be perceived as the spoiled little rich girl. They all knew my family.

"Anyway, one day I was particularly frustrated with my classes. I had a ten-page paper due the next day, and the manager was on a real rampage. I was in the store with two of my co-workers when a strange sound came from the accessories department. One of our customers, poor thing." Her face scrunched. "Got sick right in the middle of the aisle."

"No!" He was queasy at the thought.

"We drew straws to see who would clean it up. Guess who picked the shortest straw?"

He pointed at her.

"Yep. So, as I was cleaning up the mess, I thought to myself there's got to be a better future for me. If I drop out of college, what will become of my life? From then on, I was determined to succeed. The next semester, I made the dean's list."

"Look out, smarty pants." Her intelligence had been obvious to him from day one.

"That's right."

As they were admiring the tree, all the lights clicked off. The sun set only minutes ago, so there was enough light left to see her silhouette.

"The electricity must've gone off."

"Should I check the breaker box?"

She looked out the window. "Don't bother. The whole neighborhood's lost power." With the help of the flashlight on her cellphone, she went to the kitchen.

"There goes my writing schedule," he called after her, secretly relieved to start fresh in the morning.

She returned with candles. "This happens all the time," she said, lighting the pillars and placing them strategically around the room.

"We have enough light to finish decorating the tree." He hooked one of the glass balls on the tree.

"You don't have to," she said. "This was my idea."

"And a good one." When he was famous and had lots of so-called friends, professional designers decorated his house for the season. As the fame and friends dried up, he attempted to make the house festive on his own. After the broken engagement, he gave up entirely and let December 25th pass as if it were just another day.

"I'm having fun." He went for another ornament to hang.

"You are?" she asked. "After what you told me about your ex leaving you at the altar, I wouldn't blame you if you never wanted to celebrate Christmas again." She rested her hand on his arm.

He fidgeted with the ornament.

She must've sensed his discomfort because she dropped her hand. "I'm sorry."

"For what?" He enjoyed the touch more than she could know.

"Maybe you don't want to talk about the past anymore." She took the ornament from Jake and hung it on the tree.

"You're good," he said, wagging his finger at her. "We were talking about you, remember?"

"Didn't I answer your question?"

"No, you didn't. Why did you want to become a journalist?"

"For what it's worth, I'm obsessed with finding out what motivates people to do the things they do. I want to know the why's and the how's. Reporting and writing about the news allows me to understand some aspects of life."

"When you find out, let me know," he said. "It's a big mystery to me."

She sighed. "Yeah, to me too."

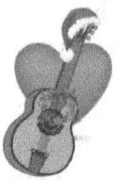

Chapter Sixteen

As much as he wanted to send a text message, it wouldn't be enough. Bodhi needed to do it the old-fashioned way. Scroll through the contacts on his phone, find the number, and hit send. He listened to the rings and silently wished to simply leave a message on her voicemail. If Kacey was interested, she'd return his call.

The problem with the plan was she would never agree to his invitation to join them in the mountains for Mackenzie's birthday. Why should she? He'd made an obnoxious fool of himself during their first so-called meeting. It clearly hadn't been a date. He wasn't completely clueless how frustrated Kacey became during his campaign to get her to influence Mackenzie. His attempt to win her over was a long shot, but desperate times called for desperate measures.

Jake counted on Bodhi. A positive story would benefit Mackenzie too. He'd have to press these points upon Kacey.

On the third ring, she picked up. *That seems just like her.* She probably didn't want to appear too anxious to find out who was on the other end of the call. His phone number was listed as private, and he was positive she hadn't put him in her phonebook.

"Hi, it's Bodhi," he said, striking a casual tone though his legs were shaking. If she knew he wanted something again, she would put her guard up.

"Who?" she asked.

He hesitated. Was she serious?

"I'm kidding." She laughed, likely at his suffering. "What's going on?"

"Do you have a minute?" He assumed she did or she wouldn't have answered the phone. The question was a good way to stall while he worked up the courage to tell her what he wanted.

"Just. I'm due at the gallery to meet with my dealer."

"Exciting," he said. "Everything okay?"

"Great. We're on track, and we may even get a few reviews out of the show."

Prolonging the inevitable wasn't an option. He sucked in his breath and finally said, "Do you have any plans for tomorrow?"

"Sure do. It's Mackenzie's birthday, and we're all celebrating at my family's house."

He could hear rustling on the other end of the line. Maybe Kacey was about to walk out the door. With only a few minutes to make his case, the situation became more complicated. It was up to him to change their plans.

"Here's the thing," he said. "Jake asked me to give you a call and suggest we drive up to the mountains and celebrate Mackenzie's birthday there…together."

There was a long pause on the other end. "We? As in you and me?"

Was he supposed to invite Kacey's family too? He didn't have clear enough instructions from Jake.

Man, this is awkward. Bodhi would have to remember to make Jake pay big time for the favor *after* he recorded his winning Christmas song.

"Mackenzie went there to check on her sister, but she was supposed to come right back. He hasn't kidnapped her or something?"

"No," he cried, desperate to deescalate the situation quickly. "Of course not. I guess they got snowed in."

"But the roads are open now."

"When's the last time you talked to Mackenzie?"

"A few days ago. She said the weather was bad, so they were staying up until it cleared. But she promised she'd be home soon."

He had feared Jake was off on some tropical island sipping mais tais and working on his tan rather than a Christmas song. Bodhi almost had a heart attack when Jake answered his call with "Aloha."

"They decided to stay a few days." Bodhi entertained the idea of a romance blossoming, but Jake was too focused on his song. At least Bodhi hoped so. His friend hardly needed the distraction.

"But she was supposed to celebrate her birthday with me." Kacey sounded hurt. Bodhi's throat clenched. He hated causing her any pain.

How can I make this better? How could he possibly ask her to abandon her family in favor of Jake and him? It was Mackenzie's birthday, though. Best friends should be together to celebrate.

Bodhi had a brilliant idea. "Why don't we *all* go up to the mountains? Jake said it's beautiful up there, and Mackenzie would love to see you and your family."

"You do realize we're talking about more than my mother and father. I have six brothers."

"The more the merrier." He swallowed a little too loudly. *Six brothers*. He was sure she heard his fear on the other end of the line.

"But only three of them are in town."

"Too bad." Picturing six male versions of her rang an alarm bell in his mind. He counted his blessings he'd only be subjected to three.

"You have no idea what you're getting yourself in to." She sounded amused, as if the new set of circumstances presented a unique way to taunt him.

"Is that a yes?" He was all in, and much to his surprise, was looking forward to it.

His parents lived back in England. A big family dinner was only something he watched on television. He'd dismissed the scenes as sentimental, but he'd missed it all along.

"Are you driving?" she asked.

His two-door coupe would never fit six passengers. He'd have to rent an SUV anyway to get through the snow. "Pick you up at ten AM tomorrow?"

"Maybe, and that's a big maybe."

He could hear the wheels turning in her head. Perhaps it wouldn't be so easy to convince her family.

"My family doesn't do well with change," she said.

"Who does?" He didn't know it before he called her, but change was something he might look forward to. Who said he had to be a bachelor for life?

"Let me give them a call, and I'll let you know."

"Thank you. I hope we can make this happen," he said, hanging up the phone and praying it would all work out.

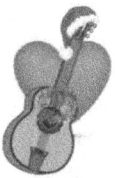

Chapter Seventeen

They were sitting around the breakfast table when Dylan shuffled in and sank into a chair. Still in pajamas and hair uncombed, he sighed heavily as he poured himself a bowl of cereal.

Jake snuck a peek at Mackenzie to see if she knew what all the angst was about. She shrugged.

"What's with the long face?" asked Abby.

Dylan crunched his cereal. "Nothing," he said in between chews.

Jake guessed it was something to do with the girl Dylan was trying to impress. He didn't have his guitar with him, and Jake grew suspicious. The two had been inseparable since Jake arrived. He felt proud he might have something to do with this kid discovering a love for playing music.

It had been a dream of his to teach children, and he even considered opening his own music school. With all the touring, even just at the small, local venues, he didn't have the time to dedicate himself to such an important job.

"Where's your guitar?" he asked. "Should we send out a search party?"

"It doesn't matter." Dylan's voice cracked.

His despair broke Jake's heart.

Abby's brows drew together. "But you've got to keep practicing. Even if you've got the song down perfect, it never hurts to keep your fingers limber."

He was impressed by her pep talk. Only last night she'd complained to him and Mackenzie she'd lost her son to a guitar and a song.

"It's over." Dylan slammed his spoon on the table. Milk splattered the placemat.

Mackenzie jumped. "Jeez, you don't have to make a mess about it. What's over?"

Jake imagined her pulling out her reporter's pen and pad. Though he hoped she'd be gentler with her nephew than she was with Jake.

Dylan wiped away the tears at the corners of his eyes. "Kyle left Lake Arrowhead last night. He won't be back in time for the ceremony."

"But that's just one person," said his mother. "Surely the show can go on without him."

"Kyle's the drummer." He rolled his eyes.

"Do you need a drummer?" asked Jake. "I could program a drum machine to play the song."

"Ethan said if it's only the three of us performing, he didn't want to do to it."

"So now you're down to two," said Mackenzie. It sounded like the reporter in her was trying to piece the facts together in the middle of the emotional turmoil. "Still doable."

"Ethan's the singer. We can't go on with only a guitar and bass player. And he even threatened to quit the band altogether."

"What about an acoustic set? You and the guitar?" Considering his own struggles with stage fright, it was a lot to expect, but Jake didn't see any other alternative.

"Can he sing?" Mackenzie asked her sister.

"He might be cursed with the Stone's inability to carry a tune," she whispered.

"I can hear you," said Dylan.

"Sorry, but it's true." Abby pinched the bridge of her nose. "We gotta come up with Plan B."

"Maybe it's not too late to find another singer." Mackenzie tilted her head in Jake's direction.

"Oh, no. I've got my own Christmas-song problems. Besides, you don't want me to steal the spotlight." He puffed his chest out in a mocking proud peacock fashion.

She threw her napkin at him. "With my handsome nephew center stage, they won't even notice you."

"You got me there," he said, slumping his shoulders. "Can you sing the song?" he asked Dylan.

"No way." The kid's face turned red. "In front of Sophia? In front of everyone? Forget it!"

He empathized with Dylan. Maybe they didn't have a choice. He'd worked so persistently Jake was compelled to do something about it.

"This might be a blessing in disguise," he said.

Dylan crossed his arms.

"Now, hear me out. You're going to be great. Sophia won't laugh at you. In fact, there's no better way to make a girl swoon than to dedicate a song to her."

"Oh please." Mackenzie snorted. "You actually think we're all that shallow?"

"I'm not saying that." Jake tried to explain without offending her even more. "A good song is the quickest way to someone's heart. Music is capable of transporting raw, emotional power."

"He has a point," said Abby. "There's a reason teenagers go crazy over their favorite musicians. Even I'm guilty of that."

"You don't say," Mackenzie teased.

"Why don't you get your guitar?" said Jake. "You can audition for us."

Dylan's eyes went round. "I'm scared."

"We'll be gentle," he said. "But honest."

While Dylan ran to get his guitar, they cleared the table.

"What if he's terrible?" asked Abby. "Don't make him feel bad."

"What kind of aunt do you think I am?" Mackenzie frowned. "Anyway, it's 'Jingle Bell Rock.' How hard could it be?" She sang the lyrics.

Jake and Abby looked at each other in horror. Abby covered her ears, and Jake howled like a dog.

"Stop it! You're just jealous because I was the best singer in the family."

"That's not saying much," said Abby.

Head hung low, Dylan returned with his guitar. "I don't know if I can do this."

"It's okay, sweetheart," said Abby. "Play the song for us."

He strummed the opening, before stopping abruptly. "Sorry."

"It's okay," said Jake. "Try again. The beginning's a little tricky, and you're only nervous about the singing part. You've got this."

Dylan sang the first line.

Abby's mouth dropped open. "Wow," she mouthed to Jake and Mackenzie.

Her son continued without looking up.

The proud aunt beamed at him then Jake. She started to sing along, but Abby put her hand over Mackenzie's mouth. It was mean, but Jake couldn't blame Abby. She didn't want anyone to steal the moment from her son. Jake's mom would've done the same.

When Dylan finished, he waited, gaze glued to the floor. He was afraid to face his judges.

Abby clapped. "That was so great." She tried to hug him, but

Dylan's guitar got in the way.

"Mom," he whined. "You better not hug me in front of Sophia."

She laughed. "Okay, I won't embarrass you in front of your friends."

"Does this mean you're going to do it?" asked Mackenzie. "Get up on the stage by yourself and sing the song?"

"Don't make it sound so dreadful," said Abby.

"Of course he is," said Jake confidently, even though they were all waiting for a confirmation from Dylan. Jake understood the importance of a verbal commitment better than anyone else.

"I guess so," said Dylan.

"You're gonna rock the Christmas tree lighting," said Mackenzie. "Girl or no girl."

An hour later, the house was filled with Christmas music. Dylan in his room singing and Jake back at the piano.

Abby entered the library where he was writing down some ideas. The morning activities had inspired him. Mackenzie followed closely behind, both wearing somber looks on their faces.

"Uh oh?" he said. *What could possibly be wrong now?*

"I just got off the phone with Cameron Finch. He's the mayor and in charge of the tree lighting ceremony." Abby collapsed on the sofa.

"Dylan can't perform. The band lost their slot when the others quit," said Mackenzie. "They booked another act. Can you believe it? And now the mayor says they're on a tight schedule and won't include Dylan. How long can 'Jingle Bell Rock' take, for Pete's sake?" She threw up her arms.

"Calm down," said Abby.

"This is ridiculous," said Mackenzie, ignoring her sister. Her face was flushed with anger. She picked up the phone. "What's Mayor Finch's number?"

"Stop," said Abby. "You're not the most charming when you're like this."

"I don't care about being charming. He's crushing a young boy's dream. I'm not standing for that kind of injustice."

"Take it easy, Ruth Bader Ginsburg." She gently took the phone from her sister. "If Dylan finds out his aunt bullied the mayor into letting her nephew play, I'll never hear the end of it."

"I'm only doing what's fair. Don't you want—"

"Of course, I do," said Abby, cutting her off. "But we have to be subtler about it. Kids his age don't always appreciate their family stepping in to save the day. They get embarrassed about the most ridiculous things. Last week Dylan asked me to drop him off down the street from the ice-skating rink. It took all my strength to do it. Then I remembered how we used to want Dad to do the same thing."

"We just let this happen?"

They ignored Jake as if he wasn't in the room. He cleared his throat to remind them though he wasn't sure how to help.

Mackenzie's face lit up. "Maybe his mom or aunt can't step in, but what about the famous guy from out of town?"

"No way," he said. Throwing his name around like some kind of super power, even if it was for good, was not his style.

"C'mon, people are putty in your hands," she said. "Look at my sister, for example. She could barely remember her own name when I introduced you."

"Shut up," said Abby, suddenly fiddling with her earring. "But it's not a bad idea."

"You want me to call up and say this is Jake Wilder, now let Dylan play?"

"Not call up," said Mackenzie. "Show up."

Refusing the Stone sisters was futile. When they set their minds to something, nobody had a chance at doing any different.

An hour later they were on their way to the village. Dylan had gone to a friend's house believing everything was on track for his solo performance. They thought it best if he didn't catch on to what they were doing. Jake prayed they wouldn't have to break the bad news. Even with the weight of the world on his shoulders, he welcomed the challenge. It came as a relief to think about somebody else for a change.

"Mayor Finch is a retired police officer," said Abby. "He can spot someone trying to pull one over on him a mile away."

"Be honest, but be firm," said Mackenzie.

They treated him like he was taking a trip to the principal's office after getting caught playing hooky.

The mayor's office was in a quaint store front in the heart of the village. Jake imagined a friendly, small town headquarters where nobody ever got in serious trouble. The visual put him at ease.

"To what do I owe this pleasure?" The mayor sat behind a large, rustic-looking desk.

Mackenzie flashed a toothy, forced smile. Abby made her practice grinning and bearing it on the way over.

"Nice to see you," she said. "I'm sure you're busy with all the festivities coming up."

"Not too busy for the Stone sisters."

Jake hid behind his baseball cap, hoping the women would warm up the mayor before being introduced.

"Speaking of festivities," said Mackenzie, in her most polite and restrained voice. "My nephew's been practicing so much, playing and singing 'Jingle Bell Rock' nonstop. It would be a shame to let him down like this."

Mayor Finch shook his head. "Sheesh, I'm sorry about that. There's nothing I can do. A schedule's a schedule."

"Could you make an exception?" Jake chimed in.

"No, I'm sorry," said the mayor, without a hint of recognition. They were asking for trouble relying on Jake's fame.

"Dylan will be crushed." Tears filled Abby's eyes. "I'd hate to break the news to my sweet, vulnerable son."

Mackenzie flashed Abby the thumbs up when Mayor Finch looked away.

"I remember when people dismissed me," said Jake. "All I needed was one chance to prove myself, one yes to open the door. I'll never forget when that person came along. He was my hero."

"Don't you want to be Dylan's hero?" asked Mackenzie.

A petite woman with charcoal-gray hair came into the office. She was holding a brown paper bag but dropped it to the floor when she saw Jake. A blush crept up her cheeks. "You're Jake Wilder."

"I am." He held onto his poker face. This common response by fans confused him as if he didn't know who he was and only needed a reminder.

Mayor Finch scrutinized Jake.

"This is Mrs. Finch," said Abby.

"Nice to meet you." He took the mayor's wife's hand in his own.

She was shaking. "What are you doing here on our little mountain?"

"We came in to ask your husband to allow Dylan, Abby's son, to play his one short song at the Christmas tree lighting ceremony."

"Look." The mayor tapped his fingers on his desk. "There's simply no time available in the schedule."

She stared her husband down. "Of course, there's time," she said. "This is Jake Wilder. And if he wants Dylan to perform, he will."

When they made it back to their car, they all busted up laughing.

"I thought Mayor Finch was going to cry." Mackenzie slapped her knee.

"I'd hate to cross her," said Abby. "Thank you, Mrs. Finch."

"As they say, the show must go on." Jake was drunk with happiness.

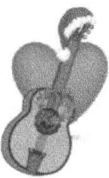

Chapter Eighteen

Kacey and her family bumped into each other as they spun around the tiny kitchen. The limited space wasn't meant for six people. Her brothers, Paul, Mark, and Andy, took up enough room to double the count. They scrambled to pack food for the party while they waited for Bodhi to pick them up.

"Don't drink the milk straight from the container," Kacey's mother scolded Paul. He wiped his mouth off with his sleeve.

"That's disgusting," said Kacey. "I'm gonna have to throw the whole thing away now."

"Hand it here." Bobby took a big swig.

She held her breath, hoping they didn't do any more damage. A cereal bowl had already been broken and a spoon accidentally ground up in the garbage disposal. Her older brothers acted more like teenagers than the twenty somethings they all were. Together, their ages added up to about fifteen.

Her father sat at the kitchen table and read the newspaper like he was all alone in his favorite diner. A magnitude 5.1 earthquake could hit, shake the apartment like a maraca, and he'd yawn and turn the page. If left to his own device, Mr. Flores would soon curl up on the couch for a nap.

Mrs. Flores ran circles in the kitchen trying to figure out how she was going to transport all the food up the long, windy hill. "Ah, *miha*, I wish you would've given us more notice."

"I only found out myself." Her request put everyone out, but in the end, it would be worth it. Lake Arrowhead was breathtaking this time of year.

"I prepared everything to eat at home. Now what am I supposed to do?" Mrs. Flores opened and closed the kitchen drawers.

"What are you looking for?"

"Tin foil to cover these bowls."

"But the food is already sealed in plastic containers with lids."

"I don't trust these flimsy things." Mrs. Flores held up the potato salad so Kacey could see.

She didn't want to argue with her mother and handed her the aluminum foil. "We're going to have fun in the mountains. You'll see."

Mrs. Flores looked doubtful. A pang of guilt shot through Kacey. *This better work out or I'll never live it down.*

"Boys, get out of my way." Her mom shoved her sons aside.

That she still treated her grown sons like children was humorous and a little pathetic

"Why don't you try helping Mom instead of making a bigger mess?" said Kacey.

"I don't see you doing anything." Bobby was the second oldest of her six brothers, and her favorite, though she would never admit it to the others.

He was an art historian at the local university and took her to museums when she was a kid. She became a painter because of him, and he taught her the meaning and value of art when the rest of her brothers were busy picking on her.

"I'm standing by in case Bodhi pulls up." She made up the bogus excuse at the last minute. Being the youngest, she learned to think quick on her feet.

"Oh, that's important," said Andy.

He was the youngest of the six brothers. Closest in age to her, he felt a special obligation to be her protector. It drove her crazy as a teenager—he was the first to tell her parents when she ditched school or broke any of the rules. She hated him back then for it but now saw he was only looking out for her.

"He's here," she shouted, justifying her post by the window.

"I'm not ready." Mrs. Flores rushed her work in covering all the containers with the foil.

Each of the Flores's kids slung their bags over their shoulders and scooped up a dish despite their mother's protest.

Once outside, they circled Bodhi's rental car.

"Sweet ride," said Paul.

He was the most boyish, the jock of the brothers. He loved cars almost as much as he loved sports. His sister didn't mind the friends he used to bring home from whatever team he was on. She kept that tidbit from Andy. He would've had a fit.

"It's a Chevy Tahoe. The biggest car on the lot." Bodhi looked tiny standing next to the huge SUV.

"Mom's going to need a ladder to get in there," said Kacey.

"I've got her." Andy offered a hand to his mother.

"I can do it," said Mrs. Flores. With surprising agility, she hoisted herself up into the front seat.

Kacey reluctantly climbed into the second row. She suffered from car sickness and wanted to sit up front. Her father slid in next to her, and all three guys took the back row. It reminded her of when she was a kid. The whole family piling into the minivan for a summer road trip.

Bodhi waited quietly as they settled in. If she wasn't mistaken, a look of satisfaction spread across his face.

Once they reached the foothill of the mountain, they stopped for a bathroom break. Kacey took a motion sickness pill and offered one to her brothers.

"I don't need one of those," said Paul. He teased Bob for taking one. "Don't be a wimp."

The roads were covered with snow, but the Tahoe glided right over them. Bodhi mostly listened to her family's banter. She figured he'd rather not get involved in the ridiculous debates her brothers were having. They couldn't agree on anything. From their favorite college football team to whether James Bond movies were overrated. Whatever the issue, if one was in favor, two weren't.

"You better pull over, bro," said Paul. He looked a little green around the gills.

"Don't be such a *wimp*," Bob teased.

"I mean it, Bodhi. If you want this SUV to retain its new car smell."

Bodhi drove to the side as quickly as he could.

Paul barely made it out the door before he threw up on the side of the road. Mrs. Flores found some napkins in one of the bags and brought them to her son with a bottle of water.

Bob and Andy doubled over with laughter. Bodhi glanced at Kacey to see her reaction.

She gave a half-smile. "Welcome to the family."

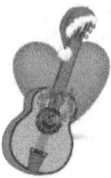

Chapter Nineteen

Mackenzie had determined she wouldn't let Kacey and her family down. The fact they'd celebrate her birthday when her own family was out of town was too generous and kind to simply flake out on them. Mackenzie would find a way to get down the mountain to be with them. If she asked to borrow Jake's car, he'd insist on going with her, but now more than ever, he needed to stay and finish his song. Her neighbor Penny had a truck she'd loan Mackenzie if necessary.

When she called Kacey to tell her she was looking forward to seeing them, she said her mother wasn't feeling well. Did Mackenzie mind postponing?

"Is there something I can do?" She bit her lip. Mrs. Flores was like a second mother to her.

"Just the sniffles," Kacey had said. "Besides, I'm so busy with my upcoming show, I can hardly spare a moment. Raincheck?"

"Sure, why not?" Disappointment sagged through Mackenzie. Spending the day with Kacey's family had been something Mackenzie looked forward to all week, but the cancellation freed her up to work on Jake and her article.

After dinner the night before, he continued to work on his song but was clearly exhausted. The sheer determination to complete it kept him hovering over the piano as he worked out the lyrics.

She wanted to help more. Perhaps try her hand at writing a lyric or two. Was songwriting so different from writing an article? Both called for evocative imagery with the goal of communicating ideas and emotions.

Assisting him with the contest would violate a professional boundary. Staying in the mountains together was bad enough. If anybody at the paper found out, especially Ross, she'd be mortified.

Had she already crossed the line? When they were decorating the tree, she had wanted to kiss Jake. They got caught up in the moment, and it probably meant nothing to him now. She was glad because getting involved with her subject was not a good idea even though she couldn't get his soft eyes out of her head. He was handsome, smart, and artistic. In any other situation, she would be tempted. In *this* situation, she was very tempted.

~ * ~

The next afternoon Mackenzie called one of the local restaurants to ask about reservations. It was still her birthday, after all.

As she was making the reservation for the four of them, somebody knocked on the office door where she'd been working.

"Can I come in?" asked Jake.

"Just a sec." She took a quick look in the mirror. Her hair was a mess, so she ran her fingers through it and swiped on lip gloss. A little voice inside her head told her to stop primping for him. Keep it professional, it said.

When she opened the door, he held an arrangement of orange roses and yellow sunflowers. "Happy birthday."

"It's like a fall sunrise." She inhaled the sweet scent.

"They go with your hair."

She melted when he smiled. "You've been out?"

"I drove into the village to pick up a few provisions."

He looked great in her father's flannel shirt. "I know you're working on the song, so don't feel obligated to celebrate my birthday. It's no big deal."

"I have a better idea," he said, his eyes flashing as though he were up to something she couldn't figure out. "Come with me."

As they approached the kitchen, whispers and shuffling footsteps came from the room. She rounded the corner half expecting to see her sister with Dylan and some of his friends.

"Surprise!" Kacey jumped up and down, clapping her hands.

"You'll scare her half to death." Kacey's mother held Kacey's hands to stop her from making so much noise.

"I can't help myself." She wiggled free from her mother. "Can you believe it? We're here."

Tears filled Mackenzie's eyes. She floated with giddiness. Kacey, her parents, and three of her brothers had driven up to celebrate her birthday.

Bodhi handed Mackenzie a bouquet of balloons. "Happy Birthday."

"What are you all doing here?" For the first time in her life, somebody actually managed to surprise her. She usually ruined secretly-planned parties with her suspicious nature.

"And Peterkins too." Jake's dog scampered to her side.

"I hope you don't mind," he said. "Abby said it was all right, and I missed my boy."

"Of course not." She nuzzled into Peterkins for a cuddle.

"Jake asked us to come," said Mrs. Flores. "We couldn't let the day go without having a big party."

"Happy birthday," said Dylan. He hugged her, and Abby joined in for a big squeeze too.

Happiness flowed through Mackenzie. Everybody deserved family and friends like these.

They gathered around the big table in the formal dining room. Abby put out their mother's best china and took pictures to send her to parents in Italy.

Bodhi and Kacey sat next to each other, looking cozy and intimate.

"What are your intentions with my sister?" Paul, the oldest, asked.

It wouldn't be long before Kacey's older brothers started teasing Bodhi.

He dropped his head, probably so nobody could see him blushing. He was lucky Kacey's three other brothers weren't there to join in. They were with their wives and families in different states, one in another country.

Bob tossed a roll at his brother. "Don't listen to him." His face grew serious. "So, what *are* your intentions?"

Mackenzie snickered. Kacey kicked her under the table.

She wasn't so innocent herself. As soon as she got Mackenzie alone, Kacey had grilled Makenzie about the *Jake situation*. "I see the way he's looking at you," Kacey said.

"It's strictly professional." Mackenzie's nostrils flared.

"Not even close." Kacey pointed to Mackenzie's face. "Besides, I can tell something's up. Your nose gets all funny when you're bothered about something."

"I don't think so," she said. "Neither of us wants the distraction. We've got important business to take care of."

"Sure thing," Kacey had said. "It's all *business*."

"Bodhi, where did you learn to make this chicken recipe?" Jake asked in time to save his friend from the inquisition. "In all the years I've known you, you've never cooked for me. As a matter of fact, you're always eating at my house."

"One can rise to the occasion," Bodhi said. "When I was younger, I entertained the idea of culinary school."

Jake's eyes widened. "You did?"

"You don't know everything about me. I wanted to be a chef."

Mrs. Flores clasped her hands together as though she was pleased her prayers had been answered. Finally, her daughter had found the perfect man.

They were already welcoming Bodhi into their family. Even with Kacey's reputations for playing the field, her family hadn't given up on finding her a steady boyfriend.

"Somebody pass me the salad," said Mr. Flores. He usually stayed out of family drama but could probably see where his wife's train-of-thought was going.

"I can't take all the credit," said Bodhi. "Mrs. Flores made the rest of this delicious spread."

"Thank you, Mama," said Kacey.

"Everything is amazing," said Mackenzie. "The food is superb, but the company is even better."

Mr. Flores picked up his glass of wine. "A toast. To family and friends, old and new."

"Cheers," said Jake.

"I'm so happy you all came," said Abby. "It probably wasn't easy, but at least Mackenzie doesn't have to spend her birthday with just us."

"What's wrong with just us?" asked Dylan.

"Nothing," said Abby. "I don't want your Aunt Mackenzie to feel too lonely is what I meant."

"She's not lonely," Kacey said. "She has Jake."

Mackenzie glared at Kacey.

"I'm afraid I'm not very good company." He drew in a deep breath.

"How's the song coming, anyway?" asked Bodhi.

Mackenzie was grateful for the quick change of subject.

"I'll play it for you later," said Jake. "But to be honest, I'm struggling with the lyrics."

"He only needs a little more Christmas magic." Mackenzie was protecting him though she wondered what was compelling her. She was supposed to stay objective, wasn't she?

"We can help," said Paul. All three brothers sang out their favorite Christmas songs. Of course, they were all different, so it sounded like a cacophony of jingle bell duds.

After dinner, they gathered in the library. It was late afternoon, but the light was low. She switched on the tree. The beautiful, one-of-a-kind ornaments refracted colorful lights around the room.

Mrs. Flores settled close to her husband on the sofa. They were wrapped in a plush blanket like newlyweds. Thirty-five years of marriage, and they were still happy. Kacey's brothers sat around the piano waiting for Jake to take center stage. The scene reminded Mackenzie of a Norman Rockwell painting. They weren't blood relatives, but they were family.

"C'mon, play 'City Lights'," Paul said to Jake. "The guys at work aren't going to believe I hung out with Jake Wilder."

"You don't want to hear that oldie." Jake rolled his shoulders. He probably knew refusing was a losing battle.

"Oh yes we do," said Bob.

Jake stretched his fingers out then laid them on the keyboard. Mackenzie gave him credit for being such a good sport.

When he finished, he transitioned into "Let It Snow."

Kacey and Bodhi brought in slices of birthday cake.

"Jingle Bells" quickly followed. Jake wasn't taking a break as he offered everybody their favorite song.

"Can I play something?" asked Andy.

"Be my guest." Jake vacated the hot seat and dug into a piece of cake.

Andy tapped out a few notes. "I've been thinking about your Christmas song," he said. "How about something like this?" He played "Santa Claus is Comin' to Town."

"Jeez," Paul yelled. "I thought you were serious."

"Move over, clown." Bob shoved Andy over.

"Yeah, make room," said Paul, parking himself on the other side. The three acted like pre-teens goofing around.

"Help me clear these plates," Kacey said to Mackenzie.

"They can wait." She was enjoying the show too much to leave.

"No, they can't." Kacey raised her chin in the direction of the kitchen.

Mackenzie didn't want to bicker in front of the guests and diligently followed her friend into the kitchen, suspecting the earlier conversation about Jake wouldn't be the end to Kacey's interrogation.

"So," she said as soon as they were out of earshot. "You're here with Jake Wilder. In this romantic setting, and you're going to tell me nothing's going on?"

"Nope." She placed the dishes in the sink and ran the water. "It's purely business."

"Uh-huh." Kacey opened the dishwasher.

"You know the story. My sister and nephew got into a car accident. Jake drove me here then we were snowed in. The rest is ancient history." She loaded the dishwasher, careful to avoid Kacey's suspecting gaze.

"The roads are clear now," said Kacey. "You could drive back to Los Angeles tonight. He writes his song; you write your article."

"You don't understand," said Mackenzie. "He doesn't have a chance at winning this contest without my help."

"Why does he *have* to win? When you took this story, there was no guarantee."

"What kind of story ends with a defeat?" Sometimes she regretted sharing every detail of her life with Kacey. She was one of those pesky best friends—the kind who tell you the truth no matter what.

"You're the journalist," said Kacey. "You figure it out."

"What's wrong with helping the story out a bit? Think of me as a Christmas elf building careers for the both of us." She was done with this conversation.

"I don't want you to get hurt," said Kacey. "He's cool and charming, but is he the *one*?"

Mackenzie threw her hands up. This was ridiculous. How did they go from writing a song and follow-up newspaper article to spending the rest of their lives together?

"At first I was excited about the possibility of you and Jake getting together. I want you to be happy." Kacey hesitated, as she seemed to search for the right words. "But I also don't want you to sacrifice your dream of becoming a big-time reporter."

"That's what I'm doing. Following my dream by doing my job."

"Are you sure?" Kacey raised an eyebrow but said no more.

It was up to Mackenzie to figure out the answer.

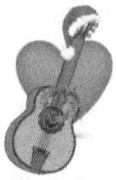

Chapter Twenty

During the next few days, Jake tried to get back to work. He mulled over several themes for his song. This was how he usually started. What did he want to say and why? The idea of being lost and found again kept coming back to him. It was too early to fully understand its significance. The music and lyrics had a way of working themselves out in his subconscious, and he wished the first line would hit in the middle of the night. His problem was he tended to overthink every word or idea that sprang into his mind. That, along with the tremendous pressure he was under, only frightened his inner muse away.

The Christmas tree lighting ceremony was just the inspiration, and break, he needed.

He'd been to the village center during the day, but at night, the experience was entirely different. The Swiss-style buildings glittered and glowed with lights. The light posts were wrapped in candy cane paper and the storefronts draped with snowcapped garland. A life-sized toy train carried children and adults from one end to another. The village bordered a frozen lake that reflected all the magnificence back to them.

"This is unbelievable," he said. "I haven't been to a tree lighting, since—"

He stopped himself from rehashing the depressing story once again. The last one he had gone to was with Samantha, his ex-fiancée, back in her hometown on the east coast. The night was picture-perfect. It was snowing, like it was tonight, when she indicated for the first time she had questions about their future together. The wedding was only weeks away.

His mistake was not paying more attention to her doubts. Instead, he brushed away her comments, wrote off her feelings as pre-wedding jitters. The honest truth was they weren't right for each other. He wanted to settle down after the wedding. Stop touring and focus on having a family, but Samantha was gearing up for a glamourous life on the road with her popstar husband.

There wasn't any point in spending so much time blaming her when she'd done them both a huge favor by not going through with the wedding. He silently wished her well and hoped she found what she was looking for.

"Since?" Mackenzie waved her hand in front of him to snap him back to the present.

"A long time," he said. "Too long maybe." He petted Peterkins.

The dog looked dapper in his new green and red Christmas sweater. His pet sitter insisted on buying something warm for the dog when she found out he'd be up in the mountains. At first he refused to humiliate his buddy, but Mackenzie insisted he was the cutest thing she'd ever seen. Peterkins liked it too.

They were near the tree when a dark-haired woman approached. She was from the shop Jake popped into when they first arrived that evening.

Abby was with Dylan as he got ready for his big performance. Mackenzie had run into an old friend and waited for Jake outside while he made the secret purchase.

"Excuse me, sir," said the saleswoman.

"Yes." He led her away from Mackenzie so the surprise wouldn't be ruined. She looked on suspiciously.

The saleswoman seemed to understand and discreetly handed him the wrapped package. "I hope she likes it."

"Me too." He tucked the gift into his pocket. "She's done so much for me I can hardly begin to repay her."

When the woman walked away, Mackenzie asked, "Another fan?"

"It happens." He widened his eyes innocently.

"I'm sure you especially hate the pretty ones." Her nostrils flared, and she looked away.

He'd never seen her act like this. She was too emotional for such a supposedly objective journalist. *Is she jealous?*

"Something wrong with your nose?" The opportunity to have some fun at her expense was too tempting to pass up.

"What are you talking about?" She gave him a frosty look and rubbed her nose. "Is there something on my face?"

"No, you seemed bothered."

"I notice you offer the beautiful fans extra special attention. I guess the plain ones like me only get an autograph or a selfie if we're lucky."

"I'm nice to all my fans." He was shocked she cared at all.

What had he done? He catalogued all the offenses he may have committed: not making his bed that morning, eating leftover cake straight from the box. He wasn't perfect by any means.

Assuming she was jealous, that would mean she might actually have feelings for him. The revelation pleasantly surprised him.

"Never mind," she huffed, buttoning up her coat tight around her throat.

Maybe he should've refuted the comment about her being plain even though it was obvious to everyone she was beautiful. She didn't seem the type to fish for a compliment.

"As you know," he said, "I have fans from all different walks of life. Can I help it some women are attracted to me?" If she was going to accuse him of being a cad, he'd work it and play up the pompous-celebrity type.

"I was one of *People* magazine's most attractive men." He gave the mysterious-angsty expression he'd perfected over the years.

"Oh, please," she said, rolling her eyes. "Of course. You keep reminding me."

He touched his hand to his heart. "Seriously, I didn't mean to hurt you."

"Don't flatter yourself." She turned away.

This tense back-and-forth came out of nowhere. Jake's feelings had grown for her, but he was sure they weren't reciprocated. He was doing his best to fulfill his obligation, to be a good subject for her story. Nothing more.

"Are you angry with me?" he asked.

"Of course not." Her expression closed, so he couldn't read her.

He fingered the package in his pocket. The plan was to wait until after he submitted his song to give her the gift as a thank you. Maybe it was better to offer it now as a way to make peace.

The crowd closed in around the tree as it was getting near time to light it up. Her voice was lowered as she said, "I'm just concerned."

He didn't expect that word. Anger he could deal with, but *concern* frightened him. People were concerned when there was bad news. Someone's health was failing or something bad was going to happen and people weren't prepared. Then there was the most frightening possibility. He'd disappointed someone, and they were concerned he'd do it again.

Concern came from his mom when she received a call from the school principal about her son daydreaming in class instead of listening to his teacher. Mom, he'd explained, I was composing music in my head. They were *concerned* he might fail his subjects.

"What about?" he asked.

"You take a lot of breaks when you're writing." Mackenzie shifted from one foot to the other.

He related to her physical discomfort. "If I sit too long, the ideas rush down my legs and out my feet." He was trying to lighten the mood.

She didn't take the bait.

"I'll admit it," he finally said. "I'm stumped by the lyrics. It's not easy writing a Christmas song, searching to say something that hasn't been said a thousand times."

She drew in a long breath. "I get it. Sometimes when writer's block gets a hold of me, I want to give up. Quit writing, quit reporting."

She's not a tyrant after all.

"It can be so challenging," she continued. "But I've listened to your music. Your songs were fresh and original."

"I wish I had as much confidence as you."

"This is what I'm talking about. If you don't believe you can do it, you won't."

"I'm afraid it takes more than confidence." He worried he never really had what it took. "It takes talent."

"You have that coming out your ears."

He let go of his pent-up anxiety and envisioned completing the song. "Don't worry. You'll get your story no matter what."

"Heck, yes I will," she said. "You have so much talent, but you keep it locked up in there." She gently pressed against his heart.

"I lost the key," he said. The crowd grew thicker, but he felt like they were the only two in the world.

"We'll find it."

Her words were like a glass of water to his parched soul. She had no idea how much they meant to him. "Does it come in a box with pretty Christmas paper? Is it in the form of a song? I don't know. I keep asking myself these questions."

"I think it comes in the form of perusing your dreams," she said. "You want to make a comeback, right?"

If he thought about it, he and Peterkins had a good thing going. A nice house in the hills, a swimming pool, and a recording studio. What else could he want? He only wanted his music to be valued.

"I do," he finally said. "I believe I have something to say and want to share it with anybody willing to listen."

"Absolutely."

His answer seemed to satisfy her, and he was pleased with the reaffirmation as well. She pushed him to look deep inside himself. For the first time since he met her, they could finally be friends outside of their professional relationship.

She glanced at her watch. "They should be starting soon. Every year, Santa comes at six PM sharp to light the tree."

He handed her the gift from his pocket. "I saw this tonight and couldn't resist."

"A present for me?"

"It's certainly not for the other, *prettier* fan."

She sighed. "Let's forget that ever happened."

"Forgotten," Jake said, even though it had been nice to think for a moment she might actually be falling for him. "Well, are you going to open it?"

"Can I?" she asked as she was already unwrapping the gift. "I love presents."

"I would have never guessed."

She handed him the torn paper. From the tissue, came a Christmas tree music box. "Oh, it's beautiful." She examined the hand-painted red bows and gold star on top.

"It plays music," he said.

She turned the miniature silver crank. "We Wish You a Merry Christmas" rang out from the tiny internal speaker.

The couple next to them hummed along.

"I love it," she said.

"I saw it and knew you had to have it." The music box was the perfect symbol to commemorate their experience. He wondered if he'd be in her life next year to enjoy it. "I hope it doesn't get lost among your other decorations."

"Are you kidding? It's going right in the center of the whole, darn village. Thank you."

"You're welcome."

The train chugged along the tracks and whistled as it approached and stopped to deliver Santa. "Ho ho ho," Santa said, as he made his way through the crowd.

On the count of three, he lit up the tree.

The glowing lights illuminated the night sky. Everyone murmured and awed. Mayor Finch said a few words, but Jake could hardly pay attention. He felt like a nervous father and wiped his sweaty palms on his pants.

"You're making me nervous too," she said.

"I can't help it." He had tried to think of everything before sending Dylan and Abby to the waiting area by the stage. "I hope Abby reminded Dylan to make sure he has extra guitar strings in his pocket."

"You only examined the guitar a thousand times. It's going to be fine."

"Knock on wood." He repressed the urge to run to the nearest tree to tap on the bark.

Abby had been just as panicky. On the way over, she made them turn back to the house. She was positive she'd left the oven on. Mackenzie, on the other hand, was as cool as a cucumber. Jake didn't know where she got the confidence from, but he could see Dylan's manager in the making.

The crowd grew as they waited for the program to begin. To ease Dylan's jitters, Jake advised Dylan to focus on one person in the crowd. "Pretend it's only the two of you."

"But not Sophia," he said. "That'd only make me more nervous."

"Excuse me," Abby said, cutting her way through the people around them. "There's not much more we can do now." She shivered, clutching the collar of her jacket.

"Pray," said Jake.

Mackenzie elbowed him. "He's gonna crush this."

"I coached him on the importance of facial expressions. I even told him to try winking." Abby fluttered her right eyelid to demonstrate.

Jake wanted to weep. *That's exactly what he should not be doing.*

"But Dylan refused. He asked me if I had something in my eye."

"Thank goodness because you look ridiculous." Mackenzie wasn't so subtle.

"I thought it would be cute." Her sister pouted. "I told him to loosen up and have fun."

"Yep," said Jake. "That's what making and performing music should be about." Taking his own advice wouldn't be a bad idea.

The duet act before Dylan sang "It Had to Be You."

Jake whispered to Mackenzie. "Is this a Christmas song?" He shook his head in response to his own question.

"It could be," she said

"Why?" He felt like an authority on the issue now. "There's no mention of Christmas or snow or anything holiday-like at all."

"Never mind." She shushed him when Dylan approached the stage.

"Showtime." He closed his eyes and said a silent prayer.

Dylan walked slowly to the microphone. His hands shook as he strapped on his guitar. "Jingle bell, jingle bell, jingle bell rock," he sang without looking up at the audience.

C'mon, Dylan, connect with one person.

"Jingle bells swing and jingle bells ring," he continued, gaze glued to the stage floor. "Snowing and blowing up bushels of fun / Now the jingle hop has begun." He raised his head just enough to make eye contact with somebody in the front row.

Abby clapped along to the music. Mackenzie and the rest of the crowd followed.

The sound of everyone joining in must've relaxed Dylan because he began moving his body along with the song. He bobbed his head and belted it out even louder.

They crowd joined in too.

When he was finished, he took off his Santa hat and threw it into the audience. A young girl caught it. Jake hoped it was Sophia.

"How'd I do?" Dylan rushed to Jake's side after the performance. He was smiling from ear to ear.

"You were incredible," he said.

Despite Abby's promise, she gave her son a big hug in public. Dylan was so elated, he didn't seem to mind.

"The best performer of the night," said Mackenzie.

"And guess what? Sophia asked me to go ice skating later."

"Okay," said Abby. "But remember, it's not always about getting the girl."

"Correct," Dylan said. "It's about the love of the music."

Jake beamed with pride.

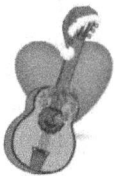

Chapter Twenty-One

Jake practically whispered the new lyrics he was working on. Mackenzie could barely hear from the other room. Not that she was eavesdropping. She was only curious about the progress he made since Dylan's performance.

As quietly as possible, she removed the ingredients from the refrigerator and cupboard. The cookie cutters had been easy to find, right on the top of the drawer as though they'd recently been used. It seemed like only yesterday her mom baked Christmas cookies for the entire neighborhood.

She lined up the jars of colored sugar sprinkles in a neat row on the counter. Her mother would frost each tree, star, and gingerbread man with the precision of a pastry chef, but Mackenzie could barely squeeze the frosting out of the pastry bag. When it did come out, the colors plopped and smeared everywhere. To her the impressionistic look was *très chic* and tasted as good as her mother's perfect creations. Tonight, she decided to keep things simple with her mother's easy sugar cookie recipe and a simple layer of sprinkles.

Making Christmas cookies would keep him in the holiday spirit. He had been so moved by the celebration in the village and Dylan's performance, Jake wanted to get straight to the piano. Far be it from her to stand in his way. Her plan was working better than she imagined it would.

As the oven heated, she forgot whether she needed to grease the cookie pan. There was enough butter in the batter to clog arteries. She opened her laptop to look it up, and as much as she tried not to, checked her work email.

Hope fluttered inside her when she saw an email from *The Sunrise Press*. Perhaps Mr. Hughes had returned from his leave and wanted to check in. She was anxious for an additional assignment she could research while waiting for Jake to finish his song. It would also keep her from obsessing over his progress or lack thereof. She clicked open the email.

"Dear Ms. Stone," it started. *Not a good sign.* Too formal, even for Mr. Hughes. Her stomach knotted as she glanced at the signature. The letter was from Ross, signed editor-in-chief. *What is that little sneak up to?* The news was as awful as she anticipated.

Mr. Hughes had retired to spend time with his family. Her heart stopped when she read the line regarding her future at *The Sunrise Press.* "We've decided to go in a different direction," it said. They were firing her.

"That's it?" Mackenzie shouted. *They can't do this to me.* Ross wrote her belongings would be packed, and she could pick them up at her convenience.

What was she going to do? Her head spun. She'd given everything to the paper, and though she hadn't planned to stay forever, she worked hard and was dedicated to its success along with her own. Over the years, she'd compiled her best clips, but she wasn't ready to apply for a new job. None of her stories had taken off like she hoped. She was depending on the Jake Wilder article to propel her to the next level.

She took a chance Kacey was near her laptop and called using a video chat app.

"Hey there." Kacey answered after a few rings. She was dressed in her painting clothes, music playing in the background.

"Am I interrupting?" It was obvious she was but was desperate to talk to her best friend.

"Yes, but I'll drop anything for you." Kacey leaned into the camera.

"Thank you." She stalled, not quite ready to drop the bombshell. "I'm so glad you and your family came for my birthday. It wouldn't have been the same without you."

"What's wrong?" Kacey raised an eyebrow. Even through a tiny camera, she could dig up the truth like the ace reporter Mackenzie longed to be.

"Why do you assume something's wrong?"

"Because you already thanked me, and besides, I know that look."

Gah! If the artist thing doesn't work out, she could apply for the FBI. "Can't I thank my friend? It meant a lot to me."

"You're welcome." Kacey wiped her hand across her shoulder leaving a beautiful smudge of magenta. "Now spill it."

"I was fired."

"By Jake?"

"No." She wondered if he could do that. "By the paper."

"You're kidding?" Kacey's face screwed up.

"I wish."

"Mr. Hughes fired you."

"He retired," said Mackenzie. "Ross is editor-in-chief now, and it seems like his first order of business was to get rid of me."

"That's the thanks you get for not going out for coffee with him." Kacey shook her head in disgust. "Want me to tweet something bad about him? I've got a bunch of followers."

Mackenzie smirked. The idea was appealing, but she thought better of it. "No, thanks. They said the paper was going in a different direction, and that direction didn't include me."

"If you ask me, he's doing you a favor."

"How do you figure?"

"It's time to move on to bigger and better opportunities."

Kacey was right, but Mackenzie figured when she left the paper, it would be her choice. Getting sacked wasn't good for her résumé or her ego. "What am I'm going to do?"

"Are you in the kitchen right now?" asked Kacey.

"Naturally. Why?"

"If I recall, there were some seriously tasty leftovers."

"Jake ate the rest of the cake."

"How dare he." Kacey put her arms across her chest. "Man after my own heart."

Her spirits lifted almost immediately. Kacey always had a way of cheering Mackenzie up with her sense of humor. "Not all's lost. I'm baking cookies."

"That's a good first step. Piled high with frosting like your mom makes?"

Mackenzie held up a jar of green sprinkles. "Afraid not."

"You can't have it all I guess."

"Seriously, I needed more time at the paper to get my portfolio in order. Nobody's gonna hire an amateur like me."

"Okay, stop right there." Kacey's forehead creased. "You are not an amateur. You are a smart, talented journalist. I've seen your articles, and nobody covers a bake sale like you. Any paper would be lucky to have you."

The fact Kacey could say "bake sale" with a serious face made Mackenzie love her best friend even more. "How did you get so smart?"

"I happened to be born both smart and beautiful. Sometimes it's a curse, but you know, I make the best of it."

"The question now is, what am I going to do about Jake's story?"

"Does he know you were canned?"

"You have such a way with words," Mackenzie said. "No, I only found out myself. What's the point of finishing the story? I don't have a newspaper backing me anymore."

Kacey picked up her computer and held the camera up to her paintings. "I can't tell you how many of these I've made without knowing what was next. That's the business. Write your article anyway. If it's good enough, somebody will publish it."

She had a point. Mackenzie was now officially a freelance writer. The realization both delighted and terrified her.

"Show that Ross you'll make it without him."

~ * ~

"I've got to tell you—" Jake startled her from her daze. "Eating raw cookie dough can make you sick."

Lost in deep thought, she hadn't noticed the music had stopped. She tried not to flick a dollop onto him. Now was not the time for playful banter.

"I need it," she said, cradling the spoon like a sugar addict.

"Rough night?" He filled a glass of water.

"Yep."

"Did you want to bake those?" He gestured toward the bowl Mackenzie was holding.

"I guess so," she said. "But I better make a fresh batch. I must've stuck this spoon in there about fifty times."

"I don't mind," he said. "Can I help?"

"What about your work?" Should she should tell him the truth about losing her job? Not that it would stop him from continuing. The Christmas writing challenge was still on.

She stuck her spoon back into the bowl and sighed.

"Are you okay?" asked Jake.

"I want you to understand this has no bearing on you. You are welcome to stay here and finish your song."

"You're making me nervous," he said.

"I was fired from the paper." She squeezed her eyes shut to keep the tears from coming.

"Have a seat."

When she opened her eyes, he had pulled out a stool from underneath the kitchen island.

Peterkins pushed his warm body into her legs and stared up at her with big round eyes. She was impressed with his intuition until she remembered she smelled like cookie dough.

"Kacey thinks I should write the story anyway." She remained positive despite her misgivings. He didn't need to fall under the Mackenzie Stone curse if she was doomed to fail.

"Absolutely," he said. "I've been working on some lines I feel good about. As soon as I get something together, I'll let you listen."

"You don't have to," she said, drawing in a long breath. The defeat was almost debilitating. "I mean, I'd love to hear, but you're not obligated to share anything with me now."

"But I want to," he said. "We're in this together."

Her cheeks grew warm. The attraction for him had intensified at the tree lighting ceremony, but she pushed it away. It was her duty as a reporter to stay objective. Falling for her subject would influence the story, she told herself. Now that she'd been fired, everything was up in the air.

"Help me whip up another batch." Another minute of contemplation and she might end up in his arms, letting him comfort her.

"I'm going to write a winning song, and you will write a great article." His bright smile was infectious.

She handed him a clean bowl. "Then we're well on our way because everybody knows the key ingredients to delicious Christmas cookies are a positive attitude with a dash of hope."

"We are both free agents."

The thought made her stomach sink again. Her expression must've given her away because he added, "It's exciting."

"Maybe," she said. "But I'm nervous and a little frightened."

"But in a good way. Life is unpredictable."

"Predictability might not be such a bad thing."

"Naw, that's boring. Life doesn't come with instructions. Sometimes you have to just let go."

Easier said than done. Focusing on her career had given her direction. A purpose. Without a steady, reliable job, who was she?

"Fine." She laid out the measuring spoons and cups. It was time to move forward. "But in this case, we're following the recipe instructions to the tee."

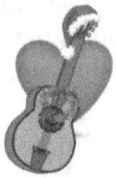

Chapter Twenty-Two

The Christmas tree lights reflected off the large picture window and bounced back into the library where Jake was resting on the sofa. He was finally alone. After baking and eating way too many cookies, he said goodnight to Mackenzie and went to work on his song.

She'd been so generous. He worried he'd never be able to fully express how grateful he was. Everything she'd done was in the interest of reviving a Christmas spirit that had been lost to him long ago. Building the snowman, decorating the tree, and taking him to the tree-lighting ceremony in the village was an act of kindness that inspired him. He once accused her of having an ulterior motive. If he didn't succeed, neither would she. Her motives were so much more. A person couldn't fake that kind of kindness.

On top of that, when he wasn't paying attention, she had hung stockings on the chimney mantle. One even had his name written on it in silver glitter. He thought back to his childhood stocking chock full of toys and candy Santa delivered. She was like his very own Santa Claus— a much prettier version.

He had so much for which to be thankful and wasted too much time bitter and angry over his fledgling career. But who could blame him? Shortly after his star dimmed, he continued writing songs. They were good, but the critics didn't have any more patience for him. They fixated on his looks and said the pretty boy was all fluff with little content.

Even when he wrote songs that were extremely personal, they slammed him anyway. The one about his dying father received almost no attention. Jake recalled their final Christmas together. His father was in the hospital, and his mother brought in a small artificial tree. They decorated it together and reminisced about their past holidays together. Against all odds, Jake wished for more time together. Fate didn't have that in mind, and the next day, his father died. All these years later, the tree sat preserved in storage.

Bodhi constantly reminded Jake that very few people experienced the kind of success he'd enjoyed. He still had fans who loved every minute of his concerts. Who knew what songs he had left in him?

Gratitude. He wrote the word in his journal where he penned his best songs in the past but had gotten out of the habit. The pages were painfully blank. Scraps of paper left in the inner hinge revealed where he'd ripped out recent lyrics. He had balled them up and tossed the paper into the fireplace, promising to press on no matter how awful the writing seemed at first.

It was do-or-die time. The deadline was closing in on him like a runaway train on a downhill track. Desperate for words, he closed his eyes. Surprisingly, what popped into his head was the first time he'd met Mackenzie. She was lost on the side of the road in that wonderful, but impractical little convertible of hers. He wrote the line: *Somehow I found you.*

It had nothing to do with Christmas, but he couldn't worry about that now.

Moments from their time together flashed through his mind like scenes from a movie. The memories were pleasant until he replayed his romance and break up with his ex. The TMZ headline, "Has-Been Pop Star Left Singing the Blues at the Altar," crept into the picture. He opened his eyes and steadied his breath. Abandoned. Lonely. That was what he felt after the record company dropped his band. The negative emotions clung like an ill-fitting shirt.

He took in a sharp breath to slow the hyperventilating. Only the piano, his trusty friend, held the answers. Melodies ran through him, down his arms, and to his fingers to the keys as he played for his life. If he were to survive, he had to replace the old, hurtful memories. Winning the contest had become so much more. The song was about finding Christmas again. Maybe it was even about finding love. He wanted to capture nostalgia, romance, and the joy of coming home. Home to his heart.

The layers of protection peeled away. For a moment, he dared to look into his heart and saw there might be an opening. He was only in his thirties but had lived a life so full of ups and downs and endured so many failed relationships. There had been other women. Blind dates he'd been set up with, professional acquaintances with common interests. On paper, they were perfect matches, but they never really clicked. He wasn't overly picky. Who was he to be so judgmental? Accepting love again meant rewiring the cynical man he'd become. It was no longer okay to simply brush romance off because it just *wasn't for him.* Or *it never worked out anyway.* These were the lies he told himself every day until now.

He stopped playing for a moment and wrote *falling* into his journal.

Inhaling deeply, he relaxed. The voice of his childhood music teacher chimed in his head. "Allow the music to whisper in your ear," she'd said.

There were images of childhood Christmases, his family at church and eating a big dinner afterward in celebration. He saw himself on stage, playing to full audiences rejoicing in his songs. Music and lyrics written by him and adored by them. He had done it once. He could do it again.

As he recalled his ex-fiancée, the hurt feelings were now replaced with a sense of gratitude for having the opportunity to love her, but he had to move on. At every level. He embraced the process of letting go of the old and letting in the new but wondered if it was too much to actually imagine Jake Wilder, the songwriter and performer, could emerge renewed.

His songwriting ritual consisted of contemplation followed by a moment in which he cleared his mind and summoned the creative muses. The blank pages of his journal didn't look so intimidating anymore. He put his pen to paper and wrote without stopping.

Line after line, the lyrics poured out of him. The damn had broken, and the pages absorbed his words. His wrist began to hurt, but he ignored it. His foot, curled up beneath his thigh, tingled. He untucked it to shake off the pins and needles but kept going like he was nineteen all over again. Nothing but the future ahead of him. Big hopes and big dreams. A superstar, the likes of which nobody had seen, was about to hit the airwaves. That was what he believed back then. Now, he knew better. There was more to success than fame.

When he was offered a role on the celebrity game show, it wasn't right because there was no soul in it. It hadn't even been a consideration since he had nothing more to offer than a somewhat-recognizable name and persona.

Writing this song, here and now, felt right whether there was fame attached to it or not.

Even in his darkest days, success was about embracing one's art, persevering when times were tough. When you're on the loser train and nobody wanted to get on board with you, you were all alone, but you kept going. You had no choice. Maybe, if he was lucky, he'd win the contest, but he'd be ready to adjust to whatever happened. If these years had taught him anything, it was how he weathered the storms that counted the most.

It was getting late, but Jake gathered his guitar and the portable recording equipment Bodhi brought him. He spent most of the night recording.

By morning, he had his song.

Chapter Twenty-Three

It had been a week since Bodhi had seen Kacey, but he couldn't stop thinking of her. Worrying about whether Jake would meet the contest deadline helped to distract Bodhi. It seemed ridiculous to miss her since they'd barely spent any time together, yet there was a connection. At least he hoped so and wondered if she felt it too.

He contemplated asking her out on a real date. During Mackenzie's birthday party, Kacey seemed receptive. Apparently she'd forgiven him after he'd made such an ass of himself at the coffee shop. Nobody could manipulate her and get away with it. He'd been foolish and selfish for trying.

The thought of her big, rowdy family put him in a good mood. In the mountains, they'd all gone outside to toss around the football, ribbing him like a brother might when he dropped the ball because his fingers were near frozen, and he wasn't any good at playing football anyway. Mrs. Flores had insisted he take some of the leftovers home and made him promise to visit if he was in the neighborhood. Kacey didn't seem to mind him getting close to her family.

With all those kids in the house, he figured they were used to feeding hungry friends and giving them a warm, loving home to do their homework or just hang out. Bodhi's heart warmed. He was an only child and ached for siblings like she had. Though like any little sister, she pretended they were a pain and scoffed when he said how much he liked her brothers.

It took all of his strength not to ask Jake to find out from Mackenzie if Kacey liked him, as if he were in grade school passing a note. *Check this box for yes, this one for no.*

When his friend invited him to the movie set she'd been working on, Bodhi immediately wanted to invite Kacey to join. His director friend was shooting a Christmastime movie, and the studio in Burbank was decked out as a Dickens-style Christmas village, complete with snow. If they went tonight, they'd have the set almost to themselves while the crew tested out the snow machines.

He lost his nerve to call, so he texted her instead. He wanted to give her an easy out if she needed one.

Surprised to hear from you. She responded right away, an excellent sign.

Thought you might be busy painting. He tried to play it cool. *How are you?*

Good. You?

Jake's still working on the song, and the deadline is soon. He wasn't sure why he mentioned it except Jake and Mackenzie were what they had in common. Bodhi would have to work to change that. With Kacey's wide interests and intelligence, they'd find lots to talk about.

Yikes.

I'm not worried.

She replied with an eye-rolling emoji.

Are you free tonight? I've got a surprise.

I'm intrigued... she wrote.

Then say yes.

Yes.

His heart skipped a beat, as they made arrangements to meet later.

~ * ~

"It's cold like real snow." She stood in the middle of the indoor sound stage and held out both hands to catch the falling snow.

"That's because it is real snow. It's made the same way." The technicians were adjusting the artificial snow machines before they called the actors back to the set the next day.

"Mackenzie should see this." As Kacey turned to point out the town inn, her long, dark hair glistened with snow, electrifying him. His breath caught.

"She'd go nuts," she said. "The buildings look exactly like they do in one of her villages."

"She has more than one?"

"Don't ask." She lifted an eyebrow.

"I can't believe they're still up in the mountains."

"What's up with that?"

He was stumped. It was all he could do not to drive back up the mountain and demand Jake play his song.

They walked to the next building, a charming house, complete with smoking chimney.

"As long as Jake's finishes and records the song, I'm happy." He hid his anxiety. This career-hinging moment shouldn't be her problem too.

"Hopefully they're working instead of falling for each other."

"Is there something I should know?" He needed his one and only client focused on writing a song not losing his head over a woman, especially one writing his so-called comeback story.

"Can you blame him? She's perfect—smart, beautiful. I hate her." Kacey stuck out her tongue.

"Jake's not a bad catch himself." Though many times Bodhi wanted to throttle Jake. The guy had so much talent, but nobody was going to come to him only on his terms. He had to get out there and show the world—again–what he was capable of.

Kacey skipped toward one of the cottages. "Can I go inside?"

"I don't see why not? Just don't break anything."

The door wouldn't budge. She walked to the window and peeked in. "Nothing inside anyway."

"I guess you'll have to use your imagination."

"Maybe if this painting thing doesn't work out, I could get into set decorating. I'd love to create entire imaginary worlds."

"I've seen your art," Bodhi said. "Your show's gonna be a smashing success."

She clapped. "You've seen my work?"

"I may have checked out your website. I love all the colors you use. Vibrant and exciting. I'm hoping to collect a piece myself." He liked to believe he was an art appreciator.

"Are you trying to buy me?"

"No." He shook his head more vigorously than he intended. *Great!* Now he looked desperate.

"Because you totally can." She guffawed as she made her way to a bench under a street lamp. The yellow glow lit up her face. "I wonder if we'll see Ebenezer Scrooge walking down the street."

"I hope it's *after* he's visited by the three ghosts."

"Not me," she said. "I want to tell that stingy old man where to go."

"Have you always been this feisty?"

"You don't grow up the youngest girl of six brothers without developing a bit of sass. I was quite the tomboy, climbing trees, skinning my knees. I'll have you know I was the fastest runner in my whole elementary school. Even faster than the older kids."

He was impressed. As the slowest kid in school, he was nearly always the last to get picked for sports teams. With his love of cooking, music, and math, he wasn't exactly popular with the cool kids.

"You're a girl jock," he joked.

"Am not." She cracked a smile. "Maybe a little."

"Strong and sensitive. I like that." He wanted to take her hand in his, but she turned away from him. The snow machines stopped pumping out snow as the techs gathered for a meeting nearby.

Had he overstepped his boundaries? Should he apologize? Though he hadn't done anything inappropriate, and she couldn't possibly know what he was thinking—he was incredibly attracted to her.

"What a beautiful church." He pointed toward a building with a stained glass rose window high above the front door.

"Hey, turn that up," one of the stage hands shouted. Music, which was little more than background noise before, filled the set.

Nat King Cole's "Unforgettable" stopped Bodhi in his tracks. He took her hand. "Shall we dance?"

~ * ~

Kacey hesitated. If she danced with him, she might give him the impression she was interested in being more than friends. This had been true until Ian called two nights ago. Her ex-boyfriend had an uncanny knack for throwing her off her game.

She loved this song, though, and the moment felt so right. Before she knew it, she and Bodhi were dancing in the middle of the set. Embarrassment stirred in her as the crew looked on. They were in show business and probably used to seeing people performing. Is that what she was doing—auditioning to be his girlfriend?

His arms encircled her waist. Her father taught her to dance and made it abundantly clear a boy's hands should never go any lower. *Ever.* Her brothers enforced the rule in case anybody got out of line. Once she got the hang of learning to dance, the basics were easy: count the steps, avoid stepping on toes, listen to the music. She rested her head on his shoulder.

He was a wonderful dancer, treading softly as he led them in a simple box step. They didn't speak. It was as if she could only hear her own heartbeat. His warm body pressed close to hers. She inhaled a toasty vanilla scent. Had he been baking? She imagined him pulling warm oatmeal chocolate chip cookies from the oven. In that moment, she could envision a whole lifetime with him.

She lifted her head.

"Are you okay?" he asked.

"Did you bring me here to dance?" The song ended, and she went back to the bench.

"I didn't plan it," he said. "I'm not that smooth, but it was a nice surprise."

Guilt crept inside her. Ian had asked if they could make things work again. Normally, she would have brushed him off. She was a forward motion kind of gal, but he was her first true love. They'd ended amicably even though there was a part of her that regretted the break up. When he'd gone off to law school, she stayed in Los Angeles. It wasn't until his recent move back to the city, that he called.

"Penny for your thoughts," said Bodhi.

"It's nothing." What could she say? *I'm thinking of another man as I'm dancing with you.* The admission would be unnecessarily cruel. She was attracted to him but didn't want to ruin any chance she might have with Ian. "Why did you ask me out?" Her annoyance flared though it wasn't his fault. Messy feelings made her grumpy.

"The past few times we've been together, it's been because I've wanted you to help Jake in some way. I was rude, so I thought I'd make it up to you."

"You're not still concerned with Jake?"

"Oh, I am. Trust me," he said. "I can hardly think of anything else. But the song's almost finished." He crossed his fingers and looked heavenward. "All I can do is let nature take its course."

"Mackenzie's going to write a great story one way or another." Kacey hoped by changing the subject back to Jake, she'd wiggle out of telling him about Ian.

"I trust you're right."

"I am." She knew her friend better than anyone in the world. Mackenzie was tenacious and would publish a great piece. "You don't want me to get involved with the story anymore?"

"I'm sorry I ever asked," he said. "I thought maybe we could get to know each other."

"My life's complicated right now." She felt like she was updating her social profile status. "I don't mean to sound so cliché."

"Complicated in terms of how you feel about me?" Bodhi gave her a puppy-dog look.

She wanted to hide in one of the cottages she felt so conflicted.

"Or is there someone else?"

She swallowed. It hadn't been her intention to bring Ian up, but now it was the elephant in the room. *How can Ian rattle me like this? I'm usually the one calling the shots.*

"I feel silly talking about this, but my ex-boyfriend contacted me a few days ago. He wants to meet for lunch."

She noticed they were standing near a church. That was probably why she felt like this was more of a confession rather than a casual conversation.

"Do you *want* to meet him for lunch?"

She hadn't decided yet. Ian was a great guy, but she once believed he wasn't her type. He was too conservative, too much of a person with his entire life mapped out when she only wanted to go with the flow. Perhaps she was different now, and the idea of making plans didn't sound so awful anymore.

Her parents would cheer if they knew what she was thinking. They'd been trying to get her to settle down. They adored Ian but getting back together with him to please everyone else wasn't a good enough reason.

"I suppose a lunch date couldn't hurt," she finally said.

Bodhi looked at his shoes. She didn't mean to crush him, but how could she know he liked her? She might pretend to be a big flirt, but she cared about hurting people's feelings.

"Thanks for being honest at least."

"Sure, that's me. Honest Abe." Kacey wanted to go home and cry. Once again, she made someone unhappy by simply being herself.

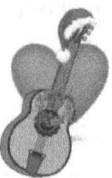

Chapter Twenty-Four

"Good morning." Jake held out a fresh cup of coffee for Mackenzie. She examined him suspiciously, probably surprised he was in the kitchen waiting for her at six AM.

"Did you sleep at all last night?" she asked. He was dressed in the clothes he wore the night before.

"I napped here and there." His eyes burned and watered from exhaustion though the big smile across his face might fool anyone into believing he was well rested. Either that or he was a little loopy. He was so happy, he couldn't help himself.

"I guess I don't have to remind you today's the deadline?"

"Always the practical one." He passed her the sugar bowl. He knew how she took her coffee and wondered what other preferences of hers he'd learn if given the opportunity. "I know what today is."

She heaped a big teaspoonful into her cup, stirred then added more. "I like a lot of sugar," she snapped as if used to defending her sweet tooth.

"Do you want to listen to what I've been doing?"

"I was afraid to ask." She took a big swig of her coffee. Seemingly satisfied with the caffeine running through her veins, she continued, "By the look on your face, I'd say you've got your song."

"I do indeed." He bounced from one foot to the other, barely able to contain his excitement.

"Don't torture me. I'm dying to hear it."

He opened his laptop and stretched his fingers out for effect like he was about to play at Carnegie Hall. "It's called 'You Gave Me Christmas'."

"Hit play already," she said. Peterkins lifted his head from a nap. "Sorry I disturbed you." She patted him.

"Patience." Jake was nervous to hear the song even though he'd listened to it a hundred times already.

When he forced himself to hit play, the song filled the room like a long, forgotten friend:

> *Snowflakes are falling*
> *And I'm falling too*
> *Slowly and softly*
> *I'm falling for you*
>
> *Here in this moment*
> *On a cold Winter's night*
> *It's Christmas, I'm with you*
> *And it feels so right*
>
> *Somehow I found you*
> *Like you were sent from above*
> *You gave me Christmas*
> *When you gave me your love*
>
> *Jingle Bells ring*
> *Angels get wings*
> *My heart starts to sing*
> *When I'm here with you*

As she listened, he watched her reaction. She swayed.

A good sign. It meant she was allowing the music to saturate her being. To go into her heart and through her soul.

She then gave him a half-smile. *What did that mean?* He was anxious to find out but didn't dare interrupt.

Even after hearing it so many times, he still liked the song. This was rare. Recently, if anything he wrote made it as far as the recording, he was scrapping and rewriting until there was nothing left but a few words and phrases.

At three AM something can sound wonderful but not hold up past sunrise. This music had longevity.

Mackenzie appeared to agree. She tapped her foot to the chorus. He needed this kind of reaction, and it thrilled him to see somebody enjoy something *new* he'd written.

With those last lines, she did more than move her head and tap her foot, she looked to be clearly embracing with her body, heart, and soul *his* Christmas song. He didn't care if he won the contest. He'd won over at least one fan, and for now, it was enough.

The song ended, and Mackenzie clapped. "Jake Wilder," she

said, "you are brilliant."

His cheeks heated. "Ah, shucks."

"I mean it. You've done it. You're gonna win!"

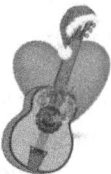

Chapter Twenty-Five

When Mackenzie said Jake would win the contest, she meant it with every fiber of her being. She had faith in her intuition even before they heard the official results. The song was amazing. Initially, it began on the slow and wistful side. There was a beauty and softness to it that gradually built into joy. It made her dance and cry with both happiness and longing for the very Christmas he depicted.

Longing didn't seem quite like the right sentiment since what he described was their experience in real time. It felt personal *and* universal. She couldn't wait for the rest of the world to hear "You Gave Me Christmas."

He had emailed the recording to Bodhi, and as soon as he listened to it, he called hollering in delight. Jake had it in him all along, he said. Their friendship and loyalty ran as deep as hers and Kacey's. No wonder her friend was crushing on Bodhi. He was a good guy.

With the song on speaker mode, Jake and Bodhi listened to it together. He was so enthusiastic he submitted it to Satellite Records right away. Now, all they had to do was wait. When Jake called his mother to tell her he'd written a song he was really proud of, it charmed Mackenzie to see a grown man, who'd seen great success before, continue to seek the approval of his mother.

Once the flurry settled, he didn't mention going back home. In fact, he didn't say much and passed on the toast and coffee Mackenzie set out in front of him. He was bone-weary tired. All he could do was stagger upstairs to bed.

There was a part of her that wanted to stay up in the mountains, but she would never suggest it. He probably needed to get back to the city. Now that he was feeling accomplished and inspired, maybe he'd want to write more songs in his studio.

On a personal level, she was thrilled to celebrate the rest of the season in the snowy wonderland, surrounded by memories of her family.

She could finish her article and find it a home with another newspaper. Maybe once it was published, editors would be knocking at her door offering a full-time position.

In the meantime, there were so many Christmas adventures in the village, and they deserved a moment to celebrate at least one more. Would it hurt to attend one of the town's most exciting events, the gingerbread house building contest? The trophy winners had always been her mother and father, who took building a gingerbread house as seriously as projects in her father's architecture business. As much as she and Abby tried, they couldn't compete with their parents' mad skills.

With the village champs out of town, maybe Mackenzie and Jake had a chance. She threw open the kitchen pantry door and searched for the special tool kit with its precision instruments. Like a doctor's bag, it held all the equipment necessary to assemble, sculpt, mold, and bring to life the house made of cookies and candy. Her mother collected small spatulas and metal wax and plaster carving tools for the occasion.

Unfortunately, she couldn't find anything and wondered if they were hidden in the safe. The tools were that important to her mother.

~ * ~

"Wake up, sleepy head." She nudged Jake awake. He was napping on the back porch overlooking the lake.

"Aren't you cold?" she asked.

He rubbed his eyes, squinting in the afternoon light. The snowy afternoon was bright and beautiful. "Not a bit."

She wrapped the last string of lights around the railing. In all the excitement of the past week, including midwifing a song into existence, she hadn't decorated the outside of the house.

"It'll be pretty all lit up at night," he said.

"I think so." She waited for him to mention going back to the city, reluctant to bring up the subject herself. Her goal was to get them to the two PM start time for the gingerbread building contest.

Wiping her sweaty palms on her jeans, she fought the urge to blurt out her plan for the afternoon. Instead, she'd have to mention it casually.

"Want to go into town with me?" She slipped him a curious glance to see if he was suspicious.

"Sure." Jake yawned and stretched his arms overhead. She hadn't seen him this relaxed in days.

Peterkins came outside to join them. "Hey, boy," she said. Relief washed over her that Jake so easily agreed. There wasn't any good reason to leave the house except to go back to Los Angeles.

"Why?" he asked.

Darn! She almost had him. "Say you'll go, and I'll explain it on the way."

Did he have her same Christmas stamina? Not a lot of people did. Kacey tolerated about half of her antics, complaining midmonth about stepping over trains and finding a place on the coffee table among all the *doodads*, as she called them, for an actual cup of coffee.

"She's always up to something," he said to his dog. Peterkins wagged his tail.

~ * ~

The roads were busy with tourists as the official Christmas season was well underway. She worried he might be tired of sleigh bells and snowflakes after writing his song. Since most Christmas songs were written in the summer in order to have enough time to record and produce by Christmas, those artists finished long before the holiday actually rolled around. Poor guy wouldn't have that kind of time to produce his song, but she was getting ahead of herself. He hadn't won the contest—yet.

Mackenzie avoided mentioning the gingerbread building contest on the ride, and he didn't press for details. Quiet solitude filled the car.

Perhaps he was tapped out of energy. Exhausted from all of the events over the past few days, he'd rather lie back and trust her. At least she hoped so.

He actually did it. Composed a song out of thin air. The comprehension of such an achievement both impressed and inspired her. She supposed the process was a lot like when she wrote her articles except on top of the lyrics, he actually penned the music too. She snuck a glance at him. *Talented and gorgeous.*

Was she suddenly star struck? Her integrity wouldn't allow shallow celebrity worship. A person needed to earn admiration. Fame, in itself, wasn't reason enough for adulation. Now, she saw him for the talented, hardworking, honest man he was. Her skin flushed.

"Are you warm?" He turned down the car heater.

She was grateful he didn't ask what she was thinking.

"Give me a hint at least," he said.

She pulled into a parking spot near the church. "What do you think of gingerbread houses?"

"I'm for them," he said, as if he were being asked to take a vote in congress.

"Of course you are." She giggled. "Who isn't? I mean what do you think about building one?"

A crowd of people pushed their way into the church.

"Must be a good sermon today."

There's no service today," she said. "That's our competition. It's the annual gingerbread house-building contest."

"I have a bad feeling."

"What? They got nothing on us." She batted her eyelashes.

"Don't play innocent with me." He zipped up his jacket as if he were getting ready for battle.

"C'mon. It'll be fun." Fun wasn't the right word. More like *fierce*, but she didn't want to frighten him with her zealous language.

"Famous last words."

Once inside, she searched for a spot near the judge's table. They were known to give clues about what a winning gingerbread house might look like. Every year, the judges were different and tastes varied. Insider information was as important as the right tools. She was tormented she hadn't found her mother's tool bag.

"I've never made a gingerbread house," Jake admitted. "But I'm sure they taste good."

She put her hand over her heart. "Don't let the judges hear you say that. It's a big event around here, and my parents always stomp out the competition."

"You think we can take their place?"

"We can try."

Abby and Dylan had set up their own table nearby. Their parents' tool bag was by her side. Mackenzie shot her sister a dirty look. Abby stuck her tongue out. It was time for the Stone sister competition as well.

Most of the other competitors were already gathered around their tables. The coveted spot near the judges was taken by a couple wearing matching Christmas sweaters.

"Are they actually stretching?" asked Jake.

The woman leaned into a runner's stretch. Her husband bent forward and touched his toes.

"The competition is brutal." Mackenzie rolled her head from side to side to loosen up her neck.

He raised his eyebrows. "In that case, I better take off my jacket." He stepped back from their table near the back and bounced up and down as if he were jumping rope.

"What are you doing?" she asked.

"Limbering up."

Each of the workstations was set with the necessary supplies: prebaked gingerbread pieces, icing, a pastry bag with various sized tips, and bowls of candy. There were a few rudimentary tools they would have to use.

The sweater couple laid out their specialized instruments. Mackenzie fumed.

The head judge explained the rules. Each team had one hour to assemble and decorate their houses. They could be as creative as their imaginations allowed but must use only the provided candy. Last year a couple snuck in Belgium chocolate curls to influence one of the judges, a legendary chocoholic. Competitors could use their own tools.

Her mouth fell open when the Sweaters tested out their William Sonoma kitchen torch.

As Jake scanned the room, Mackenzie wondered what he was thinking. Someone like him was probably used to sharing space with cool city folk lounging at sidewalk cafes or taking meetings to pitch their next big project. Gathered there was a collection of regular people anxious to build gingerbread houses.

Her neighbor Penny waved in their direction. Jake gave a small wave back, probably not wanting to draw attention to himself. It was too late. She mouthed the words "That's him" to one of the judges. Mackenzie's eyes grew wide, and she grinned enthusiastically when the judge realized it was Jake Wilder.

She silently celebrated. "I think I may have found our in," she whispered to him.

"What do you mean?"

"One of the judges recognizes you. Be super nice to her. Maybe even offer to pose for a selfie."

He put his finger to his lips to shush her, pretending he was listening intently to the rules.

"We need all the help we can get." She was not losing to her sister or the Sweaters.

He tsked. "I'm surprised at you. I wouldn't take advantage of my status just to win."

"What status?" she asked, plastering on a fake smile. Served him right for taunting her. This contest was too important to her.

"Oh, that's low. Even for you, Stone."

The Sweaters organized their tools according to size, and possibly, importance. The sunlight from the nearby window hit the metal and bounced into Mackenzie's eyes. She squinted. "It's our only hope."

"Have a little faith," he said. "We're gonna kick butt."

She appreciated his enthusiasm and was glad once again there was no mention of driving down the mountain. Maybe he was enjoying the festivities as much as she was. Without a job to rush back to and a roommate submerged in her upcoming show and possibly in a new relationship, what was her hurry?

But guilt ate at her. Keeping him like he was a hostage wasn't right.

She wanted to spend more time with him there with a million things to do like sledding and skiing the local slopes. A picture of them warming up by the fireplace after a day playing in the snow crept into her mind. Her heart thumped.

"On your mark, get set, go." The judge's command broke her from the fantasy.

Chapter Twenty-Six

Jake sorted through the pieces of gingerbread and held up one of the walls as if he was mystified to its purpose. Careful not to break it, he set it gently back on the sheet of wax paper.

"Help me hold these together while I attach the other side and back." Mackenzie filled the pastry bag and piped icing along the edge of one of the walls and front of the house.

They pressed all four pieces together, but as soon as they let go, the house collapsed.

"I thought you knew what you were doing." He became serious about winning. The competitive spirit was infectious, and after submitting his song, he was in the mood to succeed. Clearly it would please her to do well, and pleasing her made him happy.

"I'm rusty," she said. "They already have the roof on."

She tilted her head in the direction of the husband and wife team wearing matching Christmas sweaters. They'd be winning candidates in any ugly sweater contest. Competitors for sure. It was obvious: they'd come to take the trophy.

"See how they're using soup cans to hold the walls of the house together? We need to do the same until the frosting dries," he said. If she hadn't sprung this on him, he would've been better prepared.

"Sure, let me fish out those cans from my purse. Goodness knows I don't travel anywhere without my chicken noodle."

"You know what I mean, smart aleck. You must have something that'll work."

She emptied the contents of her purse. A wallet, makeup bag, cellphone, a plastic baggie full of restaurant condiments, and a toy hammer spilled onto the table.

Stroking his chin stubble, he studied Mackenzie. She might be even more eccentric than he'd given her credit. "This might come in handy." He held up the toy hammer.

"You never know," she said. "Let's surround the house to hold it together. In a few minutes, we can put on the roof."

Once the house was stable, she changed the tip on the pastry bag, scalloping the roof without rhyme or reason.

"What style would you call this house?" he asked.

How could he demand perfection when she was having so much fun? She moved the pastry bag in sweeping, circular motions like a rhythmic gymnast spiraling her ribbon.

"I'm going with the Baroque style," she said, embellishing every square inch with frosted exuberance.

"Leave room for the candy." He popped a jelly bean into his mouth.

A hissing noise coming from the direction of the couple in matching sweaters. Sugar sizzled as the man fired the small blowtorch back and forth over the house. The smell of burnt brown sugar filled the room. "Are they actually caramelizing the roof?"

Laughing uncontrollably, she shook so hard her body bumped the table, and their entire house caved in.

"Now you've done it." He suppressed a laugh.

One of the judges noticed the chaos and came over to their table. "Everything okay here?"

Mackenzie elbowed Jake in an obvious attempt to indicate this was the judge he was supposed to woo over. The judge didn't seem to notice their disastrous house. She was too busy staring at him. Her chest rose and fell with rapid breaths.

"We had a bit of an accident." Mackenzie tried to right the walls of their house. "Is it possible to get new gingerbread pieces?"

"That's not allowed," the judge snapped at Mackenzie. "Sorry," she said nicely to him.

"Can I introduce you to my friend Jake Wilder?"

Jake offered his hand, and the woman shook it heartily. He couldn't believe he was selling out to win a gingerbread house building contest.

"I'm a huge fan," she said. "I know all the words to all of your songs."

He'd heard the same line many times but never grew tired of it.

It sounded odd in the middle of an intense competition. Not to mention, the goofy apron Mackenzie insisted upon him wearing was covered with frosting. His look was a far cry from the casually cool popstar he once worked to maintain. A fit of laughter overcame him thinking about it.

Mackenzie's eyes grew wide. She probably thought Jake was

making fun of the judge.

"Here," Mackenzie said quickly to the woman. "Give me your phone, so I can take a picture of the two of you."

She handed Mackenzie the phone as the judge squeezed tight next to him.

"Let me see about getting you a new setup," she said.

Even with the fresh start, they weren't going to win. Nobody stood a chance compared to the masterpiece created by the matching sweater couple and their baking torch. They accepted their trophy with a humility some might call questionable.

"It's all just good fun," the woman said, as she held tightly on to the trophy. "We hardly knew what we were doing. We don't deserve this."

"But we'll take it," said her husband. He put his arms on his wife's shoulders, and they posed for a photo shoot that could rival any red-carpet award show.

Mackenzie's nose scrunched up. "I like our house better," she said. "It's...cozy."

He was thrilled the thing stayed in one piece long enough to make the hour deadline. "Hey, can I take this home to my niece?"

"Sure." She sounded less than enthusiastic.

He was surprised. *Did she want to keep the house for herself?* "Or, you can have it," he said.

"I guess that means you want to go home." Her smile faded.

When he woke from his nap this afternoon, he thought her bags would be packed and waiting by the door. They hadn't yet discussed an exit plan, but he needed to get back to the city.

Or did he? The song was submitted, and if he won, he'd have to record and produce it. Rehearsals for the debut and a publicity tour would follow. That was what he hoped for, of course. In truth, he needed it. After experiencing the exhilaration and reward of writing a new song, relying on his old hits wasn't an option for him anymore.

But if he lost, would it be so terrible? He'd love to stay in the mountains and spend special moments like Christmas Eve and New Year's Eve with her. Without the constraints of a professional relationship, they'd be free to pursue a romantic one. He had no indication what she wanted, but she seemed disappointed at the thought of going home. His gut told him she wanted him to stay.

"Did you see our house?" Dylan and Abby cut through the awkward silence in time to save Jake from blowing it. He had been ready to give up his whole career for Mackenzie though he didn't know how she felt about him.

"It's awesome," she said. "But we should have won." She proudly held up their lopsided concoction. "This is our house."

"Is that what you're calling it?" said Abby.

"If you hadn't stolen Mom and Dad's tools."

Abby waved her sister's accusation away. "Anyway," she said. "We're going for ice cream if you want to join."

"Are you crazy? It's freezing," Jake said. "How about a nice warm cup of hot chocolate instead?"

"We know a place that serves the best chocolate chip around. You like ice cream, right?"

"I do."

"Good, I was getting worried about your lack of a sweet tooth."

"Who ate all the leftover birthday cake?" He rubbed his belly.

"I thought maybe I did in the middle of the night. I've been known to sleepwalk my way into the kitchen." Mackenzie eyed the winning trophy on the way out.

"Show me the way," he said.

~ * ~

"I was wondering when I'd see the sisters together again." A man in his seventies greeted them as they entered the ice-cream shop.

"Here we are," said Abby. "Jake, this is Freddie."

"Pleased to meet you," said Freddie. "I've known these girls since they were this high." He held his hand by his knee. "Here's a fun fact. Mackenzie can eat more ice cream than you and I put together."

"Darn straight." She was already on the other side scooping her own.

"Now you stop that," he said. "I could get in trouble for allowing you back there."

"How's Joyce? His wife," she explained.

"As ornery as ever." He scratched his head. "And is this your boyfriend?"

She blushed. "No, just a friend."

Jake was disappointed she labeled him as a *friend* but kept a straight face anyway.

"You never know what'll happen," he said, as if reading Jake's mind. "Joyce and I despised each other at first."

"You're kidding me." Mackenzie heaped two giant scoops of ice cream on a sugar cone and handed it to Dylan.

Abby gave a disapproving look but let her son have it anyway.

"We were next door neighbors." Affection glowed in Freddie's eyes. "She'd been recently widowed, and I wasn't married. I knew she was trouble the day she complained about my overgrown hedges."

"I'll take mine in a cup," Jake said quietly to Mackenzie. He didn't want to interrupt Freddie, but the way she was piling those scoops, made him cautious.

"From there it was history," she said.

"We've been gardening together ever since." Freddie broke from his reverie. "Now get your skinny behind from behind my counter before I get Joyce. She'll run you right out of here."

"Thanks." Mackenzie handed Jake his cup.

They ate their ice cream in a booth by the window. Abby and Dylan sat at a table with some of his friends and their parents.

The ice cream was the best Jake had ever eaten despite the strangeness of eating a frozen treat when the world outside was covered in snow. Luckily, Freddie didn't skimp on the heat, and the parlor was nice and toasty.

Jake wasn't going to mention driving back to the city, but it became obvious they were avoiding the subject. If they ignored it, could they spend the rest of the day wandering around the village and acting like they didn't have a care in the world? She hardly checked her phone anymore. When they first met, her head had been buried in the tiny screen. Always in the present moment, he liked the new, more carefree woman.

"What are you thinking?" he asked.

"About what I'd write when you win the contest." She took a bite of the cone. It was nearly gone.

"Aren't you the one who thought our gingerbread house was a sure thing?" The subject needed to be changed. He was superstitious about celebrating or announcing anything before the ink dried on a contract.

"I like to project positive vibes into the universe."

"You sound like the housekeeper who saged my studio at home to clear it of the bad vibes."

"Speaking of home studio, are you anxious to get back?" She drew in a deep breath.

He took another bite of his ice cream. "Not necessarily."

"Seriously?" Her eyes lit up.

This time, he wasn't imagining it. Perhaps he could ask her out on a real date without worrying about professional relationships.

"Would you like to stay up here longer? With me?" The last question he ventured with obvious trepidation. Nothing had been declared. His feelings for her were unexpressed, and hers for him, unknown.

"Sure, why not." She reached her hand across the table.

He enfolded it with his own.

"So, what's your intention?" she asked.

Leave it to her to break the mood. Most people go on beating around the bush, but not her. That was what he liked so much about her. Her inquisitive nature and *hutzpah*.

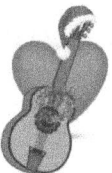

Chapter Twenty-Seven

"How do I look?" Jake exited the dressing room and modeled his rented ski outfit.

In his matching black pants and jacket, he could pass for a pro or maybe a handsome skiing ninja warrior. Mackenzie admired the way the clothes hugged his body, but she wasn't willing to say it aloud. Her desire for him became unbearable.

Afraid she might do something regrettable in private, she decided upon activities in crowded places like the local ski resort to keep them busy. "It's how you perform on the slopes that matter."

"I'll be skiing circles around you in no time, hot shot." He admired himself in the mirror. Tucking the poles under his armpits and squatting, he shifted right and left as if he were racing downhill at breakneck speed.

"But first, ski lessons for you."

He waved her off. "Not necessary."

"I insist," she said.

The first time her parents took Mackenzie skiing, she was too frightened to jump off the ski lift at the top of the hill. They practically pushed her out before she was whisked away in the chair to ride back down the mountain all by herself.

"Besides, if anything happens to *the* Jake Wilder, I'll never forgive myself."

"That's right," he said. "Who will sing the next Christmas song classic?"

"It could happen."

He doubted his song would win the contest. The competition was intense, he warned her several times since submitting "You Gave Me Christmas."

"There's a better chance I'll make the next Olympic ski team." He picked up his skis on their way outside.

The day was bright and clear. Freshly fallen snow formed a thick powder layer on the mountain.

"Skidding down the mountain on your rear end should be a good distraction," she said.

He buckled on his ski boots. "You're going to regret those words when you see me in action."

"Sure thing, I'll meet you at the bottom of the bunny hill in two hours."

~ * ~

Mackenzie suppressed a laugh as Jake skidded to an awkward halt. "Did you pass the class?"

"With flying colors. I was the best student there," he said, lifting the goggles from his face.

"You were the *only* student." She placed her hands at the small of her back and stretched. After doing a couple of runs with Abby and Dylan on the more advanced slopes, she was sore. There were taking a much-needed break outside the lodge before going back for more.

"Was it my fault nobody else signed up?" Jake said. "Anyway, the teacher said I was a natural."

"Uh-huh. Let me guess. He's a big fan."

He crossed his arms over his chest. "I won't even dignify that with a response."

"Did I hurt your feelings?" She rubbed his shoulder in a playful gesture. When he covered his hand over hers, her flesh tingled at the thought of him enclosing her whole body.

"If I say yes, will you be nice to me?" He dropped her hand.

"I'm always nice to you." Disappointment shredded her insides. Not that she expected him to kiss her right there in front of everybody, but the fantasy was enticing, nonetheless.

"The bunny hill's for beginners," he said, eyeing the intermediate ski lift.

"You're just a beginner," she reminded him.

"Not for long."

As he skied toward the lift, she embraced his good mood. Since submitting his song yesterday, he'd been lighter, almost carefree. More relaxed than she'd ever seen him. She tried not to dwell on her own uncertain future and shared in his high spirits instead.

When it came to skiing, though, his arrogance was going to get him in trouble. She'd seen lots of accidents and wouldn't let him break a limb to prove himself.

"Be careful anyway," she said. "And try not to take anyone else down when you fall."

"I appreciate the confidence."

As soon as their turn to ascend the slope came, they sat on the chair lift and headed up. Pine trees dotted the snowy mountains and shrank as they rode higher.

She tried not to look down. "I'm afraid of heights." Her love of skiing hadn't helped to alleviate the terror of imagining herself stranded on the chair lift. "My worst fear is the lift breaking, and I'm left to dangle fifty feet above ground."

"I'll be dangling right by your side," he said.

"That won't do either of us any good. Suppose I fall?"

"Then I'd jump after you. It'd be like flying."

"Best case scenario, you'd break both legs."

"So what?" he said. "As long as I'm with you."

He's really lost his mind. All day he'd been flirting with her. Once the contest ended and her story written, would they even remain friends? Perhaps he was overly tired and punchy from staying up too late.

"How would you perform your new hit song on TV?"

He rubbed his stubble, and she wondered what her face would feel like against her cheek.

"I hadn't thought of it. In that case, you'd have to wait until I called in reinforcements," he said. "You'd be okay until then."

"Yeah, right," she said. "Thanks for the effort."

"No problem." He put his arm around her shoulder.

Was it a friendly gesture or romantic one? Even in the cold air, she melted at his touch.

"Are you sure you know how to exit the chair?" She enjoyed Jake's arm around her but wanted to keep him focused on skiing. All the talk about falling made her nervous.

"We covered it in class."

"Are you scared?" she asked.

"Of skiing or are we talking about the contest?" He removed his arm from her.

"Both." She hated bringing it up, but since he was the one who mentioned it, she couldn't resist.

"Scared isn't the right word." He leaned in and whispered, "I'm terrified."

Her stomach sank. She feared as much. "If you don't win, then all of this was for nothing. A complete waste of time."

"It wasn't for nothing," he said. "I met you."

She wanted to kiss him more than anything she'd ever wanted in her entire life.

"We're here." He jumped off the seat with an ease that surprised her.

She followed, almost falling off herself. The gracelessness of the dismount reminded her of the many times she'd made a fool of herself in front of people she was trying to impress. She winced at her clumsiness.

"Are you sure *you* know how to exit the chair?" He mimicked her.

"My leg cramped up."

Her nostrils flared because she was caught in lie. Just a tiny white one to save her ego.

They looked down the mountain. The intermediate hill could be intimidating to anyone, especially a beginner like him. She was sure they were making a big mistake.

"Ready?" she said.

He lowered his goggles and positioned himself. Pushing off immediately, she regretted not letting Jake go first to keep an eye on him. She slowed. Thank goodness the mountain wasn't too crowded. They easily had enough space to negotiate their own paths, but she wished he would follow in hers more closely.

She considered waiting off to the side. *That move might kill his confidence.* He should enjoy the day at his own pace.

Last night she had asked him if he wanted to go skiing. The proposal was risky considering they hadn't decided when to go back home. Shouldn't she have enough information to write her article? Relying on conducting more personal interviews to keep him close was an excuse he'd see through in a minute.

He already finished the song, and searching for inspiration in the mountains wasn't a reason for him to stay anymore.

Was she using him to avoid reality? The thought of starting all over, applying at a new newspaper, knocked her off-kilter. Hadn't getting a job at a big-time organization been her goal since graduating from college?

Insecurities flooded her mind. She'd gone far down the slope before remembering Jake was supposed to be right behind her. Panic seized her, and she stopped by the side of the run. He effortlessly skied by her, waving his pole as he passed.

"Keep your eyes on the road," she yelled after him.

Maybe he was a natural skier like his teacher said. He could chop wood, make snowmen, and ski, but he definitely needed practice building gingerbread houses. Perhaps by next year they'd both improve.

There her mind went again. Making plans when the future was so uncertain. Why was she setting herself up for disappointment?

A family of skiers wedged themselves between she and Jake. He yelled, "Eat my dust" to them.

They didn't respond and quickly skied by him.

"I'm sorry. I thought you were somebody else," he said.

Jake assumed he was talking to her. "Haha! Show off," she said.

The embarrassment must have thrown him because he wobbled to the left, then the right, before overcorrecting himself. The jarring was too much, and he went down. When he tried to stand up again, his skis got in the way, and he fell face first into the snow.

"Didn't they teach you how to stand in class?" Mackenzie skied over to him and offered her hand.

He brushed the snow from his jacket. "I didn't need help. Just wanted to hold your hand."

Before she could respond, he took off. Instead of slowly going from one side to the other, like he'd been doing, he pointed his skis straight down the hill.

"Turn," she yelled. He was going way too fast.

"Bomber," a teenager cried out, as Jake whizzed by seemingly out of control.

He ignored everybody and tucked his poles in like he was about to do a 360° jump.

She sped up. "Hey," she said even though he probably couldn't hear her. "What do you think you're doing?" Was he trying to show her up?

Hooting and hollering, he picked up even more speed, and luckily found his own lane. Good, he'd be the only casualty if something happened. As if that thought helped soothe her anxiety.

She saw it all before it happened. His body flying in the air. Putting his hands out to break his fall and busting both arms. His career would be in jeopardy, and the accident would be all her fault. What was she thinking by taking him up there? She should have kept him safe.

The fall didn't happen quite the way she envisioned. Instead of a flying landing, he plopped on his rear and slid about twenty yards before careering into a small mound of snow. His skies flew off, and he stretched flat out on his back.

"Are you okay?" She rushed to his side.

"That was fun," he said, lifting his head.

"You could have seriously hurt yourself. Or somebody else. That wasn't funny." She was furious.

He sat up. "You're right. I'm not sure what got into me."

"You're a fool. I should send you back to the city right now." The words came out before she realized the consequences. She didn't want him to leave even though he could use a good shaking.

"I can't go back." He laid back down and removed his gloves to show her the scrapes on his arm. "I'm hurt."

She gathered some snow and threw it at him. "I'll see you at the bottom."

She skied off, happy he wanted to stay…at least for a while.

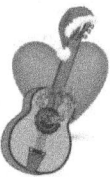

Chapter Twenty-Eight

Inside the ski lodge, the wood floor and paneled walls made Jake warm and cozy. Just the place to rest his sore body. Large groups of people sat on benches behind long picnic tables. Their excited chatter filled the large, hall-like room.

He found a seat near the enormous fireplace to relax. Perhaps he should have started with the beginner course like Mackenzie recommended. After the fall, he hobbled the rest of the way downhill. His ego was bruised more than his backside. There were a few bumps and scratches on his arms and legs, but nothing too severe. Both his body and ego would eventually heal.

The hot chocolate went down easily as he waited for her to finish skiing. Though she complained about being exhausted, she was back on the advanced slopes with Abby and Dylan. Mastering the art of skiing would take longer than Jake predicted, but he was willing to try if it meant spending winters with her and her family.

There was no denying it anymore. After he finished the song and submitted it to the record company, he realized how much she meant to him. So singularly focused on writing the song, it had been difficult to appreciate their developing relationship. He wanted to see what path the spunky, take-no-prisoner journalist took. If he was lucky enough, he'd be by her side along the way.

He resolved to tell her how he felt about her as soon as possible. If she rejected him, it would hurt, but at least he tried.

His phone chimed with a text from Bodhi. *Skiing! What are you thinking?*

He was right. Jake should be more careful in protecting his limbs and livelihood, especially if he had to put those arms to use playing his new Christmas hit on television. Bodhi didn't mention the contest, though, and Jake specifically had asked about in an earlier text. Patience certainly wasn't his strong suit, but the decision needed to be made soon.

They were taping *A Poppin' Christmas* in only a few days. He carefully put the phone back into his pocket. It was his lifeline.

A group of twenty-something guys sat at a table across from him. They were staring, so he raised his mug and toasted. As if they didn't notice his gesture, they quickly looked at their phones. Had they recognized him? He couldn't tell these days, and wearing a full ski suit wasn't exactly his signature style.

Speaking of style, would the television producers make him wear a Christmas sweater if he were to appear on their show? He remembered Peterkins' goofy sweater. *Poor pooch.*

Entranced by the fire, he startled when he felt a tap on his shoulder and spilled hot chocolate on the table.

"Sorry," said a young girl's voice.

Sophia, Dylan's friend from the tree-lighting ceremony, smiled shyly. She wore a matching baby-blue ski outfit and was probably ten times the skier than Jake.

"My fault," he said, wiping his hand. "I was spacing out."

Her nose crinkled. "You were in another time zone."

"Practically another universe." He threw up his hands.

"Anyway." She looked down. "Would you mind if I took a selfie with you? Dylan says you're super famous, and I want to post our picture."

"Sure." He took her phone. His arms were longer, so he could get the better picture while posing and snapping.

She examined the picture and seemed satisfied. "Thanks."

"What did you think of Dylan's 'Jingle Bell Rock'? Pretty good, right?" He was proud of Dylan's performance. They hadn't worked together since, but if Jake stayed in Mackenzie's life, he would be sure to spend more time with the kid.

"I loved it." She beamed. "But I think Dylan's mad at me."

"What? No." She was so adorable, his heart ached at the thought of her hurt feelings.

She picked at her nails. "He was telling me all about you, and I'm afraid I didn't act liked I cared enough."

"I'm sure that's not it at all." He recalled Dylan mentioned something about the two not having much in common. He'd have to talk to Dylan about being more open to different perspectives. "You shouldn't have to act at all. Be yourself. You're perfect as you are."

"My mom said the same thing."

"She's smart," he said. "Besides, who cares about me anyway? I'm boring."

"No, you're not!" Her eyes lit up. "I listened to all of your songs on YouTube. Dylan's right. You *are* cool."

He hadn't felt this flattered by a fan in a long time. "Maybe I used to be."

"You still are. My mom says you're a babe."

"That's nice of her." Sophia's mom might have been one of his original fans.

"Well, I gotta go," she said. "Thanks for the picture."

"I see your fans are getting younger and younger." Mackenzie came up from behind. She removed her coat, shaking snow on the floor.

"Have a seat." He gestured to the bench across from him. "Bodhi's always telling me I've got to reach across generations."

"You've reached Dylan and his friends. That's for sure. How are you, anyway?"

"As limber as a gymnast." He groaned as he stretched his arms overhead.

She smirked. "That's what you get for showing off."

"I feel great." The last time he stood, he was stiff and his muscles ached. An Epsom salt soak would be in order if he could sneak one in later. "Can I get you something?" He hoped she'd say no. Walking back to get her a coffee would wear him out.

"I've ordered us lunch," she said. "You could probably use some sustenance after your epic tumble downhill."

"Very funny. If you were so concerned, you wouldn't have left me all alone." He didn't blame her for walking away, but he may as well play the sympathy card if possible.

"Are you kidding? I could barely keep up with you." Her face turned red. "You don't need me."

He wanted to hold her close to him and tell her he did need her. It had only been a couple of hours since they parted, but he missed her. The thought of going home and leaving her left him miserable. It'd been years since he needed someone like this.

When he opened his mouth, nothing came out. Even though he was scared, time was running out if he was going to confess his feelings to her. There were no more excuses to stay longer. If he didn't have to rush back to Los Angeles, would it be inappropriate to stay with her family? Unless he had his own place up in the mountains. The fantasy of buying a winter chalet drifted into his head. They could be neighbors, exchanging nights by the glowing fireplace at each other's houses.

Ridiculous! She would never want to settle down with him, especially after she'd seen him at his weakest and most vulnerable. He wasn't the cool popstar but a human being made of flesh and blood like everyone else.

He snapped backed to the moment. "I guess I was trying to show off," he finally said.

"For me? Why do you care what I think?"

This was his moment to spill everything. He wanted to tell her though it had only been a few weeks since they met, he was connected to her. She was his inspiration. His muse. He only attempted to write a Christmas song because she wanted him to. Now, he was filled with the spirit of the season, the love and the brotherhood of the holiday community, and he thanked her for all of it.

A young man from the table across came over to him. "Excuse me. Are you Jake Wilder?"

"As far as I know," said Mackenzie.

He narrowed his eyes at her as if to say thanks a lot. He liked to please his fans, but these interruptions were getting to him. Now wasn't a good time.

"Would you like a selfie?" he said, wanting to be polite but asking with less enthusiasm than usual.

"Maybe later," said the guy. "But we were wondering if you might play a song to kick off the open-mic session."

Jake only now noticed the other guys setting up a makeshift stage in front of the lodge.

"I don't have my guitar with me." Even if he did, he was reluctant to participate. Sure, he could be nice and help them out, but he didn't like making a scene or taking the attention away from other acts.

"You can use mine," one of the guys called out from the stage.

"That's okay," said Jake.

"Are you sure?" He held up his guitar, as if it might help convince Jake it needed to be played.

"He's got a new Christmas song." Mackenzie revealed the news to the gathering audience.

Always on the job. Reporting must be in her blood.

"That's top secret." Jake pressed his finger to his lips. Undoubtedly somebody would record the song and release it to the world before it was ready.

"Hey, it's Jake Wilder," cried out a woman in the audience.

He inwardly groaned. This intimate moment ruined once again by his so-called fame. An outright *no* was out of the question when he noticed Mackenzie's prideful expression. She wanted this moment in the spotlight for him. Not as a reporter, but as a supporting friend.

The idea of playing "You Gave Me Christmas" for the first time in front of a live audience appealed to him. He pictured her glowing face lit up by the Stone's Christmas tree. The handmade tree ornaments and the other details of their time together encouraged him to write a song he hoped would become a classic. If he could convey all of those emotions through music and lyrics, then he'd done his job. Contest winner or not, he could hold his head high.

"'City Lights,' 'City Lights,'" a chorus of people chanted.

Once again, saved by an old classic. Jake could keep his new song under wraps for now. Hopefully the record company would reveal it soon enough.

As he took the stage, the words flowed like honey. Gone was the pesky stage fright that had been daunting him for the past few years. He was as comfortable as if he were sitting back at Mackenzie's house eating cookie dough straight from the bowl.

His mind and heart floated above the room, outside the lodge, and merged with the universe. Finally, he was at one with his music.

When he finished, the audience applauded enthusiastically.

They called for more, but he waved them off. "I'll see you soon," he said, silently praying he was telling the truth.

Back at the table, Mackenzie gave Jake a standing ovation.

"Stop that," he said.

"Do you see how much they love you?" She beamed.

Now, he was finally ready to lay it all out on the line and tell her how much he loved her when they were interrupted by his ringing phone.

"It could be about the contest," she said.

"I doubt it." He played down his expectations though it wouldn't be impossible for the decision to be made so quickly.

Record executives were impulsive. It was one of the traits that annoyed him the most. Listening to music took contemplation and time to digest, he'd argued when they shooed him out of their offices without listening to the rest of his album. Ironically, the very conduct he despised was the one he now hoped for.

It was Bodhi. Jake answered on the second ring, careful not to set himself up for too much disappointment.

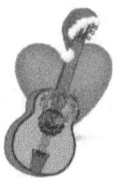

Chapter Twenty-Nine

Studying Jake's body language and using all of her best face-reading skills, Mackenzie speculated about whether the news was good or bad.

He bobbed his head and wasn't smiling nor frowning. "I see," he said.

It could be a robocall for all she knew, but by the way he answered so quickly, he most likely recognized the number.

"Who is it?" She couldn't stop herself from interrupting the phone call.

He held up his index finger in a just-a-minute gesture. Without a moment to spare, she was dying to know what the call was about.

How can he keep such a straight face? If it were her, she'd be jumping up and down if her song had been selected or crying into her hot cocoa if it wasn't. The first time her college newspaper published one of her stories, she told every single person she'd ever met they were looking at the next Pulitzer-prize winning journalist.

Kacey even threw a party, which wasn't such a stretch considering she needed very little excuse to put on her dancing shoes to celebrate. Still, the accomplishment was exciting, and Mackenzie never took the opportunity to publish for granted.

He ended the call. He threaded a hand through his hair, and his face went blank.

"Well?" she asked, trying to break the ice. He clearly wasn't going to quickly reveal the news.

He frowned. "That was Bodhi."

"I thought so." Her palms were sweating. The contest meant as much to her as it did to Jake and not because her article depended on it. She'd become invested in his career and wanted to see him win.

"I got it," he said. His eyes lit up. "I got the gig. They loved 'You Gave Me Christmas.'"

"That's what I'm talking about," she screamed. "I told you."

"Everything all right over there?" a man sitting next to them asked.

"You happen to be in the presence of the next Christmas-song-writing sensation." Everybody turned, as Jake slid down in his seat to hide. "Wave to your adoring fans."

He lifted his hand to the people in the ski lodge.

"We should celebrate." The words came out of her mouth before she realized he would need to get back to start recording immediately. "Of course, if you have time."

"I always make time for the little people." He puffed out his chest like he'd just thrown the winning pass.

"Okay, big shot."

"What do you have in mind?" he asked, gathering their coats. He stepped so lightly, it was like he was floating on cloud nine. She had never seen him this elated.

"It's not a big deal," she said, regretting she'd set it up as if it were a post-Grammy award party. "I'm sure you'll have a lot of events to get to once you're back home." As he helped her with her jacket, she avoided looking him in the eye, fearing her insecurity would damper his joy. This was a happy occasion. All positivity, all the time.

"I'd be happy to go anywhere with you," he whispered in her ear.

Her knees weakened. She wanted to kiss him on the spot but hesitated. If he reciprocated, she might always wonder if he kissed her back because he was excited about winning the contest rather than having genuine feelings for her. The other scenario was even more frightening. That he'd reject her outright.

"There's this store down the street." She swallowed her concerns. This was Jake's moment.

"Not another ice cream parlor."

"What are you insinuating?" She put her hand on her hips and faked offense. "It's a gallery that sells hand-blown Christmas ornaments. I saw the perfect one for you. I think you've earned it."

They strolled to the gallery only a short distance away.

"Are you cold?" she asked.

"Are you kidding?" he said, shivering. "This is nothing."

"I hear there's a heat wave next week in L.A." She'd eventually have to part ways with him, but the countdown until that happened was almost unbearable.

The selfish side of her wanted him all to herself, but winning the contest and singing his song to a live TV audience was good news for her too. A profile on Jake might have been enough to land publication, but now with a winning song to accompany it, the story would be picked up by major newspapers for sure.

All of this great news, and still a weight settled on her heart.

"So, what's next?" She left the question purposefully vague on the off chance he'd mention something about her. Where she might fit into his life.

"Production, publicity, then the performance," he said so casually it reminded her he'd been through this before.

What she really wanted to ask was what's next *with us. Will this be the end?*

"The song's gonna be huge. I can feel it." She focused on what was best for him.

"I don't want to get my hopes up, but it could open a lot of doors for me."

"The comeback kid," she said.

"You've finally got your underdog story."

She shoved her hands into her pockets. What started as a desire for a newsworthy story had turned into a longing for more of him in her life not only in a professional way, but in a personal one as well. Lust, and maybe even love, blindsided her.

"Here we are," she said, as they entered the gallery.

Photographs of local eagles and scenic paintings of the lake hung on the wall. There were cases of handmade jewelry and shelves lined with pottery. The best part was the display of glass-blown ornaments. Mackenzie had spotted a guitar ornament that was perfect for Jake.

"Here it is." She held it up for him to see.

"It's perfect," he said. "I love it though I'm afraid I might not put up a tree this year."

"What?" She couldn't believe he said that after all they'd been through. His Christmas spirit had been revived only to be forgotten once he was in the limelight again.

"I'll probably be busy recording and promoting the song."

His excuse made sense, but it irritated her. She refrained from letting out a big sigh, realizing it was only her despair at the thought of them parting ways.

"Look at this painting." He pointed to one of the fishing boats. Perhaps he noticed her disappointment and was trying to change the subject.

"Oh no," she said, ducking behind a rack of postcards.

"What's wrong?"

"It's Ross, the new editor-in-chief at the paper and my enemy," she reminded him. "He must be here to get an interview with Senator Kelly." As if somebody that important would bother to speak to Ross, but it was just like him to try to finagle a meetup anyway. "I just read the senator was here on a skiing vacation with his family."

Jake didn't appear to grasp the severity of her situation.

"The guy who fired me." A vein throbbed out in her neck.

"You're going to hide from him? Get out here and face him. He's the one who should be hiding."

Jake was right. Ross didn't have the nerve to even come up with a reason for her dismissal. He let her go over petty jealously because he wasn't half the journalist she was.

She emerged from her hiding place. "Hello, Ross."

His companion, a beautiful blonde he probably pursued using his new position scrutinized Mackenzie. He scowled.

"There she is. Mackenzie Stone on holiday, again." He chuckled.

The nerve of him. Assuming she was on vacation and not working on the assignment Mr. Hughes had given her.

'I'm busy on my story," she said.

"I'm sorry," he said, eyes blazing with triumph, hardly looking apologetic. "Like I told you before, we're going in another direction."

"Right." Asking him to elaborate would only waste her time. Besides, she didn't want to give him the pleasure of detailing why her work wasn't good enough for *The Sunrise Press*. They both knew that wasn't true.

Jake came around the corner. Ross obviously recognized Jake but wouldn't dare let himself be star-struck. "This must be your friend," Ross said.

"Friend," she said. "And story." She counted on Jake understanding the latter description without meaning to belittle him or undercut the status of their relationship.

"Jake Wilder." He extended his hand. "Did Mackenzie tell you she just landed an exclusive with the winner of the Christmas Song Challenge? I'm not talking to anyone else."

"Congratulations." Ross thrust his fist into the air.

His overreaction stuck her as phony. He was obviously jealous since he'd been pestering Mr. Hughes about doing celebrity profiles from the first day on the job.

"I hope you'll consider giving us an interview," said Ross. "*The Sunrise Press* may not be the *Times*, but we have a respectable circulation."

Trying to steal my stories to the bitter end.

"I only work with the best reporters," said Jake. "It's a shame you let Mackenzie Stone get away."

Before Ross could respond, they walked away. She held back her desire to gloat and paid for the ornament instead.

Outside the gallery, she whirled around. "Did you see his face? That was the best. Thank you."

"I meant every word."

She had an overwhelming urge to hug Jake. To run her fingers through his hair and tell him she didn't want him to go back to the city. The truth was he didn't have a choice. He had to start recording his new song right away.

Since he'd found out he'd won, his phone rang nonstop, but he hadn't answered until now. "It's Bodhi again. I better take it."

"Of course."

While he was on the phone, she pictured her story printed in one of the big time newspapers.

He slipped the phone back into his pocket. The color had drained from his face.

"What now?" She assumed he was faking it again. "They want you on *Dick Clark's New Year's Rockin' Eve*?"

"Not exactly." He hung his head.

"What then?"

When he didn't answer, she waved her hand in front of his face.

"It's not your problem."

His abrupt tone startled her.

"I'm sorry," he said quickly. "I'm acting like a jerk, and it's not your fault. Bodhi just got off the phone with Satellite Records. The executives met and discussed the direction they want to take the song."

"Don't you get a say?" She didn't know anything about the music industry but assumed the artist made those kinds of decisions.

"It's not unusual under these circumstances. They played my recording for some of the producers they like to work with, and the good news is, they loved it."

"That's why you won." She didn't understand why they were discussing the creative direction without him.

Jake sighed. "They want to try another singer."

"Another singer?" She stepped back. "You mean, your song but without you?" Ross's lame phrase "going in another direction" played in her head. It burned her up all over again.

"What can I do? They want the artist Tabitha to sing it."

"It's your song, and you should be the one performing it." Tabitha was a megastar who would certainly bring attention to his song, but stealing the spotlight from him wasn't fair. He'd worked his tail off, and to be treated like a nobody was an insult he shouldn't stand for.

"It doesn't always work out like that." He rubbed his temples.

"You can't let them do this." Mackenzie stomped her foot in protest in an immature gesture. It felt good to physically release her frustration, nonetheless.

"I need this," he pleaded.

"How does this help *your* career?" This was his last chance. If his face wasn't the one in front of the camera, he'd be forgotten about forever.

Jake's face twisted. "Don't you mean, how is this good for *your* article?"

After everything they've been through, how could he accuse her of selfishness? "This is just like the corporate party." She shot back, fuming mad. "You're selling out, plain and simple."

The insult was a low blow. She actually enjoyed the concert at the Sheraton but suspected he wasn't so proud of shows he had to do simply to pay the bills.

"Easy for you to say. I don't have Mommy and Daddy's fat income and mountain chalet to escape to when things get tough."

Anger swept over her. The old familiar accusations were delivered by someone she thought actually cared for her. It was a rotten thing to say, especially since Mackenzie secretly feared he was right.

"I have to make a living and keep my name and reputation," Jake continued. "There's no shame in being a songwriter. Most would kill for this opportunity."

"I thought you were different than most. This is your song." *Our song* she wanted to say. When he sang the words, "Somehow I found you," she believed he'd meant he had found her. That she had been the one to give him Christmas and love. Now, she realized he didn't care for her at all.

"I need to get back to the city," he said after an awkward pause. "I have to sign the agreement."

She handed him the glass ornament. "Don't forget this."

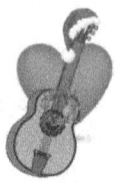

Chapter Thirty

Back at the house, Jake tidied up his bedroom and packed up what few things were his own. The portable recording unit Bodhi had delivered and Jake's guitar were already in the car. He stripped the bed and cleaned the bathroom. Mackenzie had done enough for him without having to clean up his mess too.

He was angry she'd accused him of selling out. Even if it was true, she didn't have a right to judge him so harshly. What did she understand about his business anyway? Having your song recorded by a multimillion dollar record label was a big deal. There was no shame in that.

If he played his cards right, he could parlay the opportunity into a decent deal for himself. Once again, he was in the good graces of the record company. Not exactly the way he planned, but what did they say about planning anyway? Life was what happened while making other plans.

This didn't excuse his reaction. He was frustrated and embarrassed he'd lashed out at her. Humiliated he wouldn't be allowed to sing his own song and annoyed she called him out for it—the two emotions didn't mix well in his stomach. Peterkins whined as if his tummy hurt too.

Her self-righteousness burned Jake up inside. He was infuriated to see how unsympathetic she was. Imagine if she was given the same opportunity. Would she throw it all away because hers wasn't the face looking into the camera or voice playing on radios across America? The words and music filling family living rooms on Christmas were still his. He owned them now and forever.

To think, he actually wrote the lyrics with her in mind. They'd never outright discussed what he meant when he said, "It's Christmas, I'm with you / And it feels so right." It was an acknowledgement between the two of them the song was dedicated to her. So he thought. What a relief to never have confessed his love for her. It would be easier to move on.

Peterkins circled the room while he figured out what he would say to her on the two hour drive home. Neither said a word on the short ride from the village back to the house. What more was there to discuss? She simply didn't respect his decision to sell the song to another artist and made that crystal clear. He winced at the idea of what she might write about him in her article. Thank goodness it didn't have a home, as of yet. She would have to find a new newspaper to pick up the story.

He could deny everything when the paper called to do a fact check. The article would die, but she would be ruined too. That was out of the question.

Negative thoughts sabotaged what could be a crucial turning point in his career. When Bodhi called, he said the situation wasn't as dire as it sounded. Tabitha was huge, adored by millions of fans across the globe. The song would get more airplay than they both dreamed, and that meant a big payout. "It's everything we've wanted," he said.

Once the room was clean, Jake walked Peterkins down the long hallway to the kitchen where Mackenzie was clattering about. Hopefully Abby and Dylan were still out. This situation was hard enough without having to say goodbye to them. Would they be disappointed in him too?

"Hey." Mackenzie didn't look up from the dishwasher as she was unloading the dishes.

"Ready to go?" It was too late to admit he cared for her. The moment passed. Theirs was another relationship better left undeveloped. They didn't all work out. Experience taught him that much.

"I've changed my mind." She finally faced him. Her eyes blazed defiantly.

"I have to get home," he said, irritated she was being purposely obstinate.

"Precisely." She bent to pet Peterkins and maybe avoid eye contact. He licked her hand. "I'm not stopping you."

"You're staying up here?" The moment he left her up in the mountains, he'd be empty inside.

"Why not?" she asked. "It's not like I have a job to go home to, and my parents will be arriving in a few days. I'm looking forward to some downtime."

He visualized her entire family sitting around the beautiful Christmas tree opening presents, and it crushed him. What a fool to allow himself to believe he might find a spot among her family.

"Sure," he said. "As long as you'll be okay."

"I'll be great." She crossed her arms.

It was obvious she would be fine without him. Alone and not occupied with recording sessions and rehearsals for *A Poppin' Christmas* like he expected, he'd be the one suffering. The record company promised him he'd have some input on the song, but he knew how it really worked. Tabitha and her producers could do with the song whatever they deemed necessary as he watched helplessly from the sideline.

"I hate to leave like this." Jake wanted Mackenzie to apologize. If only she'd say she supported him no matter what, he could forgive her.

"Like what? I'm a reporter, you're the subject, and now the interview is over."

"Just like that?" Her coldness chilled him to the bone. "I'll go." He picked up his bag. "Are you sure you'll be okay?"

"Don't worry about me. I'm going to stay here, do some writing, maybe search for a job, and wait for my parents."

It struck him how alike they were. She was a survivor like him. Mackenzie Stone didn't need him or anybody else for that matter. A weight settled on his heart.

"To be honest, I'm excited Tabitha's agreed to sing 'You Gave Me Christmas'. He wasn't sure why he needed to continue justifying the situation. "I've been listening to her music and am confidant she'll make it even better."

"Sure thing." Mackenzie glared at him as if she saw right through his rationalization.

They both knew he should tell Satellite Records he was performing the song himself, and if they didn't like it, they could take a hike.

"I gotta go." He plastered on a fake smile. "Nice knowing you."

~ * ~

When Jake arrived back in Los Angeles, Bodhi was waiting in the driveway.

"You don't waste any time." Jake carried the equipment to his studio.

Bodhi drew the recording contract from his briefcase. "You've got to strike while the iron's hot."

Jake understood why Bodhi might be nervous. It wouldn't be the first time Jake walked from a deal. A few years back, he was close to signing onto a comeback tour, but when he found out the promoters were more interested in using him and the other retro artists as background musicians for the label's up-and-coming artists, he turned it down.

As they entered the studio, the pungent scent of sage overtook them. Peterkins ran outside for some fresh air.

Bodhi didn't seem to notice, so intent on handing Jake the contract. "Everything looks standard."

"It's like I'm making a deal with the devil."

"A well-paying one." Bodhi's eyes flashed dollar signs, but he grew sympathetic when he saw Jake's reluctance. "Don't sweat it, man. This is a great opportunity. Do you know how many fans Tabitha has? Millions! More than you had at the height of your career."

"Thanks," he said. "I feel so much better now."

Bodhi patted Jake's back. "What I mean to say is your music is going to reach a whole new audience. Isn't that what we've always wanted?"

"Yeah, but I imagined my music would be coming from *me.*" There was no consoling him. No making it better. It became a business deal. Pure and simple.

"This is only the beginning," said Bodhi. "Satellite Records agreed to listen to a new Jake Wilder album when it's ready to go."

"That's comforting." *Listening* to a new record was not the same as promising a recording contract.

"I don't mean to change the subject." Bodhi shifted from one foot to the other, clearly uncomfortable. "I promised Kacey I'd ask about Mackenzie."

"What about her?" asked Jake.

"We heard things didn't end too smoothly."

"There was nothing to 'end.'" They'd ganged up on him by talking behind his back. Mackenzie, Kacey, and Bodhi discussed Jake's private life and dissected it as if it were on a slide under a microscope. "Look, can we stick to business, please?"

"Okay." Bodhi held up his hands. "This isn't a police inquisition."

"Not gonna lie, I've been getting cold feet."

"Hold that thought," Bodhi said at the sound of a car pulling into the driveway. He cleared his throat. "Did I mention I've got a surprise for you?"

"What now?" Jake was done with surprises for one afternoon.

"You'll never believe it, but Tabitha wanted to meet you."

He barely had a chance to get used to the idea of the twenty-year old pop sensation singing his beloved Christmas song. Now, he'd have to face her?

"Her manager says she's a huge fan."

Doubtful. Bodhi was known to be strategic with his flattery.

"You've got to be kidding me. This doesn't feel right." Jake paced the room.

"Give her a chance." Bodhi adjusted the lapels of his jacket and stepped outside of the studio to greet Tabitha and her manager.

Jake reluctantly followed.

Tabitha's jet-black hair hung in thick waves below her waist. Long paisley bell bottoms brushed the tops of her bare feet. A white poet's blouse completed the ensemble. She was straight out of the 1960s, compete with headband and round wire-framed glasses with blue mirrored lenses. Jake tried to look into her eyes to say hello. His own image reflected back at him.

She stepped forward and gave him a great big hug. "You're a sight for sore eyes."

Was this a compliment? He wasn't sure what to make of her strange greeting.

The manager, a slick guy in his thirties, introduced himself and Tabitha as they entered the studio, a place that had seen more action in the past few weeks than in years.

"I've listened to your song." She made a steeple of her fingers and bowed her head. "I adore it. The way you say 'Snowflakes are falling / And I'm falling too' makes me think of sparkling snowflakes covering my hair and face. I dance around in a snowdrift then collapse on the ground to make a magnificent snow angel who becomes my spiritual guide."

Jake glanced at Bodhi. He didn't dare look at Jake, or they'd both lose it in a fit of laughter.

She kept her sunglasses on even in his dim studio. Not all that unusual for a celebrity type, but it bothered him. He needed to find out if she was sincere in the caretaking of his song.

"I want to play you something I've been working on." With a small nod, she set her manager into action. He opened a laptop and plugged into Jake's sound system.

He was impressed she'd worked so quickly, considering they had the song for less than twelve hours.

"I never spend more than a day on any project. Otherwise, it gets stale. Do you get me?"

"Sure," he said, not knowing at all what she meant. It sometimes took him a day just to find the single right word or note. Maybe her technique was better. She must have something on him. Who can argue with millions of adoring fans?

"Ready?" asked the manager.

Jake kept an open mind. A fresh take might be what the song needed.

A deep base beat played over the speakers. She tossed her head around as she belted out the words so fast they piled on top of each other like a bad car accident. The mood of the song went from his blissful intention to her nerve-racking interpretation.

The spectacle stunned Jake. When she finally finished, he forced down a sick feeling. He was stunned into silence.

Bodhi's face twisted into a smile. "Powerful," he said, breaking the uncomfortable silence.

Jake numbly nodded in agreement.

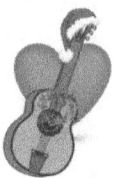

Chapter Thirty-One

A package of Oreos, Netflix, and the sofa was all Mackenzie needed for the afternoon. She wiped the crumbs from her chin and contemplated starting the next season of a series she'd been binging since after breakfast. The idea of cleaning the house and getting ready for her parents' arrival simply overwhelmed her.

Sadness crushed her. Christmas had always been her favorite time of year, but this one she wanted to forget as soon as possible. With no job and no inspiration, she found it impossible to continue writing the Jake Wilder story. *What a failure.*

Kacey had offered to make the drive again to cheer her up, but Mackenzie lied and said she'd be home soon. Asking her friend to leave the city to babysit was not an option.

The job search turned out to be futile as well. She couldn't bear looking at her resume one more time. Organizing all of her accomplishments had once been a source of pride. Now it seemed like a big waste of time. Why was she trying to make a difference anyway? Nothing mattered.

"I'm lucky to have such a great life," she shouted at her conscience. This feeling sorry for oneself followed by guilt for feeling sorry for oneself was a vicious cycle.

She pictured Jake in his funny sock hat pulled so low she could barely see his eyes. Initially he hated the cold weather but later embraced it. Maybe even enjoyed it as much as she did. A weight settled on her heart. She actually missed him.

Every hour or so, she scrolled through his Instagram page until Abby accused her of stalking him.

"I'm only looking for word about his new song." Mackenzie defended herself though it was obvious Abby was right. "Or should I say *Tabitha's* new song," Mackenzie added to throw her sister off topic.

It burned her up inside. He might have protested the song was his, but everyone would come to think of it as Tabitha's Christmas song, and Mackenzie didn't regret for one minute calling him a sellout. According to Abby, though, a more subtle expression would have been better.

Could Mackenzie help it if sometimes she was brutally honest?

"Are you going to feel sorry for yourself all day long?" Abby barged in with a shopping bag full of Christmas gifts.

Under normal circumstances, Mackenzie would want to see the haul. Instead, she ate another cookie.

Dylan plopped down at the end of the sofa, forcing her to move her feet to make room. "What's wrong?"

"Auntie Mac's just sitting on a pity potty." Abby confiscated the Oreos. She popped one into her mouth. "These are good."

Mackenzie wanted to continue feeling sorry for herself. Hadn't she earned the right? It wasn't every day a person got fired from her job *and* rejected by a guy in the same week. "I'm tired."

"Or madly in love." Her sister settled into the arm chair.

"Am not." She stood up long enough to grab the Oreos back from Abby and went back to the couch. This was *her* pity party, and she wouldn't have it ruined by a couple of intruders, family or not.

Dylan's phone buzzed. He picked it up, read the text then put it on the table without responding.

"Is that Sophia?" Mackenzie was happy to change the subject, even if it meant putting her nephew in the hot seat.

"Nope, a friend."

"I guess Sophia's out of the picture," said Abby.

"Mom," Dylan pleaded, clearly uncomfortable by their attention.

"All the work he went through learning 'Jingle Bell Rock' was for nothing," said Abby. She sounded more disappointed than Dylan.

"It's not about getting the girl. I liked playing in front of all those people."

The comment made Mackenzie proud on Jake's behalf, and she wanted to tell him what Dylan said. Then she remembered she and Jake weren't friends anymore. It would be weird and inappropriate to contact him about something so personal. It was strictly business from here on out if he was still willing to talk to her.

"We don't like the same things," said Dylan.

"That's all I'll get out of him." Abby frowned.

"I played some of Jake's music for her, and she didn't like it. She said the songs sounded like old people's music."

"Definitely a deal breaker," said Mackenzie. Sophia was

probably a Tabitha fan and would be impressed she was singing one of Jake's songs. "Did I ever tell you about your mom's first boyfriend?"

"He wasn't my boyfriend." Abby put her hands on her hips. "Besides, Dylan doesn't want to hear this."

"Mom had a boyfriend before Dad?" he asked.

"Many."

Abby tossed a throw pillow.

Mackenzie ducked and let the pillow bounce on the floor. "Your mom had a huge crush on this guy named Chris. But she was a nerdy freshman, and he was a popular junior. Much older than your mother."

Dylan's mouth hung open. He looked at his mother as if she were a person he didn't recognize anymore.

"I wasn't nerdy," Abby protested.

"She was. Anyway, he didn't know your mother was alive. But one day she came up with a plan to get Chris's attention. She dressed up in a fancy dress, high heels, and heavy makeup. We weren't allowed to wear any of that, but she snuck out of the house before your grandparents could see. She memorized Chris's schedule and happened to be right outside his math class when they let out."

"Mom!" He smirked. "Did he see her?"

"Not at first, but as she was walking away, she smacked right into a pole and fell down."

Abby turned scarlet. She covered her face with her hands, as if to hide.

"He came running to her rescue," said Mackenzie.

Dropping her hands to reveal a big grin, Abby added, "But we didn't live happily ever after. It turned out he wasn't my type at all either."

"I can't believe you did all that for a boy." He eyed his mother.

"Yeah, imagine that," she said.

The front door swung open, and they all jumped. Cookie crumbs rolled off Mackenzie's leggings and T-shirt onto the floor.

"Anyone home?" shouted her mother.

"Grandma." Dylan ran over and fell into her arms.

"Sweetheart, I'm so happy to see you."

Their mother had a way of brightening a room just with her presence. She'd only returned from Europe, but her beautiful face and rested eyes didn't show a hint of jetlag. Not a hair of her perfect bob was out of place. Mackenzie inhaled the scent of her mother's favorite perfume, a subtle blend of citrus and spice.

"Brenda," their father called from the driveway. "Send one of the girls out to help with the bags."

Knowing their mother, there would be plenty of them.

"I'll go." Mackenzie hugged her mother.

Brenda smoothed Mackenzie's tangled hair. "Are you okay?"

"She'll be fine." Abby squeezed her sister's hand.

Outside, Mackenzie squinted in the bright sun. It seemed like days since she'd seen it. She grabbed the heaviest-looking suitcase.

"That's your mother's," said her father. "Don't blame me if you have back problems in the morning."

"I won't." She heaved the suitcase to her parents' bedroom. Brenda and Abby followed. "We had the loveliest time in Italy. Wait until you taste some of the recipes I learned to cook."

"Mmmm." Mackenzie rubbed her belly. "Can't wait."

"Mackenzie lost her job at the paper," Abby blurted out of nowhere.

"Thanks a lot, Abby." Mackenzie wanted to break the news to her parents after they settled in.

"You're kidding? You want me to call the publisher?" Brenda searched her coat pockets. "Where's my phone? We're both on the board at the hospital."

"No way." She'd be mortified if her mother used her influence to beg for her job back. If she went back to the paper under those circumstances, she'd never hear the end of it from Ross even though he was editor-in-chief precisely because of family connections himself.

Brenda unpacked while Mackenzie lazily reclined on a comfortable side chair. Abby promised to help but hadn't returned from wherever she'd gone. She usually found an excuse to wander off when there were chores to be done.

Mackenzie asked to help, but her mother waved her away.

"Why don't you take some time off from working?" asked Brenda. "This seems like the perfect opportunity to travel. I could enroll you in the culinary institute."

"Have you ever seen me cook?" She never had much talent in the kitchen. "But I'm happy to be your taster."

"Why do you have to find another job so soon? Dad and I will help you with rent if that's what you're worried about."

She appreciated the offer but wanted to make it on her own. "If I don't get another job soon, I'll be yesterday's news. I can't have any gaps in my resume."

Her mother inclined her head as if contemplating Mackenzie's future. While she appreciated her mother's concern, she had no idea what the real world was like. She'd never held a paying job in her life. Dedicating herself to volunteer work was noble, and often, stressful work, but it wasn't the same as facing the pressure of a newspaper deadline. Anyway, her mother was so perfect, nobody would ever fire her.

"Aren't you working on an article right now?" asked Brenda. "Something about a singer and a Christmas song?"

"Jake Wilder."

"Yes." Her mother blinked. "Who is that anyway?"

"Nobody." Mackenzie didn't mean to sound so dismissive. "He was a popular singer once. Now he's trying to make a comeback with a Christmas hit."

"Will he?" Brenda asked.

"Make a comeback?" She contemplated this same question since Tabitha entered the picture. No doubt it'd be great for the singer's career, but Mackenzie seriously questioned what it would do for Jake's future as a performer. "I don't know."

"I hope so. In that case, you'll have a pretty good article."

"I guess, but how am I going to write it without telling the whole truth?" asked Mackenzie.

"Truth about what?" Brenda burned more calories putting away her clothes than Mackenzie had in days. She promised to exercise later.

That he sold out to the record company and their shiny popstar instead of being true to himself. He wasn't who she thought he was. "Nothing."

In Mackenzie's reporting career, she'd found some of the most heroic deeds were performed by ordinary people just trying to do what they believed was right. Like when ten-year old Ella wanted to start a lemonade stand to raise money for the children's hospital. Or when a group of high school students spent Thanksgiving at a homeless shelter serving dinner.

She expected Jake, of all people, to rise to the occasion.

Mackenzie's father lumbered in with another heavy suitcase, interrupting her thoughts.

"Harry, put that down," said Brenda. "You have a bad back."

"I wonder where I got it." He winked at Mackenzie. "How's my little girl?"

She wanted to fall into his arms and whimper like one. Tell him being a responsible adult was too much work. Instead, she straightened her posture. "I'm far from a little girl anymore."

"She was sacked," said Brenda.

"Mom!" It was evident where Abby got her bluntness.

"Well, no use beating around the bush."

Her father was a thin, dark-haired man. No matter the time of year, he always looked like he'd just returned from a Caribbean vacation. His blue eyes set against a golden tan complexion made most of her friends swoon. All she could do was roll her eyes, but her father was undeniably handsome. Her mother, who was a beauty herself, said she melted the first time she saw him across the restaurant where they met. She was on a date with another guy, but she felt this handsome stranger would be her forever sweetheart.

Harry threw his hands in the air. "Who would be foolish enough to fire the best reporter *The Sunrise Press* has ever seen?"

Mackenzie wanted to tattle on Ross as if he were the bully on the school playground who pinched her. He should get in trouble for what he'd done. Sadly, he was going to get away with it, and there was nothing she or her parents could do about it. They could call friends and acquaintances, persuade them to at least interview her, but she promised herself no matter what, she would make it on her own.

"I don't care." She balled her fists. "I needed to move on anyway. I was getting too comfortable covering fluff stories."

Her father placed his hand on her cheek. "Your dream is to work at a big paper."

"And write stories that reach a wider audience," she said. It was nice to be with family, people who loved and supported her unconditionally. "I want to make a difference."

"The piece you did on our charity event two years ago made a huge impact. We raised a lot of money for cancer research because of your article." Brenda was unpacking Harry's suitcase. She had more stamina than Mackenzie and her father put together.

"I care about local issues too." Mackenzie couldn't sit still anymore. She rolled her mother's suitcase to the doorway to store away later. "I only want a chance to spread my wings."

"Of course she does," said her father. He was her most vocal advocate, wanting the dream for his daughter just as much as she did. "I've got a friend—"

"Who?" Mackenzie and her mother both asked at the same time, cutting him off.

"I know everybody," said Brenda.

"I've still got a few tricks up my sleeve." He picked his cellphone up from the dresser. "I went to school with a man who happens to be the editor-in-chief of the *Boston World View*. How does that sound?"

"Amazing. Though I suppose I'd have to move to Boston." *Not to mention let my father bail me out.* Mackenzie didn't want to seem ungrateful, but considering the offer was against her principles to accept help from her well-connected family.

Brenda's eyes welled up. "Boston is a lovely place to visit."

Just as Mackenzie was going to say no, thank you, she got a text from Kacey with a link. *Drop everything and read this now. You won't believe what that no-good Ross has been up to.*

Her stomach knotted. *What now?*

She clicked open the link to an article in *The Sunrise Press* and gasped at the headline. "Has-Been Popstar Seen Canoodling with Wannabe Journalist in Romantic Wintery Mountain Resort."

That creep! And his choice of words—canoodling, wannabe—how tacky. It was a new low, even for Ross. Mackenzie scanned through the article only to read a bunch of nonsense about Jake, the contest, and his indiscretion with the reporter who was supposed to be profiling him, not *bedding* him.

Her face burned.

"What's wrong?" her mom asked.

"Dad, call your friend in Boston. I've got to get out of here."

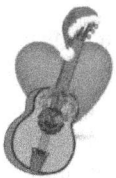

Chapter Thirty-Two

"Gorgeous." Kacey ran her hand along the smooth granite countertop.

The kitchen island alone was bigger than her kitchen and living room put together. Everything was practically new in the house though it retained the old-style charm the neighborhood was known for. A suburban retreat right outside of the city.

"It's been completely gutted and remolded," said the realtor.

The cabinets were so bright they gleamed, and the backsplash glittered with specks of gold. The place was clean and modern. A dream home for somebody who could afford it with their new salary at a fancy law firm. Somebody like Ian.

He inspected the kitchen appliances. "Top of the line," he said.

Not that he'd be using those much. From what she remembered about him, he wasn't big on the domestic front. People changed, however. It'd been five years since they dated. Maybe he had learned his way around the kitchen.

"You like to cook?" asked Kacey.

Men who cooked held a special place in her heart. She remembered Bodhi had wanted to be a chef. Surprised he'd appeared in her head, she blinked the thought away.

When Ian's phone chimed with a text message, he put his hand up toward her. She supposed he was only asking her to wait a minute, but she felt like the in-her-face gesture was abrupt and rude. If one of her brothers was there, he wouldn't have liked seeing a guy get in her space.

"I have to respond," Ian said.

"Okay." She faked a smile as he left the kitchen. Perhaps she was being overly sensitive.

The thought of getting back together with an ex-boyfriend made her question everything lately, but she had promised herself, and her parents, she'd give him a chance.

The agent continued describing the house as Kacey feigned interest. Why had Ian asked her there in the first place? After their lunch date earlier in the week, they communicated a few times. Their conversations stagnated mostly around old times.

If their interactions didn't move on from there, they were doomed. Their past wasn't solid enough to form a stable relationship.

"I'm sorry." He returned. "It was work."

She let her apprehension go. For now, he was a friend, and she could help him out by giving her opinion if he was genuinely interested in buying a house. "It's a gorgeous place."

"You always said you loved this neighborhood." He glanced at his cellphone. "The commute to work's not bad from here."

He wasn't being honest. With traffic, it might take an hour to get downtown. "Have you considered living closer to work? You'd probably love one of those new sleek condos."

"Not for me." He brushed off the suggestion too quickly. "I've lived in the city. Now, I want something more suburban, more family-friendly."

"There's a wonderful elementary school down the street," said the realtor.

"Just a thought." Perhaps Kacey should have waited to discuss alternatives when the listing agent wasn't around.

"Let's go see the bedrooms," he said.

Upstairs there were four bedrooms. Each looked out into the spacious backyard. Kacey could have lots of pets like she'd always wanted. *This isn't my house.* Why was she moving in already?

"It's perfect." His phone rang. "Sorry," he said as he walked into the hallway. "I told you the file is under Le Roux," he said loudly. "L-e-r-o-u-x."

She pretended she didn't hear his hostile tone and commented on the crown molding instead. Back at the window, she noticed a guest house outside.

"Is that part of the property?" she asked the realtor.

"Yes, it's a one-plus-one with a full kitchen."

It would make the perfect studio. She swooned at the idea of painting in this friendly, quiet setting. Again, she was mentally moving in. *This is uncomfortable.* Especially since he was acting like the type of guy she'd never tolerate. Loud, obnoxious, self-important. "Can I see it?"

"I'll follow you," said the realtor, moving toward the exit.

They passed by the guest bathrooms as Ian raised his voice on the phone. He wasn't even looking at the house. Was he depending on

Kacey to tell him whether or not he should buy it? It seemed like a careless way to invest his money if he didn't truly believe the place was right for him.

Imagining herself on one of those home buying shows, she'd be the eccentric one who wanted charm and character over the usual open-concept and brand new everything. Give her a sunken clawfoot bathtub instead of a decked out, dual-headed shower any day of the week.

His taste was a mystery to her. They'd never talked about houses or interior design, and now she felt the weight of the world on her shoulders as she explored his potential new home.

Once outside, Kacey and the realtor walked through the yard. The drought resistant landscape alleviated her worry a big yard might be too much for him. She didn't see him as the gardening type with his busy schedule.

The guest house was adorable. Decorated in a beach shack style with blue and white linens and sea shells lining the white wooden shelves, the detached space was about 450-square feet and would make an excellent studio or a perfect space to hang out with friends.

"There you are." He intercepted her back in the house.

"The guest house is charming," she said. "Worth the price of the house alone."

The real estate agent beamed. "Let's take a look at the rumpus room." She led them into a large den.

In the middle of the vast room, Kacey imagined a large grand piano. The acoustics would be outstanding. He didn't play, but perhaps he could learn. His lawyer friends would gather around to socialize and listen to music. The scene was all very sophisticated in her mind.

Out of nowhere, she pictured Bodhi in the room listening to the massive record collection he'd told her about. She saw herself cuddled up next to him but then crumbled inside remembering how she asked him not to contact her.

"Man cave! Sectional sofa here," Ian shouted, physically mapped out the plan, stepping here and there to show where everything would go.

He pointed to the wall. "Seventy-five inch TV there to watch all of my football games. Babe," he said. "I'm going to be planted right here all Sunday afternoon."

She cringed. There would be no Sundays with Ian. In fact, there would be no days with Ian at all. A weight lifted from her shoulders. Blindly following her parents' wishes and getting back with him was out of the question, especially when the only person she wanted to be with was Bodhi.

In his mind, superhero Bodhi would storm the offices of *The Sunrise Press*, slam the newspaper article on Ross Overton's desk, and demand an apology. That was what Jake wanted him to do.

Bodhi hadn't spoken to Kacey, but the sleazy article about Jake and Mackenzie hurt Kacey too. An injury to her best friend was one to Kacey. Bodhi was compelled to stand up to Ross on everyone's behalf, especially hers. He thought about her all the time. Every inch of him craved her.

This was the last place a talent manager should be. When Jake sent him the article about he and Mackenzie "canoodling" in a mountain resort, Bodhi should have celebrated. Regardless of Jake's feelings, the story was press, and most managers would see any press as good press. Something that hadn't come easily as of late.

They needed whatever they could get since there wasn't a guarantee Mackenzie would find a publisher or even finish the article, for that matter. He said she was pretty steamed at him when he left her up in the mountains.

An assistant fetched Bodhi from the waiting room. "Mr. Ross will see you now."

"Bodhi, my man." Ross leaned back in his chair and clasped his hands behind his head. "What can I do for you?"

He kept himself from scowling. The two had never spoken, yet Ross acted like they were long-lost pals.

"It's about the article." He gently placed it in front of Ross. *So much for the superhero macho act.*

"Your boy Jake's getting a little action." Ross raised his eyebrows.

Bodhi wasn't a violent man, but he wanted to smack the smug look off Ross's face. "The article's trash. Gossip of the worst kind," he said. "And completely false."

"I saw them with my own eyes." Ross took a long, leisurely drink from his coffee cup. "Sorry, buddy, but I don't make the news, I print it."

Bodhi hesitated. Confrontation wasn't his thing, so this was all new territory for him. "I'm not your buddy," he finally said.

"I can see you're upset, but don't worry. If Jake Wilder ever wants a quality profile, one written by a *real* journalist, my door's always open."

Bodhi probably would never be able to talk sense into this insecure jerk, but he couldn't have Ross hurting the people Bodhi loved. Even if it meant alienating the one and only newspaper that had covered

Jake in years.

"If you ever print anything false about Jake Wilder again, you'll be smiling on the other side of your face." He didn't understand exactly what that meant.

His grandfather used to say it, and it sounded scary to a young Bodhi. He was pleased with himself.

If Kacey found out he'd stood up to Ross Overton, she'd be proud of him too.

Bodhi turned to leave. His hand accidently brushed Ross's coffee cup, spilling the contents all over his desk.

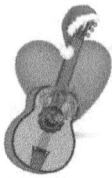

Chapter Thirty-Three

When Jake entered Tabitha's downtown loft, it was as if he walked into a steam room. The air was so thick with moisture he could hardly breathe. The crowd overwhelmed him. Not that he should be surprised there were so many people. This was a party at Tabitha's, one of the most popular singers in the world.

He preferred his alone time over this scene any day of the week, but Bodhi talked Jake into attending though they might never find each other in the chaos and confusion. The guests wore Mardi Gras masks. Feathers and glitter floated everywhere. Somehow he had missed the memo this was a costume party and figured Bodhi must've kept this information from Jake. It was difficult enough handing over his song. Doing it in a costume would be downright humiliating.

How did Christmas and Mardi Gras go together anyway? He supposed Tabitha could get away with anything. If she wanted Mardi Gras in the middle of December, she'd have it.

People threw beaded necklaces into the crowd. One of them hit him in the face. It hurt. He wanted to leave, but he couldn't abandon Bodhi, who was probably already at wit's end with Jake. The contract wasn't signed yet, and he was on thin ice with everybody, including the record company.

A Poppin' Christmas was supposed to film soon. If she didn't start recording the song tomorrow, it would never be ready for release by then. The idea was fans could buy the song the moment they heard it. His pocketbook could use the boost, but his career as a performer might tank. It was a risk. The world might soon forget Jake Wilder forever, and it certainly wouldn't bring back Mackenzie.

Not that he should care. His annoyance at her flared again for calling him a sellout. The last person he wanted to think about was her.

Somebody tapped him on the shoulder. He jumped, fearing it was the voodoo priest shadowing him moments ago.

Bodhi pushed up his mask and scowled.

"Scary."

"For you," said Bodhi, holding out a jester mask.

"Why are we here, anyway?" Jake briefly examined the mask and screwed up his face. "I can think of a million things I'd rather be doing."

"Even though you're selling your song to a megastar, we still need to network." Bodhi scanned the room. "Have you seen Tabitha?"

"Nope." Jake put the mask on. "I feel like an idiot."

"It's a small price to pay."

Bodhi wasn't as sympathetic as he'd been before, probably sick of babying Jake. Was he being a diva? He needed to pull himself together.

"Tabitha's manager said she wants to discuss a few details before they start recording," said Bodhi.

"*If* they start recording." Jake played hardball in spite of himself. Selling his song to a megastar could be a huge boost to his career, but his ego had other ideas. He wanted to be the one on stage.

"C'mon, man. There'll be other songs." Bodhi plucked a sausage puff from a passing tray.

Jake found an empty corner of the room to sulk.

Cobbling together a few more hors d'oeuvres, Bodhi followed. "I'm a bit hungry, I guess."

"Get me out of here, and I'll take you to dinner. You choose the restaurant."

"Sign this contract, and you have a deal." Bodhi dangled the document in front of Jake.

"You're relentless," he said. "You actually brought it with you."

"That's why you pay me the big bucks."

An arguing couple squeezed in next to Jake and Bodhi. The young woman's date was caught flirting with someone else.

Jake turned his back to give them privacy. "What's going on with you and Kacey?" He was glad to get back to normal, non-business, conversation. "I thought you were a confirmed bachelor for life."

I am." Bodhi put his mask back on. "But there's something special about that girl."

Jake was happy for his friend, despite the bitterness he felt about his recent failure with Mackenzie. "I'm rooting for you, buddy."

"Thanks. By the way, I arranged for you to do one last interview with Mackenzie to wrap things up."

"Is she still writing the article?" If so, she had tenacity, he had to give her that.

"Why wouldn't she be?"

"Now that she's not employed by *The Sunrise Press*, and I'm not such an exciting prospect, what's the point?"

"The point is you're a huge deal. Dude, you're in the Christmas Club. Do you know what that means?"

Jake removed his mask and motioned for Bodhi to do the same. Jake couldn't have a serious conversation talking to a silly mask. "What are you talking about?" The Christmas Club sounded like an organization his grandmother might belong to.

"Aww, man. The Christmas Club. It's an exclusive group of people who've written Christmas songs that have been recorded and enjoyed by fans around the world."

"I only wish I could sing the song *my* way."

"That makes sense," said Bodhi. "But if we're lucky, it'll be part of the Christmas cannon heard by generations of people every year."

Jake only wanted to get through one day at a time, but he liked what he was hearing.

Bodhi continued, "You've got to think big, and stop seeing selling the song to Tabitha as a failure. She can help you reach your dream."

He was grateful for Bodhi's pep talk though he'd never admit it out loud, or he might get too comfortable pitching Jake's songs to other artists. "We'll see about that."

Tabitha's manager approached the men. He wasn't wearing a mask either, and Jake was relieved he'd removed his. "Tabitha will see you now."

"It's like I've been in line to see the godfather," Jake whispered to Bodhi.

Bodhi nudged Jake to be quiet.

They were escorted to a quiet room in the back of the loft. She was seated in prayer in front of some kind of Hindu statue. He wasn't sure which goddess she was praying to. Nobody said a word, and for a few minutes he wondered if she expected them to kneel in prayer also.

Tabitha finally stood up and bowed. "Welcome. I'm so glad to see you." She embraced Jake and kissed him on both cheeks. She acted so sophisticated considering she was probably a girl in braces last week.

"Thanks for inviting us," he said. "I'm having—"

"A great time," said Bodhi, cutting him off.

Was he afraid Jake might express his reservations about her version of the song? He was too professional for that though Mackenzie would probably have it otherwise. Perhaps there was a way he could discuss it with her more tactfully. Artist to artist.

"Sometimes parties can be sooo boring." Tabitha rolled her eyes. "But I'm glad you're having fun. Stay and watch me perform."

Will she sing my *song?* He'd have to grin and bear her butchered version. "We'd love to."

"Everybody wants me to play my greatest hits, but that gets old." She had no idea she was insulting Jake's entire livelihood to his face.

"Can I talk to you about something first?"

She turned to her assistant. "Get Jake and Bodhi something to drink."

"No, thanks." Jake wanted to get this conversation over with as quickly as possible.

"It can wait until tomorrow." Bodhi fidgeted with the mask in his hand.

He had reason to be nervous, but Jake wasn't going to let it go. "I have to tell you when I wrote 'You Gave Me Christmas,' I was in an extremely reflective place."

"That's what I love about it." She placed her hand on her heart. "It moves me. I picture my own life flashing before my eyes."

That ought to take a whole five seconds. "I envision it as being emotional and moody. While I love your whole hard rock sound and energetic vocals, I don't think it suits the song."

She blinked a few times as if processing his criticism. "I appreciate your honesty," she said. "But I disagree."

Bodhi interjected, "Perhaps Jake could come to the recording tomorrow. Just for moral support." He glared at Jake, begging him with his eyes not to blow it.

Placing her hands prayer like in front of her, she bowed. "I'll see you tomorrow." As she left the room, the crowd outside swallowed her up, and she disappeared.

Whether this was a huge mistake or a career changing move, only time would tell. Fear hit him like icy water.

~ * ~

The interview with Mackenzie was arranged for the next morning. It disturbed Jake that his interactions with her were formal now. Appointments were required rather than having casual conversations. When they were together in the mountains, it was only a matter of wandering into the next room for bits of information here and there.

He continued to cooperate because he wanted her to succeed. Maybe he'd work up the courage to apologize for getting angry with her. She had a right to her opinion though the judgement was unfair. Still, they could remain friends, couldn't they?

Peterkins whined by the front door.

"In a minute," he said.

The dog was incessant, so they both trotted down the street for a quick walk before the interview. Peterkins stopped at the exact place he'd met Mackenzie for the first time. *Could he still smell her?* Of course not.

Jake loved his dog, but he wasn't exactly the sharpest tool in the shed. Shaggy and loveable was all he needed in a best friend.

The afternoon was sunny and bright. Since he'd been home from the mountains, he continued to check his weather app for Lake Arrowhead. It had become a habit, but he imagined she'd already moved on, distracted by her parents and determined to get a job at another newspaper.

Later that afternoon, he would try again to influence Tabitha and the direction of "You Gave Me Christmas." She and her manager were expecting a signed contract. A courageous man would rip up the contact and walk away. The other, more practical Jake understood the benefits of one of the most popular popstars recording *his* song. He'd eventually sign but liked the idea of making them sweat.

The days before all of this landed on his lap was a comfortable place. He shook off the thought. Hiding in one place wasn't healthy, and he knew that. Whatever happened from there, at least it was forward motion. *Forward motion right off a cliff.*

After the dog did his business, they rushed back to the house. Jake barely had time to wipe his brow before the call from Mackenzie came. Though he was as scruffy as Peterkins, he answered.

Her image appeared on the screen. She was as beautiful as ever. The snowy backdrop made him yearn for their time together.

"I see you've still got snow," he said.

"It's been snowing on and off all day."

"Are your parents there?"

"Uh-huh."

Was it his imagination or were her eyes glossy with tears?

"I bet they're disappointed in our gingerbread house disaster." He started with small talk because sorrow threatened to close up his throat. He missed her.

"Believe it or not, they asked for a rematch. Then my dad hatched this idea about getting all the previous winners together for an all-star competition. I told you they're over-the-top."

"I can respect that."

"Anyway, how's it going? Has Tabitha recorded the song yet?"

"I'm going to the studio today."

"Is that something songwriters typically do?" She acted

surprised Jake was still involved.

"I'm not sure." He wanted to remind her this wasn't his usual role. "I was invited."

"I see." Mackenzie wrote something on a pad of paper. "How will it feel to see your song performed by one of today's hottest young stars?"

The question sounded stilted and practiced, the sort of thing asked by a stranger, not by someone who shared an intimate week in the mountains.

"I'm honored, and I think she'll do a terrific job." The canned response practically choked him as it came out of his mouth. He cleared his throat. "Why don't I email you after I go to the studio today? I'll be sure to keep you updated."

She sighed. "Good idea."

"Maybe when you come back to town, we can do a follow up."

"I can't."

"Is it because of that ridiculous article Ross what's-his-name wrote?"

Even through the monitor, Jake could see her blush. "No, I don't care anymore. I'm moving to Boston next week. I got a job at the *World View*." The enthusiasm sounded forced, or maybe it was wishful thinking on his part. Of course, she'd be thrilled about it.

"Congratulations." His already foul mood plummeted. "It's everything you've always wanted."

Mackenzie avoided his gaze. "Thanks, I'll probably follow up with you from Boston."

"Good luck."

Like a trooper, he powered through the rest of the interview. This might be the last time he'd ever see her, and pain gripped his chest. On the precipice of possibly becoming a household name once again, he should be celebrating. Instead, he only wanted to sulk.

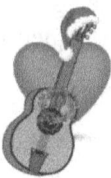

Chapter Thirty-Four

Mackenzie stretched her arms overhead. She'd been typing all morning, and despite her best effort to write something significant and noteworthy, she doubted any of it mattered. After explaining the contest, noting the particular challenge of writing a holiday song, and describing the opportunity it presented for Jake, she hit a wall. Once she mentioned super popstar Tabitha was attached to the project, Mackenzie worried the reader might not care about Jake Wilder anymore. The mere mention of Tabitha's name may not inspire Mackenzie, but ironically, it guaranteed the story's publication.

Once *A Poppin' Christmas* aired on TV, she could finish the article. Whether this was a story about an artist capturing the Christmas spirit or one about dashed dreams and missed opportunities wasn't clear.

The influence she had as a writer sometimes unnerved her. Her job was to remain objective, but she stepped back and questioned if she was too personally disappointed in him to see what an incredible break this was.

Her father was chopping wood outside, and she remembered the morning Jake stacked a big pile by the fireplace. It surprised her he had the know-how, but she had worried he hurt himself. Not that he was weak, but that kind of repetitive motion could do a number on even the most experienced outdoorsman. At the time, he needed to save his strength for strumming his guitar and the tickling piano keys. Pride shone in his eyes and his posture when he showed her what he'd done.

"Mackenzie." Her mother knocked on the bedroom door as she opened it.

"Come in." Moping in private was not allowed at the Stone residence, but Mackenzie was glad for her mother's company.

Brenda joined Mackenzie by the window and watched her husband. "He needs a haircut," she said. "Want to go into the village with us? I'll drop Dad off at the barber, and we can go shopping."

Though she would never tell her mother, Mackenzie hated shopping. It wasn't that she didn't love the beautiful clothes and trinkets Brenda showered her daughters and grandson with. Mackenzie didn't want her mother to continue spoiling her as if she were still a teenager. Abby, on the other hand, never met a shopping center she didn't love. Sometimes the two of them disappeared for hours while she and Dylan stayed home and watched movies.

"Remind me to stop by the hardware store," said Brenda. "I want to get your father a tool belt for Christmas."

"That's a practical gift."

She leaned over Mackenzie's open laptop.

"It's not done." She gently closed her computer.

"I could give you some feedback," her mother said.

"It's too early for that." She appreciated the offer, but it had been a long time since her mother proofread Mackenzie's work. Eventually having another set of eyes on the article wouldn't be a bad idea since she didn't have an editor anymore.

"So, a tool belt?" Mackenzie steered her mother away from discussing the article any further. "Are you sure you want to give him that for Christmas?"

"Whenever your dad gets on one of his home improvement kicks, he's constantly calling me to bring him a hammer or this screwdriver or that one. If he had a tool belt, he could carry it all right along with him." Brenda's eyes blazed as she described her plan.

Mackenzie had to admit, her mother was pretty ingenious to figure out how to give them both a gift with a single belt.

"He'll love it." She knew her father would. Like her, he preferred functional over frivolous.

"I think it's kind of romantic," said her mother.

Mackenzie squeezed her mother's hand. "Me too."

~ * ~

After they dropped off her father at the barber, her mother said she had a surprise.

Mackenzie inwardly groaned. The article at home wasn't going to write itself.

"Don't look so excited," Abby said to Mackenzie from the backseat.

"Ice-skating?" she asked as they pulled into the rink parking lot.

"Can't a mother take her family out on a surprise date?"

"Cool," said Dylan.

"I wish I could." It had been some time since she'd skated. "I'm out of shape."

"Don't worry, I won't go fast." Brenda opened the trunk. Everything they needed was there—skates, mittens, and heavy overcoats.

"You planned this all along."

"Don't be a spoilsport," said Abby. "If Mom didn't spring it on you like this, you'd never agree."

"You've been so melancholy lately." Brenda wrapped a dove gray cashmere scarf around her neck. "We wanted to cheer you up."

Mackenzie hadn't been herself. That was true, but how could she celebrate the season when she was preoccupied planning a trip to Boston in search of an apartment? Her job didn't officially start until mid-January, but Mackenzie had been corresponding with the editor. Her dream of writing for a bigtime newspaper was about to come true. Then why did she feel so lousy?

Dylan and Abby raced off in a speed competition as Mackenzie and her mother linked arms and skated into the ring. Brenda's glide was smooth and graceful as Mackenzie struggled to find her balance. She'd inherited her father's clumsiness.

"You were always such a beautiful skater. Can you still do the toe loop?"

"I'm not sure I'm up for it." Her mother was being modest.

Brenda let go of Mackenzie's arm and picked up speed flying past some of the slower skaters. Her mother's scarf trailed behind. After a few moments, she gently lifted off the ice, turning into an effortless landing.

In her younger days, she might've given her skater idol Dorothy Hamill a run for her money. Mackenzie cheered and hooted.

Barely out of breath, her mother skated back to Mackenzie. "Your turn."

"I don't think so." She held up her mittens. "I've got to take care of these babies. They're my future."

"Even though I'm terribly sad you're leaving," Brenda sighed, "I want you to know how proud I am of you. Your father was on the phone this morning telling everyone his daughter's going to be a bigtime reporter."

"Thank you, Mom. I'm grateful for your support. You and dad encouraged me to go to college and follow my passion."

"I only wish that passion was right around the corner, not clear across the country. I'm sorry." Brenda wiped her eyes. "I'm being selfish."

Sadness tore at her chest. Mackenzie didn't respond, fearful she might breakdown in tears too.

They skated another lap without talking.

For the longest time, she imagined seeing her name in papers across the country. With this new opportunity in Boston, perhaps she'd finally be able to report on issues that made a difference. It hadn't occurred to her that landing her dream job might mean leaving her family and everyone she loved behind.

"I'm excited to work at the *World View*." She led her mom off to the side so they could rest for a moment. "But to be honest, I'm nervous too."

"There's nobody on this planet more capable of taking risks." Brenda held on to Mackenzie's shoulders and looked her in the eyes. "You can do this."

She dreaded leaving. Many adult children moved away. This was understood, but she couldn't picture seeing them only once or twice a year. What about Kacey? Would her best friend in the whole world ever come to see Mackenzie? They'd been practically inseparable since the day they'd met.

If she was being completely truthful with herself, she didn't want to leave Jake either even though she doubted he'd ever want to see *her* again.

"Mom," she said, anxiety swirling around her. "I think I made a huge mistake."

"What is it?" Brenda's eyes filled with worry.

"I was really awful to someone who had only been a friend to me." She pictured Jake's sheepish face when Mackenzie called him a sellout. She was ashamed of herself. "He didn't deserve it. Jake needed my support and understanding, and I was a judgmental jerk."

"Can you apologize?"

"I had the opportunity yesterday, and I didn't. It's too late."

"It's never too late to apologize," said Brenda.

She doubted her mother's advice. "I need to let him get on with his life. Besides, he probably hates me."

"How can anybody hate you?" Brenda held her hand.

Her mother could never be objective, thank goodness. The love and support was like salve on a wound. "Maybe I'm too tough on people. I expect too much."

"I'm afraid you got that for me," said Brenda.

"We demand so much from ourselves and others. Sometimes, it's too high of a standard. I'm not perfect."

"I think you're perfect just the way you are," said Brenda.

Mackenzie hadn't washed her hair in two days and might've even forgotten to brush her teeth this morning. Lately her behavior had been far from perfect, especially the way she'd treated Jake. "I'll keep trying to improve."

Jake had flourished. Why couldn't she? The memory of him stammering to explain why he was the one to write a winning Christmas song though he believed the holiday had become too commercialized made her eyes glisten with nostalgia and sadness. Reluctant to get into the spirit, by the end he was building snowmen and gingerbread houses. Ones that crumbled, but still he had tried, putting himself out there once again as she hid away in the comfort of her family home. He was the brave one, she the coward.

"Are you okay?" Brenda handed Mackenzie a tissue.

"I don't think so." She whimpered at first and wanted to stop herself, but once she felt the wetness on her cheek, she couldn't stop crying. The damn had broken. "I was so mean to Jake, and the worst part is I've completely fallen for him."

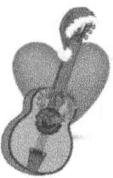

Chapter Thirty-Five

One of Tabitha's many assistants escorted Jake inside her home studio. She was rehearsing "You Gave Me Christmas." Decked out in a green leather leotard, trimmed with sequins and bells, she looked like a sexy elf, a vision that made him want to laugh or cry. He wasn't sure yet.

The music rocked hard and fast. Three musicians on electric guitar, bass, and drums backed the flashy singer. She threw her head to and fro, sending her black hair flying in all directions. Every muscle in his body tensed. It certainly wasn't his song anymore, but letting it go proved harder than expected.

When they finished, she invited him to sit with her as the makeup artist touched up her makeup. A photographer snapped pictures as she poised for the camera. There was more primping and preening than actual music making going on. Why the costume and makeup for a simple rehearsal at home? *Hey, to each her own.* Maybe it helped to get her in the mood.

"My manager said you wanted to talk." She held up a hand mirror and puckered her ruby red lips.

Jake leaned in, attempting to keep the conversation private. "I don't want to stand in the way of your creative freedom and artistic interpretation—"

"But?" she asked. "You hate it."

Had he been that obvious? "Unless it's performed in the spirit in which it was written, it loses its magic." He struggled with conveying how he felt without insulting her.

She looked into his eyes for so long, he squirmed uncomfortably. "Writing a song is like casting a spell. It seems you've written about something that's true and real for you." She clasped her hands together like an enlightened guru. "But sometimes, we write about events we'd like to *come* true."

"Exactly," he said, marveling at her insightfulness. Just because she was young and traded on her looks as much as her talent, didn't mean she was shallow.

"So, tell me, Jake Wilder. What do you want to come true?"

The makeup person stepped away. He hesitated. There were some truths he wasn't willing to admit yet, especially to someone he feared might ruin his reputation in the music business forever.

"What do I wish for?" he repeated. This stalling technique he'd used over the years when people got too close had always been successful. He tended to tell them what they wanted to hear or learned to say nothing at all.

"Who are you conjuring in your song?" she asked.

He pictured Mackenzie's face scrunched up in concentration as she asked her reporter's questions or making fun of his wardrobe while trying to be a mountain man when they both knew he was a city boy forever. The answer to her question was obvious. The song was for Mackenzie. He wished for her.

"I suppose at the end of the day, most songs are about love," Jake said with as much vagueness as he could get away with.

"That's what I'm talking about!" She twirled her hair. "Don't let all this fake bad attitude fool you. I'm a romantic at heart."

Perhaps she was capable of empathy. Realizing his hypocrisy, he'd been as judgmental of her as Mackenzie was of him. "I knew it from the moment I met you." He lied. Just a small one to cover his tracks and spare her feelings.

"You're sweet. But you're avoiding my question."

"I've been known to do that."

"I guess I should ask a different question," Tabitha said. "*Who* is the song about?"

"A journalist who was writing a story about me and the contest, if you can believe that."

"And you fell for each other?" She clutched at her heart. "That's so sweet."

He unexpectedly felt weightless and opened up to her. "She's the whole reason for the song in the first place. To tell you the truth, I wanted nothing to do with Christmas, but she showed me how to celebrate it again. And, how to love again."

"I will do my best to honor the song," she said, wiping a tear from her eye and placing her hand on his arm.

She never said exactly how she'd keep her promise, but he left Tabitha's studio satisfied enough.

~ * ~

Back home, songs flooded Jake's mind. He couldn't keep up

with the music and lyrics as he scribbled furiously in his notebook. The weight of ten years of glory and disappointment lifted from his shoulders. The irony he was relieved rather than discouraged wasn't lost on him. Maybe he needed this crazy, emotional roller-coaster ride all along.

Handing over his creation freed him at last. He wrote like he hadn't in years. Ideas came to him in his sleep, in the shower, even while he ate. Since coming home from Tabitha's studio, he didn't leave his own. He even slept there in case a critical note came to him. All he had to do was tap it out on the piano and hit record.

An idea for a theme album woke him up early. He'd been warned against producing such an endeavor. People buy singles now, he was told. Yet he believed there was an audience for an entire album, especially if it worked together like a novel. Nobody wanted to buy just one chapter.

As he was figuring out the chorus in a blues-inspired song, the phone rang. Normally he left his cellphone in the house—heaven knew he didn't need the distraction. He promised Tabitha he'd be around if she wanted to further discuss "You Gave Me Christmas." They were filming *A Poppin' Christmas* today, and soon Jake's song would be available to the world.

"Bodhi." Jake answered immediately when he recognized the number. "I was just thinking about you."

"You were?"

"No," he said, doodling on his notepad. He enjoyed ribbing his old friend once in a while.

Bodhi huffed. "You need to get to Turk Studios right away."

"The TV studio?" Jake had seen it on Melrose Avenue many times. "If this is about being an audience member at *A Poppin' Christmas*, I already told Tabitha I wasn't interested. She only invited me out of pity."

"Her manager wouldn't say why he wanted you there, but my gut tells me you better go."

"Well, if your gut says so—" He was giving Bodhi a hard time, but Jake knew his friend had his best interest at heart. Trust was an essential part of their relationship, both personally and professionally.

"Get over there," said Bodhi. "And wear something nice."

After they hung up, Jake accessed the clothes he was wearing. Jeans and a T-shirt seemed as good as anything else. He threw on a sports jacket to make Bodhi happy.

On the drive over, Jake tried not to get too excited. Why should Bodhi worry about Jake's outfit anyway? He had stage clothes in a carryon bag just in case. It was his favorite vegan suitcase. His nerves settled when he again recalled Mackenzie teasing him and his vegan jacket up in the mountains. They probably wouldn't be together the way he hoped, but he allowed himself the pleasure of her memory.

When he pulled into the lot, Bodhi met him in the lobby.

"Hurry up." He practically dragged Jake by the arm. "They're waiting for you in hair and makeup."

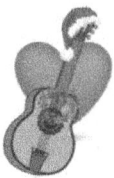

Chapter Thirty-Six

As soon as Tabitha's manager called, Bodhi knew something big was going down. His instinct told him to be on alert. Jake, caught up in the surprise and whirlwind, seemed stunned and resigned to believe miracles couldn't happen.

An optimist, Bodhi had faith in his client and the future. There was only one person in the world he wanted to share the good news with. Maybe Kacey was back with her ex-boyfriend, maybe not, but he had to take the chance she'd embrace the significance of the moment and respond to his message anyway. Was he thinking clearly? Passion took hold of him and scrambled any logic he might've possessed before meeting her. He had to win her back.

Wiping the sweat from his palms, he typed. *You might want to call Mackenzie to make sure she's watching* A Poppin' Christmas *tonight.*

A few seconds later his phone rang.

"Hi," Kacey said.

He was relieved she actually sounded glad to hear from him. "Hey, I've got great news. Can we meet?"

"How about Lucy's? It's the café on the corner near my apartment."

His heart sang, and he wanted to ask a million questions. *Is Ian still in the picture? Do I stand a chance?* Instead, he said, "See you in twenty minutes."

When he moved to Los Angeles, Bodhi learned some things about driving the freeway. If you wanted to continue moving, stay in the slow lane. A driver for an airport commuter company taught him that trick. It didn't make much sense, but Bodhi whizzed by the line of cars stuck in the number one and two lanes as he raced across town toward her apartment. The technique hadn't failed him yet.

She had been so willing to meet him face-to-face. Why? Surely not to break his heart again. He honored her request to not contact her, but it had been difficult. As he focused on getting Jake to cooperate with Tabitha, Bodhi couldn't help thinking about Kacey. It was a torturous distraction for him. He pictured her eating cake at Mackenzie's birthday party. Kacey had frosting on the end of her nose and looked so adorable, he didn't have the heart to say anything. When she finally noticed, she wiped it off with her finger and ate it without a shred of embarrassment.

There was an open spot in front of the café. He checked the time, nervous for his friend. Jake was probably in hair and makeup wondering what was going on. The producers wouldn't tell either of them why they wanted Jake there, but getting him camera ready was a good sign.

The fear they would eventually ask him to sit in the audience gnawed at Bodhi. Forcing Jake to watch helplessly as his song was ruined right before his eyes would be downright cruel.

Wearing a pair of paint-splattered reading glasses, Kacey sat at the counter eating an enormous stack of pancakes and reading the newspaper.

"Is that *The Sunrise Press*?" He eased into the stool next to her.

"Are you kidding? I wouldn't be caught dead reading that rag." She slid the plate of pancakes toward him. "Wanna bite? Banana chocolate chip."

His stomach was in knots. Between worrying about Jake and pining for Kacey, the sweet, sticky treat made him nauseous. "I'm good."

"I bet you're wondering why I called you," she said.

"Actually, I texted you first."

"Oh, yeah." She took a bite of her pancakes. "But I was going to call anyway."

His anxiety melted away. He feared she would be mad at him for bothering her. "How's the ex-boyfriend thing going?" *Why not put it right out on the table?*

She sipped her coffee. "Not great."

Celebrating a broken relationship wasn't exactly chivalrous, so he tried not to look delighted. "That's a shame."

"Don't be too sad about it," she said, smirking and punching him in the shoulder.

"Ouch." He patted the spot she'd hit. Obviously she was used to messing around with older brothers.

"I barely tapped you. Anyway, Ian's a nice guy, and he's perfect for someone else."

"Not you?" Bodhi was hungry all of the sudden and took a bite of her food.

"I already kind of like this other guy." Affection glowed in her eyes.

He could not believe what was happening. She was talking about him. This feeling was like the first time he listened to classical music or saw a whale breach. He'd had other girlfriends, but no one like this woman. She pulsated with energy and enthusiasm and was talented and smart to boot.

"*Moi*?" He gestured to himself.

"Are you going to make me say it?"

"I don't know what you're talking about." Now that he was more relaxed, he was having fun teasing her.

"Don't push it." She was going to give him another love tap, but he covered his shoulder. "Yes, you."

"That's funny." He tilted his head. "Because I kind of like you too."

"Kind of?" She leaned in for a kiss but knocked a glass of water on his lap instead. She giggled. "Sorry," she said, handing him a napkin.

"Now you've done it." He soaked up the spill.

"Why did you text me anyway?"

"It's about Jake. Speaking of—" Bodhi checked his phone to make sure he hadn't missed anything. "I can't say exactly what's going to happen, but he might be in for an exciting night."

"Are you talking about the show with Tabitha?"

"They're taping any minute," he said. "I don't want to set anyone up for a disappointment, but Mackenzie should watch tonight."

"Of course she'll be."

"I have a feeling none of us will want to miss it."

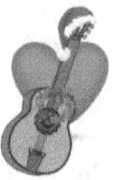

Chapter Thirty-Seven

Mackenzie sat with her mother and sister by the big picture window in the library and enjoyed the last bit of light before the sun set. Bright oranges and purples settled above the lake. Her father's Pennsylvania Flyer, the train around the tree, broke down the night before. He and Dylan worked diligently to get it running again.

It would have been the perfect holiday evening if her stomach hadn't been tied in knots. She had committed to watching Tabitha perform Jake's song no matter what. Though the pain and misery of it wasn't something Mackenzie looked forward to. He wouldn't admit it, but she knew he wanted to be the one on stage singing "You Gave Me Christmas."

She distracted herself by offering to make dinner. A simple spaghetti—sauce from a jar and packaged noodles—took all her concentration. *A Poppin' Christmas* was on in a few hours, and she couldn't think of anything else.

During the show, she didn't know which hat to put on. Was she the journalist on the job, ready to report so she could finish the article? Or the concerned friend witnessing someone she cared about throw his whole career away? Though the latter wasn't a guaranteed outcome, she worried for him anyway.

Guilt continued to torment her. She could hardly call herself a friend. Perhaps she should be more optimistic. The show and song might be a huge success. Yet, she had a bad feeling if he sacrificed his song, it would affect the rest of his life. He may never have the confidence to write again.

She stirred the sauce, her stomach growling with hunger. Between running around with her mother and sister and helping her dad with housework, she was starving. Mackenzie barely kept up with her father. If he wasn't chopping wood or fixing train sets, he made plans to repaint bedrooms and change the hardware in the guest bathroom. Her mother's tool belt idea had been a good one. Mackenzie was tired of fetching tools left and right for her father, but she was happy to be of some use. It kept her mind off Jake.

"Hello," Kacey's voiced echoed through the house.

"Hiya," Brenda's voice answered in return. "Glad you made it okay. I was getting worried."

Mackenzie wiped her hands on a dish towel and entered the hallway. "Kacey?" Mackenzie was shocked to see her friend and confused her mother knew she was coming in the first place.

"Well, look who it is." Kacey handed Mackenzie a pie box from Gerrard's.

"I'm the one who should be saying that to you. What are you doing here?" She was relieved to see the one person who knew what she needed even before she knew herself.

"I've got to have a reason to see my bestie?" Kacey hung her coat in the hall closet. "I missed you, and I brought you a fresh coconut cream pie."

Mackenzie opened the box and inhaled. "In that case, you can stay."

"I was planning on it. Get my things while I say hello to your family."

"Yes, ma'am," said Mackenzie. Only Kacey could get away with bossing Mackenzie around.

After she set Kacey up in one of the guest bedrooms, Mackenzie returned to the kitchen to find Kacey sampling the spaghetti sauce.

"Seriously, what are you doing here?" asked Mackenzie. "You shouldn't have made the drive by yourself."

"What, it's like two hours. I'm a big girl, Mom." Kacey picked up the jar of sauce nearby. "Store-bought sauce? What does your mother think?"

"She doesn't know." Mackenzie tossed the jar into the recycle bin. "I'm so glad you're here."

"Admit it. You missed me." Kacey spread her arms wide for a hug.

"So much." She'd failed everybody lately, including her best friend.

"You don't call. You don't text me back," said Kacey. "What's up with that?"

"I've been busy." Mackenzie avoided breaking the news she was moving to Boston.

She gave Mackenzie, who was dressed in yoga pants and a grubby T-shirt, the once over. "Doing what?"

"Working."

"All righty." Kacey gave a lopsided grin. "Anyway, I'm here for moral support. We're watching *A Poppin' Christmas* tonight, right?"

"Of course," said Mackenzie. "I need to finish writing the profile on Jake."

"Go easy on him."

"Are you speaking as a friend or Bodhi's representative?" Mackenzie handed Kacey napkins and silverware to set the table.

"That's low." She frowned.

"I'm sorry. I've been on edge lately. Don't worry. Bodhi will be happy with the article. And as far as Tabitha's performance goes, I'll be open and objective. I report what I see."

"Don't expect too much."

"She's a great singer and performer," said Mackenzie. "I'm sure she'll do fine." This was the right attitude she needed to adopt if she expected to be a good reporter.

Kacey found the dishes in the cupboard. "Bodhi said I shouldn't say anything, but asking a person to keep a secret from her best friend is like breaking some kind of sacred law."

"Exactly," said Mackenzie. *How many heartbreaks can I take in a week?* "How bad is it?"

"Bad." Kacey set the table before leading Mackenzie to a chair. "You better sit. Jake nearly died when he heard Tabitha's version of the song and almost walked away from the whole deal."

Mackenzie could only assume the worst. "Why would Jake let her ruin his comeback song?" Poor guy. She imagined the heartache he must've felt. Writing it meant everything to him and to witness his creation, his child, get trashed. You don't come back from something like that.

"She butchered it. Bodhi let me hear it, and it sounds like a jalopy with a busted muffler running over a perfectly good Christmas song. Wailing guitars, pounding drums, screeching vocals, which can be cool sometimes. But not here. Think death metal meets Bing Crosby."

Mackenzie hung her head. "The song you hear tonight won't be Jake's." *And it won't be mine, either.* When Tabitha sings "Here in this moment / On a cold Winter's night / It's Christmas, I'm with you / And it feels so right," who will she be talking to? Not Mackenzie that was for sure.

~ * ~

After dinner, they gathered around the television. Mackenzie tried to remember the last time they'd watched TV as a family. Her eyes welled up at the thought of leaving them behind to go to Boston. She swallowed the dreadful image, putting it off until after the new year.

Mackenzie and Kacey did their best to lower expectations of Tabitha's performance. It had nothing to do with the quality of Jake's song, Mackenzie told her family. She didn't want them to assume he wasn't a talented musician. In return, they cheered her up by making a game of it. How bad could Tabitha be?

"Will she be as bad as this?" Her father sang "Jingle Bells" in a ridiculously high-pitched voice.

"Or this?" Kacey croaked out a version of "A Holly Jolly Christmas," animating each line with a silly gesture.

They tried to top each other with the most outlandish sounding songs. The distraction worked until Mackenzie thought about Jake watching the show too. Could he stomach the disaster about to unfold?

About halfway through the program, the announcer said Tabitha was on next. Mackenzie braced herself. Butterflies fluttered in her stomach, as if she were on stage herself. She'd never felt this connected to anyone. *Be calm. Remain objective.*

When the show came back, a soft melody played. "It's the song," said Mackenzie. The camera panned to Jake sitting behind a piano. Her breath shook. "What's he doing there?"

Kacey held her palms together.

Mackenzie prepared herself for the tone switch. Perhaps Tabitha wanted to start slowly before kicking into high gear.

He looked handsome in a casual suit coat, and to Mackenzie's surprise, he seemed relaxed and happy.

"This is a pleasant song," said Harry.

"Lovely," agreed Brenda. "Is this death metal?"

Kacey snorted. "If it is, I've been missing out."

Out of nowhere, Tabatha floated to the stage in a flying sleigh. The crowd roared as she walked toward the piano and sat next to Jake. She sang the first verse of the song.

"Ladies and gentlemen, Jake Wilder." She introduced him to the audience.

Jake sang the second verse.

A duet. Perfect. The song sounded even better than before.

Mackenzie's eyes were glued to the television. Her heart thumped.

They sang the last verse together. When they finished the most beautiful song of the evening, the audience jumped to their feet to give an enthusiastic standing ovation.

"Thank you." Tabitha stared straight into the camera. "Mackenzie, this song was for you."

Her family turned to Mackenzie whose mouth had fallen open. For once, she was speechless.

Before she had time to fully process what happened, the doorbell rang.

"I'll get it." She jogged to the front door, anxious to avoid the limelight.

She flipped on the porch light to see who was there in the darkness. It might be a neighbor stopping by with a gift or to say hello, or maybe some carolers had gathered to sing to her family.

She swung the door open. Jake stood on the porch wearing the same clothes he'd performed in and looked just as gorgeous as he did on TV.

Joy overwhelmed her. "But you were on television only a minute ago."

"That's the magic of Hollywood." He waved his hand in the air like a sorcerer.

She was confused, and her face must've shown it.

"It's pre-recorded, ding-a-ling."

"Of course." Her cheeks warmed. After the performance, her logic hadn't quite kicked in yet, and she blinked a few times to clear her head. Meanwhile, he shivered in the cold air.

"Was it that bad?" He ran his hand through his hair. "Can I come in?"

"Are you kidding? The song sounded incredible." She stepped to the side to let him in. Tears formed at the corner of her eyes. She was overwhelmed with joy for his success and also surprised he was standing right in front of her.

"Who is it?" asked her father from the den.

"Shhh," Kacey said. She must've recognized Jake's voice, and like the vigilant friend she was, knew this was no time to interrupt.

He entered the foyer, but kept on his jacket and scarf, probably unsure if he was welcome.

"I thought Tabitha wasn't going to sing the song as you'd written it," said Mackenzie.

"Turns out she has a soft spot for romance."

Mackenzie wanted to confirm which romance he meant but was too shy to ask. Humiliating herself again wasn't an option. Yet, there he was, in her house.

She helped remove his jacket, and he took her hand in his. "I told Tabitha all about you. What the song meant to me. She said we had to stay true to my vision and insisted on a duet."

"And the dedication?"

"A complete surprise. I was floored, but it's true. The song is for you." He pulled Mackenzie in tight for the embrace they'd both been longing for. "It's all you."

Her heart thumped. She was breathless.

They finally transcended reporter and subject, and she wasn't scared anymore. Falling in love wouldn't keep her from achieving everything she'd always wanted. It made her stronger and even more capable of becoming the woman she'd dreamed of being.

"I love you," he said.

"I love you too." She inhaled Jake's warm, familiar scent. It was a long time coming.

He pressed his lips to hers. Desire radiated between them. She didn't want to stop kissing this man who had forever immortalized her in a song about Christmas.

Epilogue
Six Months Later

This time when Jake Wilder stepped out on stage, there was no hesitation. No anxiety. He sauntered to the microphone, guitar slung low. All rock and roll. All attitude.

Mikey tapped the cymbal. It was time to play. Jake gave him a nod, and they broke into everyone's favorite song, "City Lights."

The audience cheered. He didn't resent that they'd played the hit hundreds of times. Only pure joy.

Standing beside his friend Phil once again, they fit together like two pieces of a worn puzzle. These musicians were meant to stick together. They knew it, and the thousands of people in the audience who welcomed the band, whether they were hearing the songs for the first time or were loyal fans from back in the day, knew it too.

The Jake Wilder Trio were selling out stadiums across the country thanks to the new album. After huge sales of "You Gave Me Christmas," Satellite Records made good on their promise and let Jake, Mikey, and Phil cut a new record. It was doing well, and some in the industry even mentioned Grammy nominations.

Jake glanced to the side of the stage. Mackenzie was dancing. Happiness flowed through him.

After she finished her profile on him, the *Los Angeles Tribune* picked up the article and hired her as a full-time reporter. Much to his relief, she turned down the job at the *Boston World View*.

He couldn't believe his luck. Their romance was like a fairy tale he recited to her. She called it their origin story and made him repeat it often.

It went like this: once upon a time there was a has-been pop star named Jake Wilder who wanted more than anything to make a comeback. One day an opportunity to write a Christmas song presented itself. The problem was, though, he hated Christmas. All seemed lost until he met Mackenzie Stone, a journalist who loved Christmas more than anyone in the world. He worked hard on the song, won the contest, and the girl.

She accused him of writing an edited version. "What about the fight?" she'd ask. "There's no story without a conflict."

The following week they were going to the Montreal Jazz Festival. He planned to ask her to marry him. It might be soon in their relationship, but if they were to have a Christmastime wedding, the clock was ticking. It was only six months away.

Mackenzie wouldn't have it any other way.

Acknowledgements

Writing a hit Christmas song is not easy. Few make it into the sacred Christmas cannon—the catalog of holiday songs enjoyed by generations year after year. When I searched for the words to Jake's original Christmas song, I looked no further than friend and musician Mike Gentry. His talent and generosity continue to delight everyone who is lucky enough to know him and the beautiful music he creates.

I'd also like to thank the Champagne Book Group for bringing my sweet holiday romance to life. Cassiel Knight's insightful editorial comments inspired me to reimagine and gently guided me through thoughtful revisions.

Finally, Jack Reilly, I am so grateful for your support. Your editorial skills are invaluable, but most of all, thank you for giving me my own forever Christmas love song.

About the Author

Andee Reilly was born and raised in Los Angeles. She received her MFA in Creative Writing from the University of California, Riverside. After many years of teaching writing and literature at California State University, Channel Islands, Andee moved to Maui to pursue her dream of teaching at the University of Hawaii, writing full-time, and surfing the beautiful waves of Hawaii.

Andee loves to hear from her readers. You can find and connect with her at the links below.

Website/Blog: https://www.andeereilly.com/
Facebook: https://www.facebook.com/AndeeReillyAuthor
Instagram: https://www.instagram.com/andeereilly/
Pinterest: https://www.pinterest.com/andeereilly
Twitter: https://twitter.com/andeereilly

~ * ~

Thank you for taking the time to read *A Christmas Love Song* and hope you enjoyed reading it as much as we loved bringing it to you. If you enjoyed the story, please tell your friends, and leave a review. Reviews support authors and ensure they continue to bring readers books to love and enjoy.

DURING A MAGICAL HOLIDAY SEASON, EMMA AND ANDREW KEEP FINDING THEMSELVES SNOWED IN TOGETHER, AS THEY FACE THEIR PASTS AND FALL IN LOVE.

TURN THE PAGE FOR A LOOK INSIDE!

Chapter One

Emma Ballard hated snow. Cursing her shoe choice—leather designer boots clearly not made for mid-Atlantic winters—she stomped her feet on the frozen sidewalk under the overhang outside of the Portuguese restaurant in Newark, New Jersey. As she rocked to stay warm, she wrapped her gray wool coat, a Ballard original, a little tighter around her chest, pulled a cap from her oversized bag, and cursed all things winter.

Despite her hatred of the white flakes falling around her, the bitter air cooled her cheeks, still warm from the heat and activity of Russell Westingman's retirement party. Thanksgiving had just passed, and it was early in the season, but the weather people had been predicting a snowy winter, starting with the storm today.

Emma had insisted on keeping the party as scheduled. As CEO of Ballard Industries, she wanted to send Russell out in style, and the five-course luncheon, complete with a band and open bar, seemed to do the trick. If only Mother Nature had agreed with her plans.

She should have left earlier, but after the party cleared out, she and Russell polished off a pitcher of Sangria. With her belly full and her head spinning from the alcohol, Emma had listened to Russell's stories about her father, making a conscious effort not to let her tears fall. Russell missed Daniel "Danny Boy" Ballard, almost as much as she did.

She had known Russell all her life, since her father started Ballard Industries with a flagship store thirty years earlier, and Russell had been his first administrative hire. Later, while her father focused on building the global brand and business, Russell "kept the home fires burning," working out of the Jersey branch and focusing on human resources, office management, and technology. Their competition—Ann Taylor, Dress Barn, the Gap—had tried to lure him away, but he'd been loyal to "Danny Boy" and BI from day one.

When they finally said their goodbyes, Russell thanked Emma for the party, gushed over his generous retirement package, and cried reading the card she'd written for him. His shoes would be hard to fill.

Shoes.

She stomped her feet again, but her toes had officially become numb. They'd received word earlier that the trains to Manhattan were cancelled due to the storm. Emma debated staying in a hotel for the night. But holding onto one last thread of hope that she could get home to the city, she willed herself to be patient, and waited for the car she'd summoned.

After adjusting her wool cap over her ears, she pulled out her phone and opened her email, figuring she'd give the car another ten minutes before high-tailing it to the nearest Hilton. Snowflakes dropped onto the device as she texted the Assistant CEO, Rhonda Lewis, that she was still in Jersey. She brushed the annoying flakes off her phone as she typed, hating the snow even more.

"Ms. Ballard!" a man's voice called from the street.

"Thank God," Emma murmured, shoving her phone back into her bag. Another minute waiting, and the frostbite would have set in.

A gray, Honda something-or-other idled at the curb, while the man attached to the voice waved from the driver's seat. "Everything okay, ma'am?"

"Fine now." She walked a few careful steps toward the car. The man exited the vehicle and met her on the icy sidewalk, offering an arm to steady her. He was tall, but so was she, and she grabbed his forearm and leaned on him for support. "You can get me back to New York in this mess?"

The man quirked an eyebrow, glancing down at her with green eyes. The snowflakes gathered on his blond, unruly hair—hair that was overdue for a cut. "Oh, um." Looking across the street and then up to the sky, he finally focused on her. "I don't think so."

Her shoulders slumped. Dumb weather. She'd never make it back to the city. "Then why did you answer the call to pick me up?"

"Call?" His broad shoulders, covered in a navy dress coat, shook with his nervous laugh. "Oh, I'm not your driver. I... I work for BI. I was at Russell's party."

Her breath caught, and she groaned, embarrassed. "I'm so sorry." She hadn't noticed him inside and certainly didn't know every one of the company's fifteen-thousand employees, or even the few hundred that worked in the New Jersey branch. Still, she made excuses. "I'm a little out of it. Drank too much and I'm tired. My feet..." She stopped talking. She shouldn't be complaining to an employee, especially a stranger.

"What's wrong with your feet?" He peered down to the ground.

"They're cold." She stomped them with the hope of feeling her toes again. No luck.

Shaking his head, he pointed. "Makes sense. You're not wearing proper footwear for a snowstorm."

Ah, a know-it-all. "Aware, thanks."

"Why didn't you bring your snow boots?" He lifted his foot to show her his perfectly outdoorsy, warm and dry looking footwear. "I did."

Who *was* this guy? "Good for you. But I don't have snow boots. I don't make it a habit to be out in this awful weather."

"Not a fan of winter?"

"Not at all." She scooted back under the overhang of the restaurant before she froze to death or started babbling. Either outcome was possible. "How can I help you, Mr....?"

He held out a gloved hand. "Mooney. Andrew Mooney. IT supervisor, Jersey branch."

She shook it, the warm wool scratching her cold, uncovered palm.

"Nice to officially meet you, Ms. Ballard."

Emma smiled as she racked her brain for prior interactions with Andrew Mooney. "You can call me Emma." In her five years as CEO, she hadn't come across Andrew. That full smile. The angled jawline. Those bright green eyes. Had she met him, she would have certainly remembered.

"Okay, Emma. As much as I'm enjoying holding your hand—"

"Oh!" Her hand was still encased in his. She pulled it away as if it was set on fire.

"—we should probably not be standing in the snow on the streets of Newark. My company policy only allows for a few sick days a year, and I'm already tapped out." He let his jaw drop, feigning shock. "Did I say that out loud?"

Smirking, she wondered how many sick days employees actually received. Her Human Resources Department handled those things, and HR was Russell's end of the business. Now that he was gone, she'd have to learn that side of the company too. "You're fired," Emma barked, pointing at his chest.

The guy gasped. "For realsies?"

She tried to maintain her fake scowl but couldn't stop the grin from forming. "No, for fakesies, I guess."

His cheeks turned a cute shade of pink. "Sorry. I have little girls at home, and that's one of their favorite questions. 'For realsies?'"

Girls at home. A wave of disappointment rushed over Emma upon learning that he had a family. Not for his sake, but for her own. Their short exchange was the most non-business-related conversation she'd had with a man her age in a long time. Maybe she was even flirting? It'd been so long, she wasn't sure anymore.

"Do you mind if I start using that in my meetings? Like, when someone says something inappropriate or completely off the wall, I'll smirk at them like this," she scrunched her face, "and ask, are you for realsies?"

He nodded. "Great technique. Now if you want to add the palm in the air and the hip jut, you'd be exactly like my girls."

She tried again, following his directions. "Like this?"

"Perfect," he said, his gaze dancing. "You're a natural."

"Imagine that." She adjusted her bag on her shoulder. "Well, I hate to do this in the middle of our training here, but I kind of need to find a hotel since it doesn't look like I'll be getting home tonight."

He held his palm to the sky and caught some snowflakes in his glove, studying them like they were magical. "Oh right. That's why I stopped originally, to help you, but then I got distracted by your shoes and stuff."

The way he peered down at her, like a complete gentleman helping a damsel in distress, made her pulse race. But she wasn't a damsel in distress, she was his boss, and she was competent enough to deal with a weather inconvenience. "That's okay, Mr. Mooney. I appreciate the offer of assistance, but I'll be fine."

"Call me Andrew." He tilted his head. "Why don't you at least come wait out the storm at my place?"

She squinted at him.

"That came out weird, didn't it?" he asked, copying her expression. "I mean, you can meet my family, have a meal. I'll show you my company ID if you're worried I'm some wacko kidnapper or something."

"Funny, I didn't think that until you mentioned it." Would she go home with this man? He was a stranger, sure, but he worked for her company and was willing to help. He had a houseful of girls too, apparently. Seemed sincere. She thought for a second. "How about this? I'll ask you a company question, and if you answer it right, I'll believe you work for BI and take you up on your generous offer."

"For realsies?" He rubbed his chin. "Okay, shoot."

"What's the name of the chef from the lunch café in the Jersey branch who ran off with the V.P. of Sales?" Everyone at BI knew this story. The tale was corporate legend.

"Millicent," he answered without hesitation. "Personally, I think she could have done better."

Emma stifled her laugh before it escaped. He wasn't wrong.

"Did I pass?" Andrew asked.

"You did. Still going to text a picture of your license plate to

Rhonda, though."

He drew his hands to his chest, feigning pain. "Ouch. But smart. I'll pose next to the car if you want."

"Perfect." She dug her phone out of her bag and waved him toward the Honda.

With a huff, he leaped the two steps and leaned against the snow-covered trunk, crossing his boots at the ankle, and extending his long arms to the side. "My chariot. And my regards to Ms. Lewis."

After she tapped her phone to take the picture, he jumped back to her side, offering his arm. She held on, wobbling her way over the sidewalk, into the street, to the passenger side. He opened the door for her, and she sat in the warm car, texting Rhonda the photo while he scraped the snow that had accumulated off the windshield.

Emma: Know this guy?

Rhonda: Andrew Mooney. NJ office. Something with IT?

Emma: He's giving me a ride. Thoughts?

Rhonda: Neutral. If you go missing, I'll know where to look.

Emma: Great.

By the time he sat in the driver's seat, she'd defrosted and dried off a bit. "Thank you for helping me, Andrew Mooney."

He put the car into drive and glanced at her in the passenger seat. "It's an honor, Boss Lady."

Smiling at the nickname, she had no idea where they were going, but she didn't care. Despite Rhonda's neutrality, Emma's instincts told her she was safe with Andrew. Best of all, in the heat of the little car, she could feel her toes again.

*   *   *

Andrew pulled the Accord onto the streets, which thankfully were plowed, and pointed them toward his home, mentally reviewing his factual knowledge of Emma Ballard.

He knew as much about the woman sitting next to him as she seemed to know about him. Very little. Emma Ballard. CEO. Former model. Hired over five years ago when her father died, which would make her his boss's boss's boss. Considered a reluctant CEO, he'd heard she was a good businesswoman, tolerated by the Board of Directors as a legacy to her father but mostly as a placeholder until the Board could usher her out for a more suitable candidate of their choice. Smart. Neutral about employee issues. She didn't bother the staff; they didn't bother her.

He glanced at her in the passenger seat and added to his fact base. Beautiful. Brunette. Long, thick hair. Brown, mysterious eyes with full lashes, perfect for catching snowflakes.

At Russell's retirement party—Russell being his boss's boss—she'd glided around the room, somehow avoiding attention but at the same time lighting up the place. He vaguely recalled seeing her on the cover of magazines but had a hard time reconciling the supermodel with the CEO. That afternoon was the first time he'd seen her in person.

That afternoon was also the first time he'd had a woman in his car since Hayley.

When the silence between them became awkward, for him at least, Andrew cleared his throat. "So, Emma. Any big plans for the holidays?"

"Not really. Just working. How about you?" Her friendly tone invited the conversation.

"Hanging with my girls. They already made their lists for Santa."

"Already? But Christmas is still a month away."

He smiled. "They insisted the elves need the lists now to start making toys."

"Smart. How old are they?"

"Six."

She paused then said, "Both of them?"

"Yep. They're twins."

"The Realsie Twins?"

He liked the nickname. "You got it."

"How fun. You and your wife must have a blast with them."

Andrew gulped and glanced at her. "Oh, I'm not married."

"I'm sorry." She groaned. "I'm an idiot. You wear a ring, but I shouldn't have assumed…"

"My wife passed away." He hoped she'd leave it at that. Andrew had loved his wife more than the world but hated talking about her out loud. Even after six years, when he heard the sadness in people's reactions to her death, a vise gripped his heart.

"I'm so sorry," Emma said quietly. "For you and your girls."

She didn't ask any follow-up questions, which he appreciated. "What about you? Any kids?" He knew the answers to these questions from the company gossip hounds, but figured they'd make do for conversational purposes.

"Not married. No kids."

Andrew couldn't imagine a life so free. He had loved his wife, and loved his girls more than anything, but between work and them, he didn't have time for much else. Thankfully, his father lived next door and helped out more than he should so Andrew could do things, like attend the retirement party for Russell. "What do you do besides work?"

Emma shifted in the passenger seat. "Not much. I mean, sometimes I sew."

"You do?" He hoped the shock in his voice was indecipherable. "What do you make?"

She twisted her hands in her lap. "I love to stitch. I've been making a lot of scarves lately. It's my new obsession."

"Really?" He tapped his fingers on the steering wheel. "Wasn't your mom a clothing designer? I vaguely remember something in our company's history."

"She was." When he peeked at her, her eyes lit up. "She created the first designs my father sold for BI."

"Such an amazing story. I'm proud to work for the company." He smiled and gave a curt nod.

"That's a nice thing to say."

They drove in silence for a few more blocks. Traffic slowed as the sun set and the roads iced up. "Only a few more minutes, and we should be there." He tapped the wheel.

"What about you?" she asked. "What do you do besides work and parenting?"

Andrew pressed his lips together, unsure whether or not to confide in the fancy pants boss lady sitting beside him. He glanced her way. She may look fancy, but she didn't act fancy, and he could probably trust her with personal information. "Promise not to laugh?"

"I'd never," she insisted.

"I like theater."

She gasped. "Me too! Are you an actor?"

"I was, in another life. I still love Broadway. Musical theater is my passion. I've memorized every song in *Heatherby*."

She reached across the console, grasping his upper arm. "Wasn't that a wonderful play? I loved it so much."

He flinched, surprised at the feel of her touch on his body. "I never saw it. I don't have much time to get to the theater with the girls' schedule. It's expensive too."

Placing her hands back in her lap, she nodded. "That's true. Well, I hope someday you get to see it. *Heatherby* is…," she sighed, "…absolutely indescribable."

He smiled. "I bet." He pulled up to the duplex, his tires crunching over the snow in the driveway he already dreaded shoveling. "This side is me. The other side is my dad. He's babysitting tonight so I could attend the party. Want to come in and meet everyone?"

"Sure," she said. "Beats being home alone."

If it weren't for the sadness underlying her tone, he may have taken that as an insult. Instead, it almost made him feel sorry for her. As if he should be feeling sorry for a rich lady, his boss, while he struggled to make ends meet.

Andrew helped Emma over the slick driveway, and then opened the door to his home, the feeling of relief washing over him. He always loved walking through that doorway. Whatever happened on the outside always faded away as his girls ran to give him hugs and tell him about their days.

That evening was no exception. The soft lights and the crackle of the fire had created an orange glow through the house, and a smell of winter and Christmas wafted toward him.

Devon and Bella darted into the room, screaming, "Daddy!" but then stopped short when they saw Emma.

"Devon, Bella," he said, in his best "dad" tone, "this is Daddy's boss, Ms. Ballard."

"Hi, Ms. Ballard," Devon said.

His father hobbled over to join them, extending a hand to Emma. "Jeffrey Mooney, Andrew's father. Nice to meet you, ma'am."

Emma shook his outstretched hand. "Please, call me Emma. I'm sorry to intrude on your evening."

The girls circled Emma as she spoke, inspecting her like she was a great mystery they had to solve.

She addressed them directly, obviously not intimidated by their scrutinizing glares. "Your dad was kind enough to offer me shelter from the storm. I hope that's okay with all of you."

Bella stopped in front of Emma, crossing her arms. "You're my dad's boss?"

Emma nodded.

"She's more like my boss's boss's boss," Andrew added. "And I expect you all to be polite and respectful."

"Yeah, yeah," Bella said, waving an arm around. She turned back to Emma. "Why can't he have more days off?"

"Bella!" he yelled, then looked at Emma. "I'm sorry—"

"It's a fair question." She pressed her lips together and side-eyed him, clearly trying not to laugh. She turned her attention back to Bella. "What would you do if he did?"

Devon joined her sister, striking the same pose. "Go to the zoo. I like elephants."

Emma exaggerated a gasp. "I like them too. I got to see some when I was on a safari in Africa."

"For realsies?" Bella asked.

Andrew's heart clenched at her sweet tone. Even though the

girls' schedules were just as busy as his own, he had to find a way to spend more time with them, outside of carting them around to their various activities. He made a mental note to research season passes for the zoo.

Without missing a beat, Emma jutted a hip and lifted her chin, in the pose he had coached her on. "For realsies." She winked at Andrew. "How about this. Since you've all been so nice to me, I'll do my best to get your dad more days off, okay?"

Bella flashed Emma a thumbs up. "And you have to tell us about your safari."

"Deal." Emma offered Bella a hand, and Bella shook it.

Amused, he shot a grin over the girls' heads to his father. Jeffrey raised his brows and nodded toward Emma, clearly impressed.

When Devon waved her down to eye level, Emma squatted before her. "You have a nice nose," Devon said, reaching out to touch it.

"Devon!" Andrew barked. "Leave Ms. Ballard—"

"Emma." Emma smiled and stood up. "Ms. Ballard makes me sound old and official."

Official maybe. Old? Not so much. He vaguely remembered reading that she was thirty-something. He threw his stern dad look at Devon. "Leave *Miss* Emma, alone please. Can you let her take her coat off and get comfortable?"

His father shooed the girls into the living room and directed his attention to their house guest. "How about a cup of coffee, Emma?"

"That sounds perfect," she answered, as she slid her coat off over her arms. "You'll join me?"

Andrew wasn't sure if she was talking to his dad or him, but they both jammed their fists into their front pockets and answered in unison. "Sure."

Something about Emma Ballard had turned the Mooney men to mush.

Chapter Two

Emma woke to the sound of whispers from the other side of the bedroom door. Confused, she glanced around and remembered that she was in Andrew Mooney's house.

"Why is she in your room, Daddy?" the little voice whisper-shouted.

She smiled at the girl's attempt to be quiet. The clock on the nightstand read six-fifteen, and sat next to a picture of a woman, presumably Andrew's wife, on their wedding day. She was beautiful—smiling, beaming, in a long, lace-covered, A-line gown. Emma wondered how she died. How this family had survived without her.

"Because she was tired, and the blizzard would have made it hard to get her home." Clearly, that was Andrew's whisper voice.

"But where does she live?"

"In New York City. I think. Quiet. We don't want to wake her."

"Like Eloise?" the little voice sang.

"Huh?"

"You know, the book? She lives in New York City too."

"I thought Madeline was from New York?" he asked.

"No, Madeline lives in Paris."

"Oh, that's right. Come on. Let's get moving. Go get Devon, and we'll have breakfast."

"But I need my library book. I left it in there."

Emma sat up, focusing as she scanned the room. Books covered the dresser, mostly adult sci-fi, except for the one pink book.

"You'll get it later," Andrew's tone was hushed but stern.

With a long stretch, Emma dragged herself out of bed and grabbed the book with the illustrated elephant on the cover. She looked down at her attire—a long, black, men's T-shirt with a spaceship on it, and a pair of flannel pajama bottoms rolled up at the ankles. She barely remembered changing out of her party clothes the night before, after Andrew convinced her to stay the night.

She shuffled to the door and opened it, as the two stunned faces turned to her. "Good morning. I think this is yours." She held the book out to Bella.

"Thank you," Bella said, as she grabbed the book. Then, in a flash, she stuck her tongue out at her dad and ran down the stairs.

"Hey, you. Watch that attitude." Andrew's loud, deep "dad" voice couldn't scare a fly, as he called after Bella.

Emma took the opportunity to check him out. He was showered, shaved, his messy hair tamed with gel. He wore the typical IT outfit of khakis and a button down. "These kids," he muttered, turning back to her. "Sorry. It's only a little after six, but that's like noon around here. We didn't mean to wake you."

"Please. It's your house. There's no need to apologize."

"Did you sleep okay?" he asked.

She crossed her arms over the ridiculous shirt, as his eyes did a quick sweep of her. The combination of his warm gaze and the smell of bacon wafting up the stairs woke every wonderful nerve inside her body. "Perfect." She made a show of sniffing the air around them. "That smells fabulous."

"Breakfast is our favorite meal." He pointed down the hallway. "Two doors down is the bathroom. Why don't you get cleaned up and meet us downstairs?" His gaze darted back to hers. "Not that you're dirty."

She raised an eyebrow as he shifted before her.

"But, you know, women do things in the morning in the bathroom I guess. I mean, what they do I'll never know, but you'll figure it out. I think what I'm trying to say is, you look great, but, if you need..."

He huffed as she poked his arm, hoping to put him out of his misery. "Andrew. Stop. It's fine. Yes, I'd love to have a minute in the bathroom."

Clearly embarrassed, he shook his head. His blush was cute. She couldn't remember the last time she'd made a man so uncomfortable, at least outside of the board room.

"Anyhoo," he continued, rocking back on his heels, "we'll eat and then I'll drive you wherever you need to go. The roads are plowed, and the world keeps spinning so... Does that sound good?"

"I'd be grateful, but I don't want to put you out. I can call a car." Emma already dreaded the ride back in this weather. Andrew Mooney's house was so warm and bacon-y, she didn't want to leave.

"It's no problem. You may have to write me a late note for my boss though."

"Who *is* your boss?" she asked, realizing the topic of work hadn't come up at all the night before. Mostly, they'd discussed elephants, nail polish, and television shows. "I'm not exactly clear on where you sit in the company flow chart."

His laugh indicated he'd relaxed a bit. "I have three employees I supervise, so I'm sort of low-middle management. I report to Stuart, who used to report to Russell."

"Stu Borowski? Oh, no problem. I'll text him right now." She knew Stu well and would probably promote him to Russ's now-vacant position.

Andrew held up a hand. "Maybe that's not the best idea. Don't want the rumor mill to get started."

She raised her eyebrows. "Good point. You'd probably be embarrassed that I'm squatting in your house…"

"I don't mean for me, for you. They'll say you're slumming with the IT guy. It would be scandalous." He sputtered out an awkward chuckle.

With a tilt of her head, she grinned. "You've been a perfect gentleman. But whatever you want me to tell Stu, I'll respect that."

"Thanks." He ran a hand over his head, but with the gel it only made his hair stick out at weird angles. "I'm really annoying, huh? How about I go downstairs? You take your time, help yourself to what you need, and meet us down there for breakfast. Deal?"

Anticipating bacon, she nodded curtly. "Deal. And you're not annoying."

"Glad to hear that." He walked toward the staircase.

"Andrew?" she called.

He turned to face her.

"Thank you for letting me have your room last night."

He smiled a warm grin, his eyes crinkling in the corners. "You're welcome, Boss Lady."

※   ※   ※

A few hours later, after Andrew dropped her off at home and she had a much-needed shower and outfit change, Emma made her way to BI headquarters. She spent a minute to appreciate her office view overlooking Midtown Manhattan. The snow-lined streets were busy with business people weaving around the holiday influx of tourists who'd taken over the area. She hated snow, but she especially hated snow when it painted her city that dingy-gray color.

The people rushing around in business coats reminded her that she had to send an email to Stu. She opened her inbox and composed a new message, copying Andrew. Seeing his name pop up in the company mailbox made her heart race. He really did work there. She wondered for how long.

She sent a simple message to Stu, explaining that Andrew had "assisted her with business that morning" and thanking him for excusing his lateness. Then, she called Rhonda's office, opposite hers in the executive suite, and asked her to stop by when she had the chance.

Born in Trinidad, Rhonda Lewis had started working for Emma's father at the flagship Ballard store in Brooklyn the month after she arrived in New York, shortly after her sixteenth birthday. She'd worked her way up through the corporation as she pursued her business degree and eventually her MBA. Twenty years from the exact date of her hiring, Daniel Ballard asked Rhonda to be the Assistant CEO, the position she still held. Besides Emma's late father and Russ, nobody knew more about Ballard Industries than Rhonda.

Knowing that Mr. Ballard wanted Emma to learn the business, Rhonda didn't object when Emma was named CEO after his death. Instead, Rhonda had taken Emma under her wing. *Your father gave me a chance when I started out. It's only right he should do the same for his daughter. I respect that man and his wishes more than I care about which office I sit in,* she'd said. As much as Rhonda tried to teach Emma the art of people skills over the past five years, Rhonda was the expert on sensing the tone of the company's staff. The employees often approached her with issues, feeling more comfortable with her than with Emma. Rhonda also knew how to get information on employees, and Emma needed her help.

After a quick knock, Rhonda poked her head into the office. "Hey, Emma. What's up?"

She cleared her throat. Rhonda had known her since she was a child and would be able to sense the curiosity in Emma's voice if she wasn't careful. "Could you find me a personnel file on the down low?" Her cheeks warmed as she shuffled papers on her desk in an effort to appear disinterested.

"Sure. What's the name?"

Emma folded her hands on her desk, sitting up taller and meeting Rhonda's gaze. "Andrew Mooney. The guy from the Jersey branch."

Rhonda lifted her chin, squinting at Emma. "From the party? Did he give you a hard time? If HR needs to get involved—"

"Oh no, not at all," Emma interrupted. "He helped get me home, and I felt terrible that I didn't know who he was, that's all."

"That's all?" Rhonda asked, quirking a brow and studying Emma.

"Yes." *And I want to know more about him,* Emma didn't admit to Rhonda.

"I'll have it to you in an hour." Rhonda smiled and closed the door as she left.

Later, when Rhonda emailed the file on Andrew Mooney, Emma clicked on it but deleted it before reading anything. He'd been nice to her, and she wouldn't abuse her position by stalking him through his company history.

She spun in her chair and then picked up her phone. Thinking of Andrew, she made a few calls, cashed in a few favors, and spent more than a few dollars.

No, she wouldn't stalk him. She'd be direct. She had no idea how it would play out, but one thing was certain—she hadn't felt so alive at Ballard Industries in her　✳　✳　✳　　five years.

A courier delivered the letter after work as Andrew returned home with pizza for dinner. He didn't get a chance to open it until the girls were fed, bathed, and in bed.

His jaw dropped as he read the handwritten note.

Andrew,

I can't thank you enough for helping me last night and for the hospitality your family showed me during the snow storm. I'll never forget your generosity, your bacon, or your beautiful girls' advice on life (secret girl stuff!). I came across these Heatherby *tickets and remembered how much you wanted to see it. It's late notice, I know, but I've set up a car to pick you up and bring you to the city if you are able to go. Please take a guest, maybe your father. I'd love to babysit the girls. They are welcome at my place, or I'd be happy to watch them at your place if you think they'd be more comfortable there.*

I hope you enjoy the play as much as I did. Talk soon.
Emma.

She'd signed the note and scribbled her phone number on the bottom.

The first thing he did, the first thing he always did when life threw him a curveball, was call his father.

Jeffrey hobbled into the kitchen before Andrew had a chance to put down his phone. He grumbled a greeting, then went straight for the leftover pizza, tossing a piece onto a paper plate. "What's this about a letter?"

Andrew shoved the card and the tickets toward his father. As Jeffrey scanned the card, Andrew paced the kitchen. He'd read the thank you note from Emma twice and barely recovered from the shock at the feel of the *Heatherby* tickets between his fingers. "Do you believe this? Is this even real?"

"Nice penmanship." His father held the tickets to the overhead light, as if he were an expert on counterfeiting. "They look real to me."

"Not the tickets, the...the...sentiment."

Jeffrey handed the card and its contents to Andrew and grabbed his slice of pizza. "I think it's appropriate for her to send a thank you to her employee who helped her out. You gave up your room and drove her into that horrid city in the ice and snow. She's a classy lady, with a good upbringing—"

"She's a corporate viper." He tossed the card onto the counter.

"A damn pretty one—"

"Dad! You can't say things like that. It's not the sixties."

Jeffrey scowled and pointed the tip of the pizza slice at his son. "If I think a woman is pretty, I sure as heck can say so."

Andrew rolled his eyes, brewing a cup of coffee as his father bit into the cold slice. After Jeffrey finished, he stood next to Andrew, who focused on the coffee streaming into his "World's Best Dad" mug. He reached for Andrew's shoulder. "I think maybe your...jitters...toward Emma come from a different place than you think."

"A different place?" He felt like the twins snapping at his own father like that. All he needed was to put a hand on his hip and stick out his chin. "So it's not because she doesn't care about her job? It's not because she has no clue how to run a company?"

Jeffrey growled and turned away. "You know that's not true. The woman has an MBA, and the company's doing fine. The stock has held since she took over for her father. Listen, son, it's been six years since Hayley—"

Andrew held up a hand to stop his father's words, words he didn't want to hear because they hurt his heart. "This has nothing to do with Hayley." He picked up the note and tickets and waved them at his father. "It's not like she wants to date me, Dad. She wants me to take you."

Jeffrey huffed. "So then why are you so upset?"

Andrew peeked at the envelope. He didn't know why he was upset. Maybe because he'd never have been able to score *Heatherby* tickets on his own, and all Emma Ballard had to do was bat an eyelash and they fall from the sky. Maybe because she'd assumed he'd leave his girls with her, a practical stranger, while he gallivanted around the city. Or, maybe it was because, like his father had said, she was gorgeous, and had been sweet and nice to him during her stay in his home.

Emma Ballard scared him. Not so much as his boss's, boss's, boss, but because she was likable. He didn't want to like her.

"I should have never stopped to help her yesterday. I should have left her to her own devices."

Jeffrey grunted in disapproval. "That is not how you were raised. Don't you lose your manners because you're out of your comfort zone, young man."

Young man. His father hadn't called him that since he was a teenager. The whole situation with Emma was completely out of his comfort zone. "I'm sorry."

Jeffrey snatched the note and pulled out the tickets again, studying them. "Friday night. I'll be around to watch the girls."

Andrew furrowed his brow. "I'll call Mrs. Fletcher to watch them. You're coming with me, remember?"

His dad laughed. "Oh heck no. I hate that city, and you know I can't sit through that musical stuff. I fall asleep, and my hip gets sore." Jeffrey hated Broadway, a bone of contention between him and Andrew for years. It didn't help that he'd had hip surgery after his time in the Army, which made it difficult for him to sit for long periods without stiffening up. "I'd rather have a movie marathon with Dev and Bells."

Andrew sighed. "Well, who am I supposed to take?"

His father held up the card, tapping his thumb over Emma's signature.

"Are you insane?" He grabbed the card from his chuckling father's grasp. "She's my boss, Dad. And she doesn't want to go. She said she'd seen it already, and the card says to take you."

"Of course it does. A classy lady like Ms. Ballard wouldn't invite herself out with a man she barely knows, especially one who works for her."

"Exactly."

"But I bet if you asked her, she'd say yes."

"Well, I'm not asking." Andrew huffed again, proving to himself that he was his daughters' father. He sounded just like them. He glanced sideways at his father. "And what makes you think so?"

Jeffrey shrugged. "Just a feeling. The way she looked at you like she needed a friend. The way she poked around the house after breakfast, picking up the picture of you on the mantel, like it was the most fascinating thing ever."

"Oh please," Andrew sang, feeling his cheeks heat. He hadn't noticed any of that. Did Emma really look at the picture of him with his prize-winning tuna catch? "You make her sound like a schoolgirl with a crush. She's an ex-model, a spoiled princess turned CEO of a major corporation. She's a vi—"

"A viper," Jeffrey finished. "Yeah, right. She really seemed viper-ish and spoiled when she let Devon paint her fingernails orange last night."

Andrew ignored his father's sarcasm, taking a minute to think while he cleared the table and crushed the pizza boxes for recycling. Sure, Emma had seemed nice, sweet. But he'd heard stories about her tearing things up in the board room. Stories about how the Board constantly challenged her and tried to force her out, and how she'd never been able to move her agenda. She wasn't strong enough to fight for the company, but that didn't mean she hadn't tried. At least from what he heard through the gossip that filtered from headquarters to the Jersey branch.

Jeffrey stood next to him, leaning his bad hip against the counter. "It's a play. You don't have to marry her. Heck, you don't even have to talk to each other. It would be a common courtesy to ask the person who got the tickets if they wanted to accompany you. Just like you do when Uncle Sal gets you Yankee tickets."

Andrew scowled. Why did his father have to be so smart? He glared at Jeffrey, then sputtered out, "Fine. I'll think about it."

Out Now!

What's next on your reading list?

Champagne Book Group promises to bring to readers fiction at its finest.

Discover your next
fine read!
http://www.champagnebooks.com/

We are delighted to invite you to receive exclusive rewards. Join our Facebook group for VIP savings, bonus content, early access to new ideas we've cooked up, learn about special events for our readers, and sneak peeks at our fabulous titles.

Join now.
https://www.facebook.com/groups/ChampagneBookClub/